HEART OF THE STORM

A McCarron's Corner Mystery

Sharon K. Middleton

Black Rose Writing | Texas

ISBN: 978-1-68513-107-4
PUBLISHED BY BLACK ROSE WRITING
www.blackrosewriting.com

Printed in the United States of America
Suggested Retail Price (SRP) $20.95

Heart of the Storm is printed in Adobe Caslon

*As a planet-friendly publisher, Black Rose Writing does its best to eliminate unnecessary waste to reduce paper usage and energy costs, while never compromising the reading experience. As a result, the final word count vs. page count may not meet common expectations.

Acknowledgements

I dedicate this book to the memory of a little black Skye terrier who wangled his way into my heart from the moment I resuscitated the tiny, stillborn puppy. Cucuillin Hairy Potter was never a show dog, but he was the champion of my heart for twelve years. His registration papers might have said I owned him, but Hairy owned me, body and soul.

I miss you every day, Hairy Potter. I'll meet you at the Bridge one of these days when the Good Lord decides I have finished my chores here on Earth. Until then, run brave and free, my sweet boy. Mama promises she will sing your Hairy Baby song to you when she sees you again.

I send posthumous thanks to my dear friend, Susan Parsons, for the many dog show stories she told me over the years.

As usual, I thank my beloved husband for all his love and support he gave me as I wrote this novel.

Cast of Characters

Sara Winslow Talbott - the daughter of Melanie Henson and Richard Winslow, born before either married. We met her in *Path of the Guiding Light*.

Francesca 'Fancy' Winslow - Sara's stepmother. We met her first as a child in *Home to McCarron's Corner*.

Melanie 'Mellie' Henson – Sara's mother. We met her in *Diary of the Reluctant Duchess*, and she became important in *Path of the Guiding Light*, when we learned about Sara.

Camilla De Rosini Henson - Sara's maternal grandmother, who married Nick Henson. Sara knew her as Camille Henson. She died years ago and left the Morgan Point house to Sara. We met Mrs. Henson in *Diary of the Reluctant Duchess*, but knew nothing else about her. She was a very private person.

Dr. Ari Hotep - Sara's brother-in-law, who is married to her stepsister, Elizabeth. Ari is from Egypt. We met him in *Love You Forever*.

Elizabeth Winslow Hotep - Kirk's daughter, who Fancy adopted while married to him. Her biological mother, Anya, died in childbirth. Kirk was presumed lost at sea during the Dreadful Hurricane, and Fancy subsequently married Dr. Richard Winslow. We met her first in *Diary of the Reluctant Duchess*. Elizabeth was the heroine in *Love You Forever*. Liz owns Nefertiti's, a supper club in Galveston which Kirk bought for her. It is now run by Dave. At the beginning of this story, Sara is staying in the apartment over the club since she fled her abusive husband.

Dr. Richard Winslow – Sara's biological father. She met him when she was twelve in *Path of the Guiding Light*. Richard adopted Elizabeth along with Bella and Charles, and they all call him Dad.

Theo Hotep - Liz and Ari's adopted son. We met Theo in Love You Forever. The Hotep family lives in Cairo where Ari works for Biozyme. We met him in *Love You Forever*.

Isis Hotep - Liz and Ari's biological daughter, the Miracle Child which Liz conceived after her tubes were tied. We first met her as a newborn in *Love You Forever*.

Kirk O'Malley - Sara's stepfather and Liz's biological father. Fancy adopted Liz while she was married to Kirk. Later, Richard adopted Liz when he married Fancy after Kirk was presumed dead at sea. Kirk showed up years later and is now married to Melanie Henson O'Malley. They have one child together, Callan. We met him in *The McCarron's Daughter*.

Bella Vargas - Sara's stepsister, daughter of Fancy and her first husband, Calvin Hobbs. Calvin died many years ago. Richard Winslow later adopted Bella. We met her in *Beyond McCarron's Corner*, as an infant.

Dr. Miguel Vargas - married to Bella. They live in Cairo, where Miguel is the head of Biozyme, International. We met Miguel in *Path of the Guiding Light*. They have two children, Carlos, age 4, and toddler Caridad.

Dara Winslow - Sara's half-sister and best friend who co-owns and shows Skye terriers with Sara. We met her in *Diary of the Reluctant Duchess*.

Davis 'Dave' Hamilton - the bartender who now manages Nefertiti's, Liz's club in Galveston, Texas. We first met Dave in *Love You Forever*.

Captain Jolly Johnny English - known as Jay Fitz Simmons in an earlier life. We first met Jay in *Home to McCarron's Corner*. I mentioned him in *Diary of the Reluctant Duchess* and *Path of the Guiding Light*. There was a key role for him in *Love You Forever*. He returns here as our friendly ghost.

Tamsin Fitz Simmons - first met in *Home to McCarron's Corner* as a young woman. She is now an angelic entity.

New Characters:

Ralph Morrissey - a forensic accountant.

Philip Martino - the Senior Assistant District Attorney of Galveston County, Texas. Philip becomes Sara's love interest.

Cory De Leon - the Galveston County District Attorney, who is Philip's boss.

Senator Jim Martino, retired - Philip's father, a former US Senator.

Jackson 'Jack' Talbott - Sara's husband, a forensic accountant, Jack of All Trades, and General Jack Ass.

Robin Cangelosi - Sara's former friend and client, embroiled in a child custody case with her ex-husband, Sonny Cangelosi, who has known ties to the *'Ndrangheta*, the Calabrian mafia. Robin and Sonny have a son, Mikey, age 4.

Sonny Cangelosi - Robin's ex-husband. Straight out of the penitentiary and seeking custody of Mikey.

Ray La Rosa - a mob boss from New Jersey.

Maggie Henson - Sara's Aunt Maggie, a top-notch attorney in Galveston County

Roberto Franchetti - Sara's uncle in Calabria, in Southern Italy.

And of course, **Hairy Potter**, AKA Grand Champion Morgan Point Hairy Potter, Sara's coal-black Skye terrier 'special', the true hero of the story.

HEART OF THE STORM

Chapter 1
Sara

What do you do in the middle of a trial when you learn your husband is having an affair with your client? Neither suicide nor murder were options. I sighed as I stared into the liquor cabinet. I just finished the last two fingers of Scotch, after being out of Xanax all week.

"Oh, get real, Sara. Kill the sorry bastard. No one would care. Barring that, drink gin." My older sister, Elizabeth, thought she had the perfect solution.

Liz is always the pragmatist. Kirk O'Malley is her bio dad and Anya was Liz's bio mom. Anya died in childbirth, and my step-mom, Fancy, adopted Liz while married to Kirk many years ago. Liz is tall, svelte, and she dances like a dream. Her fabulous, dark brown hair creates the perfect foil for her startling grey eyes, which Liz inherited from her Irish father. Her skin has a touch of color, inherited from her Egyptian mother. She has a wonderful figure I would kill to have. Men grow glassy-eyed when confronted with Liz's 38C delights.

Once again, I wished I had a set of 34Cs instead of my paltry 32AAs. I always wondered if my Jack Ass would not have wandered if I had a mouthful instead of my tiny niblets. Then again, it is demeaning to reduce Jack's philandering to the size of my breasts, even if Robin's breasts are closer to my sister's breasts than to mine. Jack grew slack-jawed and hard-dicked more than once, staring at my sister's boobs when he thought I was not watching.

I tried to make Liz burst into spontaneous flames with my withering glare, but it did not work. "You know I am allergic to gin."

Liz held out her right palm toward me. "Psst. Silliest thing I ever heard. Whoever heard of an allergy to juniper berries?"

My stepmother nodded as she struggled not to burst into laughter. "I agree. I told you that many times."

My stepmom, Fancy Winslow, is a stunning redhead, with aqua eyes, translucent Irish complexion, and a brilliant mind. She is married to my dad, Dr. Richard Winslow, and they have five kids: Bella, Charlie, Liz, Dara, and Ronan. I made it an even half dozen. Dad will tell you kids are not cheaper by the half-dozen.

I sighed as I shook my head. "You two drive me nuts. All I know is I break out in hives whenever I drink gin. Sounds like an allergy to me. Listen, I need constructive ideas. What do I do?"

My other older sister, Dara, walked in then. Dara looks enough like me to be my twin, but she is almost a year older than me. She picked up an apple and rinsed it off in the sink. "Divorce him, withdraw from the slut's case, and give her the file. Or hell, just kill the son of a bitch, like Liz said. Grow a backbone. For heaven's sake, you are a strong woman. You are a lawyer, not to mention you raise terriers. I have told you all of this at least a hundred times. What more do I need to say?"

Fancy nodded. "Dara's right, honey, although I would not suggest you kill Jackson."

I rolled my eyes at them for at least the hundredth time. "I told you guys if I withdraw while we are in trial –"

"She will lose. Her ex will get custody of the kid. BFD. Not your problem." Dara's killer instinct reared its ugly head.

I crossed my arms and continued to glare at her. Maybe this time she would burst into flames if I glared at her long enough.

Dara looked away before I did, and I took it as a win. "Listen, I understand your concern is for the little boy, but it would be her problem if her adulterous behavior with your husband resulted in her losing custody of the kiddo. It would be on her head, not yours. She should have thought of the logical consequences of her behavior before she put your husband's dick in her pretty little mouth."

I cringed and rubbed my hand across my forehead. Again. "I should never have told you about that."

"But you told us, sis. You've been in the trial for a month. It's the craziest thing I've heard at a trial. How can a judge stop a trial?" She rolled her eyes in disgust.

I shook my head and rolled my eyes back at her for the umpteenth time. "Like I already explained a kajillion times, the judge called it to trial but passed it after he called it so the social study investigator could update her report."

Exasperated with the whole mess, I sighed. Dara was right: this case comprised the craziest can of worms I ever heard about at the courthouse. I wasn't aware a judge could call a case and then continue it until he did it.

Elizabeth frowned and shook her head. "Well, this Robin woman needs to hire another attorney. She was supposed to be your friend. The slut should never have slept with your husband. Yes, we know Jackson is a prime man whore, but friends do not sleep with their friend's spouses. Robin did, and what is worse, she did it while you represented her in a custody battle—which is one more reason you should never represent your friends in family law matters, Sara. This comprises a serious conflict of interest, and you have no option other than to withdraw. If you don't withdraw, you commit malpractice. Enough said."

Liz tossed her gorgeous hair back off her face to reveal her lush eyelashes framing her beautiful, almond-shaped grey eyes. Gosh, I wish I had eyelashes like hers.

I frowned and shook my head. "Elizabeth, you don't understand."

She shook her head and flipped her hand up at me again. "Enough said, Sara, I understand. I think you don't understand the seriousness of the situation. File your Motion to Withdraw, set it for a hearing, and get out of this godforsaken mess."

As I put my head in my hands, I sighed again. "Oh, God…"

I started thinking about other things to distract myself from my ridiculous dilemma. I often said I must be the only Italian American girl in the country with Average Looks. There was nothing glamorous about me, as my husband told me too many times to count over the years since we married. It always struck me as odd how Jack claimed he loved my copper-toned tresses before we married and hated them afterwards. I wondered why the Jack Ass married me in the first place, considering he told me how inadequate he considered my looks many times during our marriage.

Oh, yeah, my trust fund. Thank God Dad did not turn control of my trust fund over to Jack when we married. Of course, it infuriated Dad to learn Jack and I eloped the way we did. I will never forget the disappointment in my daddy's eyes when he learned we ran off to Vegas to get married. Dad had little to say other than, 'girl, you will rue the day you married that man.'

Boy, he nailed that one, even if he used old-fashioned terminology. I figured he picked up the phrase from my stepmother.

Maybe new highlights would help bolster my shattered self-esteem. I would have to talk to my hairdresser about it. He claims to be the Queen of the World of Hair Color. He took my hair color from ginger snap red, which Jack insisted was unacceptable for an amber-eyed Italian girl, to a more subdued strawberry blonde shade that worked well with the odd eye color I inherited from my dad. Yes, some new highlights might help. Maybe I would go all the way to blonde this time. Mom is a natural blonde. Perhaps I could find out if blondes really have more fun. It would be an improvement to have some fun in my life. I studied what I perceived as my nondescript reflection in the glass pane in the kitchen cabinet door. It might be interesting to be an amber-eyed blonde. Fancy says the first time she met Dad, his hair was sun bleached so blonde that he looked like he had golden hair, golden eyes, and a rich, golden tan. Dad laughs when she tells that story, his beautiful, golden eyes sparkling. Yes, I thought, I want to find out how I might look blonde and golden.

Hmm… I wonder why I think Dad's eyes are beautiful, but mine are odd. Come to think of it, Jackson, you got some explaining to do. Why did you praise my 'intriguing, unusual, amber eyes' before we married, and now you call them 'weird, freakish aberrations?'

The man makes me crazy.

My shoulders slumped, and I sighed as my mind went back to The Problem. "How do I get myself into these crazy jams?"

Fancy shook her head. "You didn't force that woman to have an affair with your husband, and I doubt you forced Jackson to hop in the bed with her."

"Fine, whatever. How did Robin Cangelosi wangle her way into our lives so much that I accepted employment as her attorney in this blasted case? And how did she and my husband become lovers? Why do I feel so guilty? And why the blazes can't I walk away from the damned girl and throw her to the legal wolves?"

Sighing again, I shook my head in frustration. I loved Liz, Dara, and Fancy, but they could be royal pains in the northbound end of a southbound mule. None of them appeared to grasp the urgency of my dilemma about my client. How could I legitimize pulling out of a trial already in progress?

I winced as I raised my aching, stiff body off the couch as I struggled to ignore the knowing glances between my step-mom and my sisters. Tumbling down those blasted stairs combined with the freaking Custody Battle from Hell had triggered pain running from my low back and extending down my leg in double time. It felt like a family of minor demons occupied themselves by sticking their pitchforks down my leg. "I think there's a bottle of Patron downstairs in the bar."

Liz frowned as she turned to me. "I thought you gave up margaritas."

I stopped walking towards the elevator. She was right. I love the taste of the high-priced liquor, but I hate the way tequila makes me feel the next morning. "Oh, shut up."

Bite me." She tossed her hair over her shoulder again as she glared at me.

I grinned. Elizabeth can always make me smile, no matter how dire the circumstances. "Yeah, sure, you wish. I'll let Bianca bite you."

Dara and I co-own Bianca, a gorgeous silver Skye terrier. Bianca is a temperamental little bitch and will bite when pushed. Fancy and Dad have owned, raised and showed Skye terriers for over twenty years now. We say it was Dad's fault we became obsessed with these silly dogs. His family owned Skye terriers when he was a kid growing up in Boston, and he bought two about the time he married my stepmom.

Fancy taught all of us how to handle the dogs in the show ring. I will always perform better in front of a courtroom judge than a dog show judge, but I have finished several champions. Three of our dogs received group placements with me at the end of the show lead. Fancy, Dara, and I co-own several beautiful Skyes, but only my beloved Hairy Potter lives with me.

Last year, Bianca was in the whelping box with six puppies at my house. Believe me, that created a lot of shit to shovel, especially when one considered the shit my marriage had become. Jackson Talbott offered anything but support of me or the litter of puppies while they lived with us. To make matters worse, Bianca had the audacity to snap at Jackson when he tried to pick up one of her puppies. My god, I think it was the only time he ever showed an interest in one of my dogs, and the mama dog snapped at him. Jack blew a gasket over her snap, even though it comprised nothing more than a warning. Her teeth never connected with his flesh. If she meant to draw blood, he might have lost a finger. It upset her when the mean man tried to steal her puppy. After those puppies went to their new homes, Dara took Bianca home with her to keep peace in my family.

Dara sniffed and shook her head at me. "Bianca bites no one unless they are mean to her or to me. Like Liz says, 'enough said.' When will your trial resume?"

"It resumes in a month. I still can't believe the judge granted the other attorney's request to supplement the social study. And for the record, I still want a margarita."

Hell, I wanted a whole pitcher of margaritas, maybe a boatload.

I glowered at my family. Fancy struggled to bite back laughter with surreptitious glances at Dara, Elizabeth, and me.

Elizabeth burped her baby on her shoulder as she frowned, rolled her eyes at me, and shook her head. "No margaritas for you, Miss Sara. You can't stop drinking them once you start."

"That's right, sis. How about a glass of wine instead?" asked Dara with a worried glance at Fancy and Liz.

I rolled my eyes again and shook my head as I walked over to the window. "You make it sound like I am an alcoholic. Fine, I think I will go downstairs and snag a bottle of Scotch from Dave."

Then it was Fancy's turn to frown at me. "No one said you are an alcoholic, Sara. Don't be so melodramatic. However, we all know you have a weakness for tequila. Look, go downstairs, and ask Dave to give you a drink. You don't need an entire bottle."

"Amen to that," said Liz. "Besides, you always want the good stuff. You could not drink Johnny Walker Red to save your soul if Glenlivet is available."

I glowered at her. "Sorry, not sorry, but I prefer Talisker to Glenlivet, and I prefer single malt Scotches to blends. My step-dad owns an Irish bar where I worked during summers while in college. Kirk taught me to appreciate fine liquor. And you own this bar—oops, fine eatery. So what?"

The baby let out a hearty burp as Elizabeth smiled. "What a good baby girl. You prefer tequila and like you mentioned before, you prefer Patron, to be specific. Please do not drink up the profits from my club while you stay here. I know we are just here visiting, and I realize Dave runs the club now, but there is no reason for you to dip into my profits. Slow it down, sis. I understand you're upset with Jackson, but don't take it out on me or yourself."

Dara nodded, her face grim with concern. "You know she's right."

As I shook my head again, I sighed. I took a deep breath and rubbed my hand across my forehead. My dog lolled his tongue out as he grinned at me, doggie-style.

Liz moved to Cairo when she married Dr. Ari Hotep. Ari is this drop-dead gorgeous, tall, dark, and sexy Egyptian man with an unexpected British accent from a British education. Dave Wilson inherited management of Elizabeth's fancy-schmancy Galveston restaurant and bar when she moved to Cairo, and Dave does a fabulous job. Elizabeth and Ari came home to visit family and to check on her bar. Oops, Liz said not to call it a bar anymore. She wants us to call it 'an exclusive eatery and supper club.' My sister caught some flack in a court case in Cairo about owning a bar, so she changed the place's name. Now, it is 'Nefertiti's,' replete with Egyptian artwork. Yes, sure. The joint still looked like a bar to me, even if it serves upscale food and fine liquors, but if Liz wanted to call it an upscale eatery and supper club, so be it. Who was I to question her?

Last month, Dave notified my stepdad, Kirk O'Malley, that there seemed to be some financial discrepancies he could not explain between his books and the bank account. My dad, Richard Winslow, never married my mother, Melanie. Dad married Fancy, who used to be married to Kirk. My mother,

Melanie, is married to my stepdad, Kirk, who used to be married to my stepmom, Fancy, who is now married to my dad, Rick. Typical blended American family, right? Let me tell you, it put me into therapy for two years. If that didn't give a person a headache, nothing would—unless it was this freaking mess with Jackson and Robin.

Dave urged my stepdad to send in a forensic accountant to figure out the issue about the missing money. Since I was the attorney in the family, who majored in accounting in my undergrad studies, Dave and Kirk recruited me to figure out the financial situation of Nefertiti's. Busting my hump reviewing bank records failed to reveal to me the source of the blasted problem. Kirk authorized me to hire a forensic accountant if I deemed it necessary. If I had not learned about my husband's skank-assed affair with my client, I would hire my husband, reputed to be one of the top forensic accountants in Texas. Now, it looked like I had bigger fish to fry, at least in my personal life, and damned if I intended to fork out good money to pay my husband to do forensics on my sister's bar. Oops, her exclusive eatery and supper club. She insists we no longer call it a bar.

I went downstairs to the office and stared at the spreadsheets again. My preference would be to do this work in the quiet of my home or in my private office in Clear Lake. At least, the house was quiet whenever Jack took off on his freaking sailboat, and there was never loud music coming from the next room like at Nefertiti's. If I played music at my office, it put me and my clients at ease. The music in the bar gave me a headache, and I was sick and tired of having a damned headache.

Like Dave, I was at my wit's end over the forensic mess. His records seemed impeccable. The bank records looked correct, yet they did not reconcile to his records. I shook my head again, disgusted that the problem lay right in front of me and yet somehow I missed it. Dammit, why did Jack have to pick now to cheat with Robin when I needed a blasted forensic accountant? With a sigh of unmitigated disgust, I pushed back from the antique oak desk with a sigh, arose from the chair, rubbed my forehead again, and entered Nefertiti's through the office door.

I took a deep breath and shut my eyes as the music assailed my ears. Why did they always have to play the music so damned loud? I knew it was Krazy

Kilt Karaoke Night, but the level of noise went way beyond ridiculous. As I shook my head in frustration, I walked over to Dave as he tended the antique bar Kirk had imported from Ireland, and I rubbed my forehead as I leaned against it. "Hey, Dave, could I have a Coke? I have a killer headache."

He nodded as he popped a cap off a bottled Coke for me. "Sure, boss lady, here you go. Still trying to reconcile the accounts?"

I tried to smile. "Yes, but I think the task is impossible. The error appears to be hiding in plain sight, and I fear I'll never find it."

"Never say never. See if the Coca-Cola helps. Hey, some guy came in here looking for you earlier."

I shook my head as I took a sip of the ice cold Coke. "You are the boss, not I. Things are supposed to go better with Coca Cola, and I hope they do. The man must want Liz."

Dave grinned as he shook his head at me. "Nah, I told him Liz married and moved out of the country. I didn't bother to tell him she's here visiting right now. The dude gave me bad vibes and I would not give out much info to him. Anyway, he said he meant the youngest sister, Sara. I told him you might be in later this evening, but I didn't tell him you were in the office or that you were staying upstairs."

My eyes narrowed as I frowned and peered around the restaurant. "Thanks, Dave. Hmm, the man wasn't my husband, was he?"

Dave shook his head again. "No, I know Jackson, and this guy was not him. This fellow had dark hair, slicked back with way too much Brilliantine, kinda like men wore their hair in the '50s. His hair alone was enough to set me on edge. The dude kept his shades on when he came in, even though it was dark outside this evening. He was a big, burly guy dressed in a dark suit, but without a tie, and his shirt appeared rumpled. The dude sounded downright angry, and I thought he was looking for a fight. He kept slugging one fist into the palm of his other hand. He didn't give his name, and he scowled when I told him you were not here. Oh, yeah, he said 'youse' instead of 'you,' and 'da' instead of 'the,' that kind of accent. I figured he was from the East Coast, New York, or maybe New Jersey. The dude scowled and stormed out without another word when I said you weren't here."

The description sounded a lot like Sonny Cangelosi, Robin's ex-husband, but I shrugged and feigned ignorance of the unknown man's identity. It freaked me out to think Sonny could track me down to the bar. The man gave me a severe case of the Willies. "That's weird. Who would look for me here? No one should know I am here except my family and my blasted husband. Hey, what's the latest storm doing in the Gulf?"

Dave grimaced. "It's still way off the coast of Yucatan, but the meteorologist on the news tonight said it could bounce off from Yucatan and come north to hit anywhere from Brownsville to New Orleans, or it could surprise us, sail across the Gulf, and hit Florida. Who knows what it will do? It's hurricane season in the Gulf of Mexico."

I sighed. "Oh, great, that means we could wind up smack dab in the middle of the storm path. Well, it's September, which means it's prime hurricane season. Kirk and Liz can tell us what to do in case a storm makes landfall here."

Dave nodded again. "That's what I figured. Listen, tell your sisters that you girls shouldn't go out alone. They still haven't caught the Rosenberg Ripper. I know Liz likes to go walking in the evening, because it's cooler then."

My shoulders sagged as I shook my head in disgust. "Well, wouldn't that just figure? A hurricane barreling down on us and a serial killer on the loose."

Dave smirked as he shrugged. "He's only known to have killed four women."

My frown deepened as my foot tapped with impatience. "Oh, yes, that makes me feel much safer. He's only killed four, to our knowledge. I wonder how many other young women he killed. Where is our friendly psychic tonight? He could ask the spirits what we need to do."

Dave laughed. "Now, that's funny. Mr. Jones is over in the corner. It's downright pathetic to watch that poor man keep asking his spirit guides to send Johnny back. What the heck are 'spirit guides,' anyway?"

"Beats me. The best I can tell is they are like guardian angels. Jonesie needs to give up the pipe dream of getting Captain Johnny back here as resident ghost and to search for another spirit to chat with about things on the other side. I understand Johnny 'moved on,' as Jonesie puts it. Hmm,

Jonesie appears to be talking with someone… or should I say something?" I rubbed the furrow in my forehead as I continued to frown. "I hope this ghost is friendly. It terrified me to awaken when that last ghostly clown screamed 'boo!' in my face."

Dave chuckled. "Yeah, Jonesie says it was a helluva mistake to talk to Lafitte, much less to invite him in to stay awhile. He did not realize Jean Lafitte had such a dad-blamed nasty streak. Jonesie thought Lafitte would be the perfect replacement for Johnny since the two were involved in all kinds of shenanigans together when they were alive. Now, he realizes Lafitte was a pirate."

"Like Captain Johnny wasn't a pirate while he lived? But I agree. I never dreamed I would say it, but I miss Captain Johnny. He scared me witless when I first met him, but Johnny became a cool, friendly ghost by the time he left to watch over Elizabeth in Cairo. We could almost have called him Captain Casper. Liz says Theo misses the old reprobate something terrible."

Dave burst out laughing at the idea of how Captain Johnny would have responded to be called Casper. "Call Jolly Johnny English 'Casper'? Oh, I do not think so, dear heart. I would not dare to call him Captain Casper. Why don't you go over and introduce yourself to the spirit Jonesie is interviewing?"

I took a long sip of my Coke. "Oh, this tastes good. Maybe the caffeine will help my headache."

Dave's eyes narrowed. "Do you want some aspirin?"

I shook my head. "No, thanks. My mother told me to never take drugs from a handsome man in a bar."

Dave laughed as he handed a fresh beer to one of the UTMB residents. "Handsome, huh? I knew I loved your mother. Well, thank you, ma'am, and your mom, too. 'Handsome' is the nicest thing I have been called all week."

I rubbed my forehead again. "You know, on second thought, I'll break Mom's rule. Please give me a couple of aspirins, handsome. Listen, could you turn the music down just a little? The noise is killing me."

He laughed again. "I will turn the volume down for you. Just remember it's Saturday night, a hurricane may blow into this area, a serial killer is on the loose, and the natives grow restless. Heck, they feel terrified. I can't turn the volume down too much on Krazy Kilt Karaoke Night."

I glanced down at his military-styled kilt and gave him a wry grin. "Okay, I understand. I'll check how the ghostly interviews are going."

Mr. Jones grinned as I walked up to the table in the corner. It used to be Captain Johnny's favorite spot in the house. Mr. Jones often sat there in the shadows as he chatted with local spirits. "Hey, Jonesie, how's it going? Did you find a replacement yet?"

Mr. Jones beamed at me, his blue eyes twinkling. "Yes, my dear, I believe I found the right fellow."

I arched a brow at him, a trick I learned from my stepmom years ago. "Oh, you do? Well, do you think this spirit might talk to me?"

"I think he might do better than talk, Sara." Mr. Jones leaned back in his chair and grinned again.

It surprised me to see the air shimmer. I had not expected Jonesie's interviewee to appear for me. As the features materialized, I gasped. "Captain Johnny! We thought you were, uh, well, gone."

I felt my cheeks redden with embarrassed heat.

Captain Johnny chuckled. "As did I, but the Big Man Upstairs gave me choices. I could be reborn, but Tamsin and I would never reunite if I chose that option. Or, based on the help I offered to Kirk, Theo and Elizabeth's family, I could try for my wings. If I gain them, Tammie and I shall be a team, together forevermore."

I thought my eyes might bulge out of my head. "Get your wings? You mean to say you could become an angel?"

The ghost chuckled. "Yes, Sara, a guardian angel. Amazing, isn't it? Despite my despicable behavior as a human, I won points protecting Elizabeth and Theo and for pulling Kirk out of the drink all those years ago. I chose the second option. Of course, the Lord allowed Tamsin to come along to assist me. One might say she is my personal guardian angel."

Captain Johnny beamed with ghostly pride at the beautiful, dark-haired, blue-eyed woman who materialized beside him. "Oh, go ahead, my love. Show Sara your beautiful wings."

Tamsin Fitz Simmons smiled up at Johnny. "It would be my pleasure, darling."

I gasped as the angelic entity before me spread her arms to reveal her wings, the same exquisite color of blue as her eyes. My step-mother called the eye color 'Selk blue' because so many of her Selk relatives possessed eyes the same color. "It's a great privilege to meet you, Lady Tamsin."

The pretty angel smiled at me. "I think I met you long ago when you were born at Waterside Estate."

My cheeks reddened again. "No, that was my older sister, Dara. She is upstairs. I hail from Atlanta. I'm a Georgia girl by birth."

Tamsin blushed. Her reddened cheeks surprised me, because I never suspected guardian angels could blush. "Oh, merciful heaven, I didn't realize my daughter, Fancy, had six children!"

"I'm her step-daughter, although she has always treated me like the others. I was the surprise awaiting Dad—Richard—when he came home from his time travel adventure. Dara and I look like twins. Oh, yes, and Mom— Melanie—married Kirk O'Malley some years later when he came forward in time. Our family is uber weird."

Tamsin's brow wrinkled as she frowned. "Uber?"

Surprised by her question, I laughed. I figured Tamsin would have questions about Dad's affair with Mom, or that Kirk married Mom after he came here and learned Fancy and he were no longer married. "Oops, my bad. Uber means outstanding or supreme."

"Oh." Poor Tamsin still looked confused.

I bit back my laughter. "It's a way to say our family is extremely weird."

Tamsin's mouth fell open. The angelic entity looked offended by my comment. I covered my mouth to keep from laughing at the confused spirit, and I left the table, chuckling. Pleased to discover my headache had all but disappeared, I walked over to the stage by the karaoke machine.

"Welcome back to Nefertiti's for Krazy Kilt Karaoke Night! How many of you guys are repeat offenders?" I shouted.

The audience laughed as over half of the crowd raised their hands.

"I know a brilliant lawyer if you need one," I said in an exaggerated stage whisper as I imitated Groucho Marx and his cigar. The crowd howled with laughter again.

"And how many of you are 'fresh fish' tonight?"

About two dozen people raised their hands as the crowd chanted, "Fresh fish, fresh fish!"

In prison lingo, 'fresh fish' meant 'new meat.' We use the term to refer to newcomers to Nefertiti's.

With a glance towards my office, I grinned and started 'strutting my stuff,' as Liz called it. "Oh, it's a live crowd tonight! Then, I'm going to start tonight's frivolities with an oldie but goodie."

I started the karaoke machine with the old theme song for 'Welcome Back, Kotter.' As the music played, I did my best imitation of Dara Winslow as I sang. Dara sings like a proverbial angel, but I do not. However, I can carry a tune unlike our brother, Charlie, who could not carry a tune in a bucket if his life depended on it.

Welcome back.
Your dreams were your ticket out.
Welcome back.
To the same old place you fussed about.
Well, your name has changed since you hung around.
But their dreams are the same, though most skedaddled town.

The audience laughed and clapped. I grinned and kept singing my twist to the old Kotter theme song. It was like the original, but different enough, as Liz put it.

At that point, Liz, Ari, and Theo walked into the restaurant. Ari carried Baby Isis, who blew kisses to the people who were waving to them. Isis never met a stranger and already knew how to work the crowd, and the girl was only nine months old. As they came up to the karaoke stage, the audience went hog wild crazy. When I thought the volume could not get any louder, Bella, Miguel, little Carlos, and baby Caridad came to the stage as well. It surprised me Dara did not come down from the apartment to join the fun. After all, she was the singer in the family, and she was usually the first one on the stage.

Everyone jumped up to give my family a standing ovation, as Elizabeth struggled not to cry. I hugged everyone, and then I stepped forward to begin, 'I Called the Witch Doctor.' When we reached the refrain, Theo stepped forward in a grass skirt he grabbed from Dave to sing the refrain.

"Ooh, eee, ooh, ah ah..."

As the youngster sang, the crowd again went crazy.

At the end of the second verse, Ari stunned us all as he grabbed a second grass skirt and joined in with Theo to sing the Witch Doctor refrain. The audience broke into hysterical laughter as the distinguished Dr. Hotep joined his son to sing, each clad in a grass skirt.

After 'Witch Doctor,' we moved on to the Jackson Browne song, 'Doctor My Eyes,' which Liz and her husband sang. He's an ophthalmologist, for heaven's sake! They had to sing it. It became their song years ago when Ari began doctoring my sister's eyes to help control the Stargardt disease which threatened her vision. Next, Bella and Miguel sang 'Addicted to Love' before we all sang 'Bad Case of Loving You' to the audience. As the thunderous applause ended, we made our way to the reserved tables in the corner, where Theo let out a whoop of delight as he ran to greet his favorite ghost.

"It's wonderful to see you. No one told me you would be here," Theo said to Captain Johnny.

The ghost smiled at the youngster. "Well, lad, I had to come when I heard you would be here."

I sighed. It must be nice to have your own guardian angel in training, I thought with a wry smile. I hope the Good Lord knows I could use a guardian angel of my own about now.

People began moving to the karaoke stage to sing while we huddled around the corner table and visited. Later, we went upstairs with our ghost and his angelic companion to talk more freely. Theo wanted to show Johnny photos of everything they had done since the day Ari and Liz adopted him.

"And here is the interior of the Great Pyramid, Johnny. Remember how frightened I was the first time I went there?"

Johnny shook his head. "No, lad, I did not accompany you that day. We met later that evening. I believe my appearance rather alarmed you."

Theo flushed red with embarrassment. "Oh, that's right. I had forgotten we did not meet until later."

Captain Johnny twirled one end of his mouse ache as he nodded. "Aye, lad, you seemed quite kerfuffled when we first met."

Theo's cheeks turned a darker crimson. "Well, yes, but we soon became the best of friends."

Johnny's blue eyes beamed with affection as he smiled. "Indeed, we did, Theo. Oh, look, Tamsin, Theo brought photographs of the sea life in the Red Sea."

Tamsin bent over the photos, voicing amazement at the diversity of sea life. "I never saw creatures like these."

Theo nodded, eager to tell her all about the unusual sea creatures. "They call them 'dugongs,' and they look very much like the manatees found in Florida. Johnny told me sailors sometimes mistook them for mermaids, but we both think the sailors had been at sea too long if they mistook dugongs for beautiful maidens of the sea."

As they became lost in conversation about Egypt, I glared at Dara. "Why didn't you join in the family fun tonight? You usually grab any chance you have to get up and sing for a crowd."

Dara shrugged and continued filing her nails. "Not that it is your business, but I had my reasons."

I frowned and shook my head again. Years ago, I learned Dara won't talk unless she wants to talk, so I dropped the subject. She can throw a mean left hook, and I did not need another headache.

We went upstairs to the apartment, and I squealed with excitement when Mom, Kirk, and my younger brother, Callan, came in about 11 p.m. "I didn't know you were coming, too!"

Mom hugged me tight. "It was a surprise. Why are you wincing? Does your back hurt?"

I shrugged. "Yes, I think I must have pulled a muscle. My back aches."

I did not miss Dad nod to Kirk, or that the two of them slipped outside with Miguel and Ari.

The men all stood on the balcony overlooking the bar patio below. I stood back inside the living room where I could hear them without them realizing I listened to their conversation.

"What's wrong with her back?" growled Kirk as he cracked his knuckles.

Miguel shrugged and took another swig from the longneck in his hands. "She claims she pulled a muscle, but she has a black eye, too. It's hard to see the black eye because she covered it with concealer and her makeup. Bella and I suspect Jack roughed her up. Again."

"Pulled muscle, my ass," snapped Dad. "Sara admitted to Elizabeth and Dara that Jack shook her until she fell down when she confronted Robin and him. The fool girl is much like that little dog she loves so much. She does not know when to walk away from an impending fight. When she arose, she got right back in Jackson's face, and he shoved her. She claims she lost her balance and fell down the blasted stairs. It's no wonder she has a black eye. She's lucky the fall didn't kill her."

My eyes widened with shock as Kirk turned purple with rage. Fancy told us he used to have a horrible temper. Liz and Bella remember some arguments Fancy and Kirk had back in the day. I observed he lost his temper rarely since he fell in love with Mom. She seems to have a calming effect on Kirk, which we all appreciate. However, when he lost his temper, it was never pretty. "Did you say the sorry bastard shoved our girl down the stairs at the Morgan Point house? Damn, they built that old mansion over a hundred years ago. It's older than your house in San Antonio. Those stairs are freaking steep."

Dad nodded. "Yeah, the stairs are steeper than the ones in our Del Monte house in San Antonio. Sara should have called the police and had Jackson arrested for domestic violence, especially since he already shook her before he knocked her down the stairs. Let's face it: the sorry bastard terrified her. She grabbed her dog and ran for safety."

"She wouldn't go anywhere without Hairy Potter," Kirk said, his voice soft and thoughtful. "Do we need to pay a wee visit to Mr. Talbott?"

Dad glowered again. "Unless we go now, we would miss him in the morning. He'll be out on his damned sailboat with his little tart."

"I could pay him a visit," suggested Johnny, with a naughty grin.

The men glanced at each other, savoring the idea of a ghostly visit to Jack Talbott from Captain Johnny. The idea of Captain Jolly Johnny English paying a visit to Jackson Talbott appealed to me, and I figured I would have a chat with our friendly ghost about that possibility.

It seemed like an appropriate moment for me to walk out onto the deck. I cleared my throat, and the men all fell into an awkward silence. "Are you guys doing okay out here?"

Kirk smiled and reached over to tousle my hair. Mother says he does this when he wants to lighten the mood or to distract you. "Aye, lass, we're fine. Hey, did ye hear how to get to heaven from Ireland?"

I must have heard this story at least a hundred times, but I grinned and feigned ignorance. "No, tell us how to get to heaven from Ireland."

He beamed at me, winked, and tousled my hair again before he bent to kiss my cheek. "Well, long ago, when I was a wee laddie going to confirmation classes in Ireland, Sister Mary Margaret grilled us one Sunday morning to see if we understood the concept of getting into heaven. She asked us, 'If I sold my house and my carriage, had a big sale, and gave all my money to the church, would that get me into heaven?' 'No!' all the children shouted."

I giggled; we have heard this story so many times any of us could tell it by heart.

Kirk grinned before he continued his story. "Sister Mary Margaret smiled. 'If I cleaned the church daily, maintained the garden, and kept everything neat, would I get into heaven?' Again, the answer was a resounding 'No!'"

I laughed, and Kirk winked at me again. "'If I gave sweets to the children and loved everyone, would I get me into heaven?' We yelled at the top of our lungs, 'NO!' Sister Mary Margaret was bursting with pride for us. 'Then how can I get into heaven?' So, of course, I shouted, 'Sister, you've gotta be feckin' dead.'"

Everyone burst into laughter. I know the story by heart, but the story never gets old.

"Good one, Kirk." Dad's amber eyes, so much like mine, twinkled as he grinned at me.

Kirk beamed at us, delighted by our response to his story. "We're an interesting people, the Irish. Brings a tear to your eye, doesn't it?"

Still laughing, my brothers-in-law, Ari and Miguel, wandered back inside. Miguel ambled over to the fridge to grab another beer.

I remained outside with Dad and Kirk. They are great dads, and I love them both. Dad stood on one side of me, rubbing my aching back as Kirk stood on the other side, puffing on his pipe as he gazed into the starlit night. My Skye terrier, Hairy Potter, came out on the deck and sighed as he laid down beside my feet.

Don't you love the play on my dog's name? I named him Hairy instead of Harry because Skye terriers have lots of hair. The lady in registration at the American Kennel Club called me to make sure I meant to spell it that way. She laughed as I assured her I did.

"Are you still planning to go to the big dog shows in Pennsylvania with Dara?" asked Dad with a worried frown.

"Yes, of course. Hairy Potter is the top-rated Skye terrier in the country and the number two terrier overall. Dara's drop-eared ball of goof is the number five Skye in the nation, and he's not even a champion yet."

Dad chuckled as he relaxed again. "Better not let your sister hear you talk about her dog like that."

I shrugged and flipped my hand in the air. "Whatever. I call all Skyes 'balls of goof,' including my Hairy. They are all delightful, quirky balls of goof. Anyway, I'd be a fool not to go, assuming the judge honors my vacation letter and allows me to go."

Dad frowned. "Why on earth wouldn't the judge let you go? You filed your vacation letter in January."

"It's a technicality, but I'm in a trial. The case should resume the week of the specialty. We have a status conference a week from tomorrow, and I'll know then if the trial will go forward the last week in September or not. I'm hoping he will not resume the case then. We scheduled the case for mediation the week the judge set it to resume. It was the first date available for mediation, and this judge wants cases mediated before they proceed to trials."

Dad stared at me for a long minute. "Uh, isn't that the case with what's her name?"

Nodding, I sighed. "Yeah, it's Robin Cangelosi's case. I'm going to talk to Aunt Maggie about taking it over tomorrow afternoon."

Dad lifted on eyebrow. I figured he learned it from Fancy, like I did. It has proven to be a nifty little trick in the courtroom. "Oh? Aren't you going to talk to her about anything else?"

I swallowed hard and nodded. "Yeah, I'm going to ask her to file a divorce for me in Harris County. The Texas Family Code mandates attorneys file divorces in the county where the people live, and the Morgan Point house is in Harris County. Thank heaven I don't have any cases there right now. It would be embarrassing to have to file my divorce before a Judge in whose court I have active cases."

Kirk nodded as he took another puff on his pipe. "Do ye want us to go with ye tomorrow?"

I shook my head. "No, sir, I got myself into this mess and I can get myself out of it. Aunt Maggie will take fabulous care of me. She's the best attorney in Galveston County."

"Except for you, right?" My dad grinned at me.

I chuckled. Dad always thinks his children are the best at whatever they choose to do. "Well, duh. Listen, I appreciate you guys all coming this weekend. It's great to see everyone, and it means a lot to me to know you care this much about me and want to support me during this. But please, let the little gal handle her divorce on her own with no interference from the Dad Brigade. Okay?"

Both men looked embarrassed. As Dad shuffled from foot to foot, Kirk stammered. "B-b-but that's what fathers are for..."

I nodded. "Yes, I understand, and I appreciate you guys want to help me. Really, I do."

"Heck, I just want to bite the ears off the sorry bastard," Dad answered as he glowered at me.

Coca Cola snorted out of my nose as I struggled to bite back laughter. As I wiped off my face and shirt, I struggled to control my laughter. "That would be a big 'no,' Dad. I don't want you to wind up in prison over the likes of Jackson 'Jack Ass' Talbott. Listen, when I need help, I promise I will ask for it. My family did not raise an idiot."

They both chuckled in apparent embarrassment as they shuffled back and forth from foot to foot again.

"Good to know, but by damn, I would still like to bite his ears off." My dad sounded disgusted.

Kirk chortled. "Let me help you do it, Rick."

I shook my head. "Prison is not a good place for a board-certified cardiovascular surgeon. We need you out here saving lives, not in the Big House. And yes, God knows I realize I don't look like the sharpest tack in the box right now. Jack is in my separate property house while I sit here in Liz's bar. Oops, her fine eatery. And I am the one who fell down a flight of stairs."

Both men quit laughing and stared at me. Hard.

I gulped as I glanced away from them. "Okay, yeah, he pushed me."

"He claims she's clumsy," muttered Kirk.

"Uh-huh, that is how she won all those dance competitions," answered Dad, his voice low and steady but ripe with anger. "Clumsy."

"Ah, that must be it. The dancing made her clumsy. All those wins slipped my mind." Kirk said as he took another draw on the pipe.

"They didn't slip my mind, but I paid the dance tuition and entry fees," muttered Dad.

"Oh, stop it, you guys. Yes, Jackson shoved me. I fell against the wall and lost my balance as I tried to keep my dog from attacking the Jack Ass. Anyway, as I started tumbling down the stairs, Hairy freaked out and came after me. My dog stopped my fall about halfway down."

"Thank god for the wee dust mop," said Kirk.

I rolled my eyes as I bit back the chuckle. "Yes, and thank god the wee dust mop did not attack Jackson when I fell. I had to hang on to my darling little dust mop with all my might because Hairy intended to go back up those stairs and eat him some Jack Ass for supper."

Dad nodded his head as he continued to rub my back. "What a good boy. I understand Hairy wanting to take a bite out of Jack. Especially considering that I—"

"Want to bite his ears off. Yes, we understood that the first time you said it, Daddy."

Kirk nodded in agreement as he exhaled a long string of smoke rings. "I understand the sentiment, too. I want to help Rick bite the ears off of the sorry bastard. He can have one ear and I can have the other. Good laddie, Hairy, good laddie indeed."

My dog grinned at Kirk as he reached down to tousle my dog's hair. Once again, I noticed my dog always loves Kirk's attention. Maybe it was the Irish brogue, who knows?

Later, everyone left for the night except for Liz's family, who all settled down in the bedroom. After all, it is her apartment located atop her bar. Oops, her fine eatery. Baby Isis hunkered down in her porta-crib, Theo fell asleep on the rollaway, and Ari and Liz snuggled into the king-sized bed. Hairy and I settled down on the queen-sized sofa bed in the living room. My gorgeous, coal black Skye terrier snuggled up close to me and slurped his tongue across my face, and I chuckled. "I love you, Hairy Potter. Kirk is right: you are a good laddie."

I love you, too, Mama.

I smiled as I heard my dog's words in my head. My family teased me whenever I told them Hairy and I could communicate by telepathy, but Hairy and I have had a special link since he was a puppy. Nonna, my maternal grandmother, now deceased, admitted to me she could hear the voice of one of her dogs years ago, too, but it had only happened with that one dog. Nonna described that long-ago canine as her 'heart dog.' I figured I inherited the tendency from Nonna. Hairy's tail thumped as I bent over to push his hair from his face to kiss his brow. Hairy smiled his doggie smile at me again, slurped another kiss across my cheek before he yawned, made a circle on the quilt, and then laid down beside me to drop asleep. A smile flitted across my lips as my dog snored.

If only I could fall asleep with such ease. Let me tell you: insomnia sucks.

I lay there, counting the stars through the window, and 'pondering the esoteric,' as my dad puts it. Could I have done anything differently, so Jack and I would not have arrived at this point in our marriage? Mom always told me, hasty to wed, repent at leisure. God only knew I had been repenting of my rash decision to marry Jackson Talbott for at least the past four years of our six-year marriage. He was a Jack Ass, but he was my Jack Ass, at least until Robin claimed him.

Perhaps this was my reward for calling him 'Jack Ass' for all these years. No, I thought with a shake of my head, that was not true. I caught him cheating long before Robin, just never with a friend. You would think a man would have some limits, wouldn't you?

Sighing, I tossed over to the other side. Fine, Robin could have the sorry excuse for a man. Mother always taught me to give away my used toys to more needy children when I was through playing with them. It sure looked like Robin needed Jackson more than I did. Even Jack Ass Talbott was a better catch than Sonny Cangelosi had ever been. At least Jack was not involved with the Mafia. Still, it hurt like hell to know Jack tossed me over for my friend. Oops, my former friend.

Was it my fault he cheated, like he said during our quarrel that last day? Did I pay too much attention to my law practice and dog shows, and not enough attention to poor little Jackie Boy? I loved my job and my dog. In contrast, I hated to sail because I always got seasick. Jack wanted to be on the water sailing his blasted boat every minute he was not working. He made it clear from the start after we bought his boat he resented me for not enjoying his favorite sport. I never pointed out I resented all the time he spent away from home to be on the water, or because he refused to step foot in a dog show. Robin loved to sail, and like a fool, I encouraged the pretty young woman to go sailing with my Jack Ass.

I sighed as I flipped over again. Jack and I drifted away from each other so early in our marriage. Maybe this result was inevitable.

It looked like he would soon be hers. She would figure out soon enough that once a cheater, always a cheater. I thought she figured that out with Sonny Cangelosi. But, hey, Jack made much better money than Sonny Cangelosi, and at least, Jack's earnings were legit. Jack appeared to love Robin's clinginess and dependency upon him. Nothing like enabling behavior to prove you love her, you know.

It must have been close to 4 A.M. before I fell asleep.

Chapter 2
Robin and Jack

"Where have you been all morning?"

Robin's heart galloped with anxiety at the belligerent sound of Sonny's anger-filled voice on the phone. She loathed it when Sonny adopted that tone with her. He always sounded irritated just before he knocked her senseless. She realized Jack would not tolerate Sonny striking her again, but Sonny could still frighten her with a single word. She struggled to draw a calming breath before she responded to him. "I have been right here all morning. Why?"

"You bring Mike over here at noon because the social study gal comes today to supplement her report."

"Wait a minute, Sonny. The court requires you to see Mikey at the Safe Center. The judge directed me not to take him to your home, and this is not your weekend to see him." Robin's voice quivered. The prospect of disagreeing with Sonny always caused her to feel nauseated. She motioned for Jack to pick up the extension phone so he could listen to the call.

Jack narrowed his eyes, and as he grasped what she meant, he nodded and lifted the receiver.

Mike, four years old but already aware of his father's temper, began sucking his thumb as his mom continued to speak with Sonny on the phone. Mike cringed as his father's voice thundered out again.

"Fuck da order. I don't give a flying rat's ass what dat order states. Dat cursed woman will be here at noon, and she wants to observe Mike with the little woman and me. You carry my boy over here so she can observe us together. Make certain you have him here before noon, *capisce?*"

Robin felt far too terrified to tell Sonny what she wanted to say. If she told him what she longed to tell him, he would come right over and beat the life out of her. She raised one hand as if to beg Jack, "What shall I tell him?"

Jack shook his head 'no' as he mouthed the word.

Robin drew a deep breath and squared her shoulders. "Sonny, I'm sorry, but I can't bring him over there. You may not care about breaking the law, but I do. The judge said-"

"And I said fuck da judge and his stinking order. Who does that bastard think he is, telling me when and where I can see my son? That I can't see my son in my home? Never heard such *merda* in my life. That *testa de cazzo* knows nothing. Listen, Robin, if youse knows what's good for you, youse have dat boy here at my house before noon today, or youse gonna be damned sorry."

Robin jumped as he banged the phone down. For heaven's sake, Sonny called the judge a *testa de cazzo,* a dickhead. He did not use the phrase often, and when he did, he was damned angry. Her pulse raced like a runaway stallion, and she still quivered from fear. After a pause, Jack and Robin hung up both phones as well. She wrung her sweaty palms together. "My god, Jack, what do I do?"

Jack frowned, his mouth tightening in frustration. "Babe, you cannot capitulate and take Mike over there. Sonny wants you to throw down the towel and accept defeat."

She gulped as she continued to wring her hands together. "But, Jackson, you heard him. If I don't…"

"Darling, there is no 'but' here. You cannot take Mike over there, period. Call the social study investigator and advise her what he demanded, and the thinly veiled threat that you would have hell to pay if you don't comply. Oh, and be sure to tell her whatever he called the judge in Italian, *testa* something or other."

"He called the judge a dickhead," she answered, her voice soft and trembling.

"Yeah, that's it. Be sure to tell her. Helen Broward will know what he's trying to pull. She is an objective, well experienced reporter, and she will see right through his abusive bull. I tell you, babe, Helen will understand what Sonny is trying to pull. Explain Sonny called and demanded you bring Mike over for her home interview, and he warned 'you'll be sorry' if you don't take Mike. Apologize and remind her the judge's visitation order states Sonny gets supervised visits at the Safe Center only. Explain you cannot take Mike over to his dad's house for an interview with his dad today because it would defy the judge's explicit orders, and you fear what might happen if you take Mike there as well. Hell, I bet he would run with him."

She nodded, as if excited Jack understood. "That's my concern, Jackie."

He pulled her into his arms for a hug. "Sonny realizes the Center won't allow anybody except parents to visit there, and he wants to squeeze in an unauthorized visit."

Mike tugged on Jack's pant leg. "Can I have my donut now, Uncle Jack? I'm hungry."

Jack sounded uneasy as he chuckled. "Sure, tiger. Do you want a glass of milk with your donut?"

Mikey nodded and watched in silence as Jack poured a cup of milk for him. The sweet little boy beamed as Jack gave him the donut and helped him get the cup of milk to the table so Mikey could eat his breakfast. "Thank you, Uncle Jack."

The phone rang again, and Robin glanced at Jack, nibbling her lip. "Oh, Jack, this doesn't look good."

"Maybe not so good for him. Where's the tape recorder?" Jack answered.

She grimaced. "It's in the bedroom, same place as always. Why?"

He headed for the bedroom. "I'll make sure it's hooked up. We need to use it when Sonny calls."

"Why on earth would we record his calls? And isn't that illegal?" Robin continued to frown as she followed Jack.

"It's not illegal to record phone calls in Texas as long as one person on the call knows the call is being recorded. Sara will need recordings of these calls so she can use them against Sonny in court."

Chapter 3
Sara

Elizabeth stood shaking my shoulder as she tried to awaken me. "Sis, wake up. You need to get a move on if you are supposed to meet Aunt Maggie at her office in Clear Lake City at 3."

I pushed her off the first half dozen times she tried to rouse me, but I awoke enough to raise up at last. "Huh? Oh shit, what time is it?"

"Half-past twelve. I know you want a shower before you meet with Aunt Maggie today. Here, I brought you a cup of coffee."

She handed me a piping hot cup of coffee, and I took a long sip. "God bless you, Liz. I might live now that I have a cup of coffee."

"Rough night?" she asked with a worried frown.

Nodding, I swallowed another sip of coffee. "Yeah, I tossed as much as I turned. It had to be after 4 before I fell asleep. The coffee hits the spot. Thanks, sis."

I hustled to the bathroom for a quick shower. The hot water pelted on my aching muscles and helped me relax for the first time in days. Once out of the shower, Liz handed me a glass of orange juice and a homemade breakfast taco. I devoured both as I blow dried my hair, put on makeup with care to cover the remaining discoloration around my eye, and pulled on clothing appropriate to meet a fellow attorney. Hairy sat by my side, watching for errant crumbs that might fall from my breakfast taco as I dressed. Once dressed, I squared my shoulders, took a deep breath, grabbed Robin's case file, and headed out the door with just enough time to make it to Aunt Maggie's office by 3.

Maggie Henson was my Grampa Henson's niece, my mother's cousin and my second cousin. However, I grew up in the south, where children call everyone older than themselves 'Aunt This' or 'Uncle That.' Southern children do not address their elders by their first names without the requisite 'Aunt' or 'Uncle.' By the same token, we learn at an early age to say 'yes, sir' or 'no, ma'am.' Our parents reprimand us if we fail to address our elders with proper respect. I worked for Aunt Maggie during law school at Bates College of Law and for two years after I graduated until the Jack Ass convinced me to go into practice on my own. That was the biggest mistake of my life, other than marrying my personal Jack Ass. As Mom says, marry in haste, repent at leisure.

Aunt Maggie grinned as I opened the door and entered her plush Clear Lake offices. She halfway arose from her chair at the conference table and motioned towards the coffee pot. "Come in, Sara, and grab a cup of coffee. Let's talk about this mess."

My cheeks reddened, and I forced a grin. "Thanks, Aunt Mags. I appreciate you are helping me."

She poured herself another cup of coffee and walked over to the conference table. "Tell me what's going on."

I took a deep breath. It is difficult to tell someone you respect as your aunt, as a fellow attorney, and as a former employer that you are a royal dumb ass. "The same old, same old. Jack cheated on me again."

She nodded as she leaned back in her chair. "Yeah, I figured as much. Go on."

Aunt Maggie took another sip of her coffee and waited for me to weave my tale of woe.

I put my requisite two sugars and a dollop of my favorite flavored creamer into my cup before I took a seat at the conference table. Aunt Maggie knows my preferences and bought the Irish Cream Delight creamer just for me. I took a sip of the coffee, along with a deep breath to steady my nerves before I spoke. "Last Sunday afternoon, I worked in the loft upstairs, preparing my exhibits and questions for the Cangelosi trial. They had been out sailing most of the day. We have the social study and the other evidence in our ball court. Robin's ex, Sonny Cangelosi, is a complete and total loser. Sonny got out of the state penitentiary a year ago, and that was his third trip to the joint, mind you. The big goon still reeks from his latest stay in the state's rehab unit for drug offenders. Sonny is six foot one, two hundred sixty pounds, all solid muscle, beefed up from the jail yard and covered in jailhouse tattoos. He shaves his enormous head smooth as a baby's ass..." My voice broke off as I realized my unknown visitor from the preceding night could not have been Sonny. Who could it have been? I cleared my throat. "And Sonny has a five o'clock shadow that never quits. I figure he looks like he needs a shave a few minutes after the big palooka shaves. Sonny Cangelosi is the scary, chronic, repeat offender who always kept me from becoming serious about criminal defense practice. I wouldn't want to meet the man on a dark street. Heck, I never want to run into him anywhere, period. Sonny scares me enough when I encounter him at the courthouse. He still does not have a steady job a year after his release from prison, and still lacks a safe, stable home environment for Mike. That he reappeared and sought custody of this child a couple months after his most recent release from prison for drug possession and trafficking always struck me as beyond bizarre, if not downright ballsy. It is incomprehensible to me that he wants the child. He never paid an iota of interest in Mike before this. Since his release, Sonny shacked up with an adorable little drug-addicted hooker named 'Buffy.' She gave birth to his baby six months after his release from prison. Yes, sure, like I believe little Maybelline could be his baby."

"They named the poor child Maybelline? Good grief, Sara. But maybe she conceived the baby on a conjugal visit," said Maggie, as her finger tapped on the side of her coffee cup.

I rolled my eyes and took a big breath and another sip of coffee as I noticed my hands trembled. The tremors were not from the caffeine. They were from the adrenaline rushing through my veins as I recalled the events of that horrible afternoon. I took another deep breath and continued. "Yeah, so they claim. I've still got my doubts Sonny fathered the baby, but, oh, well, not my problem. Anyway, Sonny never tried to see Mike when released from prison until the Attorney General's office socked him with a child support order. Now, he wants Mike to live with them. Oh, give me a freaking break. He wants custody of Mike so he can avoid paying child support, and it would tickle the sorry lout silly if he could control Robin. In contrast, Robin has a steady job as a phlebotomist at UTMB. She won't get rich in her job, but it is honest, steady work. Robin has a safe and stable home. In fact, she rents one of our rental properties, a nice three-bedroom brick home overlooking Clear Lake."

"Sounds nice," said Aunt Maggie.

I nodded. "It is. We remodeled it before she moved in. The previous renter did a helluva job damaging the place."

Maggie leaned forward, nodding. "I remember that. They took a hammer to the fireplace, kicked in all the doors, and left the water running when they left."

"Yes, and they knocked the faucets off in the shower and tub after they turned the water on full blast. It cost us $30,000 over what the insurance paid us to fix the place up. Believe me, it pissed off my ever-frugal accountant husband to the tenth degree to pay for those repairs."

She let out a low whistle. "I bet it pissed him off. Did you file criminal charges on them?" she asked.

I shrugged and shook my head. "Neither the insurance company nor I could find the sorry asses. We hired private investigators, but the people hid well. I figure they use an alias name now."

"Well, that's a bummer," murmured my aunt.

"You reckon? Anyway, to get back to my story, Robin supported Mike throughout her pregnancy and the entire time Sonny has been in and out of prison. Jeez-Louise, how could we lose with these facts? Oh, yeah, maybe because Robin forgot to mention she is balling my husband."

I winced as she arched a brow and 'tsked.' "Wait a minute. Do you mean Jack's latest conquest is Robin Cangelosi?"

I nodded as unbidden tears welled up in my eyes and I took another long swig of coffee. I pushed back from the conference table to walk over to the picture window overlooking the lake before I answered her. "Yeah, like I said, they often go sailing together."

"It looks like your plan bit you on your petite derriere, big time. Go on."

I gulped. "Yeah, pretty much. This sordid mess bit me square on my ass. Listen, Aunt Mags, I have other serious, life-altering issues with Robin, but

I'm the first to admit she is a decent mom. A dozen collateral contacts substantiated her parenting ability in a rock-solid social study. I told Robin she had this in the bag a jillion times. She would get all freaky and hysterical, telling me she knew she would lose Mike to 'Cagey,' as they know Cangelosi in the mob. Oh, Sonny is a far sight better than his brother. I understand Bruno 'Il Bruto' Cangelosi makes Sonny look like one of the Twelve Disciples."

With another sip of my coffee to calm my nerves, I resumed telling my story to Aunt Maggie. "Anyway, on the infamous afternoon in question, I sat working away on her case in the loft while Hairy sat at my feet, gnawing at his favorite Nylabone. I hung up the phone with some guy who called for the umpteenth time for Jack. I explained again to the impatient man Jack went sailing on his boat and had not returned home. The damned man called me a liar once, and I hung up on him. He called back and kept yelling something at me in a language I could not understand. Hell, Maggie, I speak Spanish, French and Italian besides English, and the ass was not speaking any of those. It might have been Arabic or Russian, I don't know. As my mama would say, 'he sounded right foreign.'"

Aunt Maggie laughed. "I can hear Melanie saying that."

I grinned at Maggie. "Me, too. I quit answering the man's calls when I grew sick of his insane ranting at me."

"What happened next?" Aunt Maggie asked as she handed me a Kleenex.

I dabbed the tissue at my tear-dampened cheek and tried to smile. "Thanks, Aunt Maggie. Hairy growled, and I refocused on the world of the living, not the distant realm of the law. You know I get tunnel vision while I prepare for trial."

She smiled. "Yes, I remember your tunnel vision. It's part of the reason you are so damned good at your job."

I felt my cheeks heat with color. "Thank you, ma'am. I looked up from the computer screen and realized my dog sat up and began growling towards the stairs. Hairy loves to imitate a rug and plop on the floor at my feet. He got my attention when he sat up and growled. I realized Jack and Robin had returned to the house, and a hot and heavy argument was underway downstairs. I bent over, scratched Hairy's head, and said, 'Come on.' He thumped his tail, jumped up, and ran to the stairs with a quick bark. As he turned to make sure I followed him, I chuckled. It seemed I could almost hear my dog say, 'let's go, Mama.' Anyway, I paused when I reached the stairs, because I realized this was much more serious than a simple argument. Jack's salt and pepper hair was askew, and he had anger on his face. Robin's always perfect Texas Big Hair stood out in total disarray like a drunken chimpanzee tried to style her hair. She looked like she had been in a Category 4 hurricane. Mascara streaked down her cheeks in tacky black runnels from her tears, and her lipstick smeared across her face. She looked like Tammy Faye Bakker on a bad makeup day."

Aunt Maggie laughed. "That's funny, Sara, but how do you know about Tammy Faye Bakker?"

I shrugged again. "Daddy uses the analogy. I looked Tammy Faye up once on Wikipedia. My god, that woman was a hot mess. Anyway, to get back to my story, I looked over the loft ledge down to the foyer, and I saw her grab Jack's shirt sleeve as she begged him to reconsider something. I did not know what she wanted him to rethink at that point. He frowned, pushed her off and came up the stairs."

Maggie tilted her head. "Interesting. What did he say when he got upstairs?"

"Oh, well, I could not make out their words yet, but she kept after him while they walked up the stairs. Jackson shoved her once, and I yelled, 'Jack, don't!' Do not ask me why, but I didn't want him to knock her down the stairs."

"It's because you're a good person. Then what happened next?" Aunt Maggie asked with a frown.

"He shrugged loose from her and came upstairs with her still tugging on his shirt. Hairy growled louder and more menacing, the growl that means, 'don't you mess with my Mama.'"

I paused, unable to continue as the events of the day replayed in my mind.

She nodded. "Go on, Sara."

As I took another deep, ragged breath, I realized I had twisted the Kleenex into a useless wad. With a trembling hand, I reached over for another tissue. "Well, my stomach flip-flopped as Robin's tear-dampened baby blues cut to Jack's steel greys. His eyes filled with expected angst and inexplicable anger. Hairy growled again as the hair on his neck raised and he positioned himself between Jack and me. Jack came over to me and grabbed my arm. 'Listen, Sara.' Uh, oh, not good, I thought. Truth be told, I didn't like the manic look in his eyes, and I pulled back, scared he might hit me."

"Again." Maggie looked grim. She had heard my stories before about Jack Talbott.

I gulped and nodded and dabbed the tissue at my still-leaking eyes again. "Yeah, again. He gets that look in his eyes before he roughs me up. Anyway, Jack kind of pushed me backwards to get away from my dog. I stumbled backwards towards my desk and kept one hand up to ward off any blow that might come my way. And then he stunned me. He said, 'Sara, we need to talk.' 'Okay. Talk, Jackson,' I said, and I tried to brace myself for the worst. He already knew what he was going to say. Robin started crying and reached out towards his arm. 'Jack, not now, not like this. Please, wait. I'm begging you.' Her voice trembled with emotions she barely kept in check. About then, I realized he reached out and took her hand to stroke it with an unexpected tenderness. 'It's okay, darling. Everything will be okay. You'll see, Sara will understand.'"

Pausing, I took another long sip of my coffee, surprised to see my hands still trembled.

"It's all right. Take your time. We have all afternoon." Maggie said, her voice soft and controlled, and she reached over to stroke my trembling hand.

I tried to smile and reached over to pat her hand before I continued. "Thanks, Aunt Maggie. When he said that, my heart shattered into a million little pieces. How could I understand? He uttered those sweet nothings to Robin, not to me. To my client, my friend. I could not remember the last time he used that caressing, loving tone with me. Of course, his track record with me was less than stellar. He cheated, and like a fool, I always forgave his indiscretions. Why would he think I wouldn't forgive him this time, too, I thought. I swallowed hard and tried to compose myself for the big revelation about to occur. I blinked as I tried to clear the unshed tears from my vision and struggled to speak. How could my mouth grow that yucky, nasty fuzz so fast? I took another deep breath. 'Jackson, what do you want to say?' He blinked as he realized what he had just called Robin. I guess when you get caught—again—you somehow find your courage to man up. 'This wasn't how I intended to tell you.' I took another deep breath. 'Tell me what, Jack?' I meant to keep my voice calm and low, but I must have sounded awful because Jack flinched, although I don't know if he flinched because of my tone or because of Robin's quiet, unrelenting sobs. He squared his shoulders as his lips thinned. 'Don't be mean, Sara.' I huffed up and put my hands on my hips. I figure I looked like Lady Bad Ass. 'Oh, give me a break, Jackson. I thought you were going to tell me about your affair with my client—oh, let me correct myself, with my friend, while we stand here in my home. You know, the same client who I represent in an ongoing freaking custody battle. Foolish me, I thought you were being mean to me. Please correct my error in judgment.'"

"Maggie, I cringed as a note of hysteria crept into my voice. I figured he would either smack me or hug me. I prayed it would be the hug. Oh, please, Jack, I thought, please tell me I'm wrong, but about then, Robin sobbed and he gathered her into his arms. I knew I was about to hurl. Yes, my words sounded mean. After all, I grew more upset by the minute. The muscle in my right cheek twitched, and I hate it when it does that because it's the sign I am upset and about to lose control. I blinked back those damned threatening tears because I would not, could not, let the damned man see me cry. He never saw me cry when he admitted his other indiscretions, and by damn, he would not see me cry this time, either. Dammit, Mags, we have been married six years, and I never cheated, and believe me, I've had some damn fine offers. In fact, I thought about it once or twice. I never cheated. Listen, I know I'm not gorgeous, but I'm a decent-looking woman, and I'm still a size two, just like I was in college when I met Jackson. I work out four times a week to stay in shape. I have pretty skin, firm if small breasts, and a nice, tight little butt, and yet he cheated over and over."

"Don't put yourself down, Sara. You are a beautiful young woman."

I reached over and squeezed her hand. "Thank you, Maggie. Well, Jack could bet his sweet ass I was upset, and I'm sure I sounded mean as a jail yard dog at that point."

She laughed, and with her blue eyes twinkling, she asked, "Don't you mean a junkyard dog?"

I chuckled. "No, I meant jail yard. Those guard dogs are downright mean."

Pausing, I relived that horrible afternoon. I dabbed my cheeks, blew my nose, took another ragged breath and resumed telling my story. "And then, Robin let out a blood-curdling screech. Jack turned back towards her, all solicitous again. 'What's wrong, babe?' I cringed and glared at my husband. Robin sniffed. 'That awful dog pissed on my foot!' Jack was about to tear into me about Hairy urinating on his little sweetums, when my darling Hairy raised his leg and urinated on Jack's leg, too. Jackson struggled to hold his temper. He clenched and unclenched his fists several times before he gave in to his anger, reached over and shoved me hard. It impressed me he didn't kick Hairy. I think he realized all hell would break loose if he hurt my dog, not to mention Hairy might have bitten him. Anyway, Jack took a deep breath before he spoke to me. 'I want a divorce.'"

"Wow, I did not expect him to utter those words. I blinked and struggled to straighten up from his verbal sucker punch to my gut. I remember I nodded. 'Fine, you can have one.' I was about to turn and retreat to my room, and I began planning a nice 70-30 split as I would Take His Sorry Cheating Ass to the Cleaners, as we divorce lawyers put it."

"Then what?" Maggie asked as she struggled to keep her poker face.

"He reached out, grabbed my arm, and got this nasty grin on his face. 'Don't you want to know why?' I shook my head and rubbed my arm where he grabbed me. I saw a bruise already forming from the pressure he exerted on my arm. I blinked back the tears burning at my eyes. Hell, no, I did not need him to tell me why he wanted a divorce, but I saw he wanted to make a big production for Robin. I remember I did not want to cry in front of Robin or him. 'No, not really. You can have a divorce if you want a divorce.' He glanced back at Robin. I struggled not to look at her. I feared what I might say if I looked at Robin right then while upset. Jack looked at Robin and said, 'See? I told you she wouldn't care.'"

My voice cracked. I glanced down and realized my hands shook like crazy again. I took another sip of my coffee and tried to center myself. Not that it worked. After taking a sip of coffee and a couple of deep breaths, I continued telling my story. "Robin just blinked. She looked stunned. And, like a fool, I responded to the blasted man. 'Who said I don't care? You can have a divorce, but I care.' Jack turned back to me, his face beet red, his nostrils pinched together like he smelled something vile, his smile thin, hard. His eyes had that crazy look he gets when he was about to tear into me. Scary, yes, he looked downright scary. It always amazes me such a handsome man can look so ugly when angry."

"Not me. I have seen him like that before, and he terrified me," Maggie said, her voice thoughtful.

I paused as I thought back to the time of the party. "Oh, yeah, the office Christmas party at the Galvez."

She nodded as a look of disgust washed across her face. "Damned straight, the office Christmas party at the Galvez Hotel ballroom. Jack got mad over some nonsense, and his entire face and his demeanor changed. He looked like he smelled something gross, and he slapped you right there in front of God and everyone at the party. The damned man slapped hard enough that it shocked me the force of the blow did not knock you over. Your hand flew up to your face and your eyes rounded in shock."

"The slap in front of God and everyone shocked me. We'd been married less than a year then," I demurred.

She shook her head. "Yeah. We all stared at him, shocked by his behavior. Ashley came over to you, took you by the arm, and took you to the ladies' room while Dean and Mike cornered Jackson. Linda and I joined Ashley and you in the ladies' lounge. I tried to get you to leave him that night, but you refused. I always said you should have left the sorry bastard after that horrifying incident, although I know he started knocking you around long before that party. Hell, I know he started hitting you before then because I remember the bruises you tried to shrug off time after time. I always figured he caused your miscarriage."

I ducked my head, overwhelmed with shame. These things should not happen to an attorney, especially one known around town as a land shark. "Well... yes, ma'am, maybe."

She stared at me like she wanted to smack me, and I must have cringed back. Her face softened, and she reached over to gather my hands into hers. "Oh, Sara, honey, I would not hit you. My god, girl, I love you."

I struggled not to cry. "I love you, too, Aunt Mags, and I'm lucky I have you in my life."

It was hard, but somehow I resisted the temptation to tell her, 'but Jack used to swear he loved me, too, and he hit me lots of times.'

"Where were you all last week? Why didn't you come in here on Monday morning?"

I shrugged. "I'm staying at the apartment over Liz's bar. He can't get to me there. I called your office eight or ten times starting Monday morning. I ran you down in the courthouse Thursday when you hadn't called me back."

She looked shocked. "I swear I am going to kill my worthless receptionist one of these days."

I giggled. "Well, don't kill Sami. Fire her, and I'll take her job."

Her shocked look turned indignant. "Honey, you are a damned fine attorney. You have a thriving law practice. You do not need to grab a receptionist's job. I'll fire Sami, and you come back as my partner. Ashley can be the receptionist and paralegal. Ashley gets along great with Linda, and together they are a fabulous paralegal team. Hell, better yet, she can be our law clerk. Ashley can join the firm as an associate once she completes law school next year and passes the bar exam. Okay, I take it Jackson has not filed for divorce yet?"

I shook my head. "No, I checked, and he had filed nothing by Friday afternoon, according to a clerk I spoke with in the Harris County district clerk's office. I haven't talked to Jack since I ran out of the house last Sunday. Do you want the rest of the story?"

"Holy Sweet Baby Jesus, you mean there is more? Yes, go on."

I took another gimongous breath. "I haven't told my family all of this. Daddy and Kirk already want to have an 'enlightening meeting' with him, as Dad put it."

She chuckled. "I can hear Rick saying that."

"Dad says he wants to bite Lover Boy's ears off. Kirk wants to help."

"Oh, dear lord, I hope you talked them out of that cockamamie idea," she answered.

I nodded. "I think I did. Anyway, Jack grabbed my wrist then. 'Ooh, poor little Sara, huh? It's always about you. No, Sara, not this time. You are a miserable excuse for a wife. My god, Sara, you're never there for me. You're always working or with that damned mutt.' Hairy crept closer to me, growling a little louder than before. 'Hairy, down,' I said. 'Behave, Hairy. That's not true, Jack, and you know it. I get seasick. I vomited on your boat the last time I went with you, so I don't go sailing anymore.' He glared at me, you know, that 'if looks could kill' look. 'You did that on purpose,' he growled at me. I shook my head. 'No, I did not. My god, why would a person throw up on purpose, Jackson? That was the reason you used to make me clean up the boat afterwards. I will never forget standing in the car wash scrubbing down your boat while I sobbed. I didn't realize you would start fucking my clients when I quit going out on the boat with you.'"

My voice broke, and I gasped for air. I realized more than my hands trembled; I trembled all over.

Maggie drew her breath in. "Oh, my god, Sara, what did he say then?"

I shrugged again. "He looked livid and his face turned red. He balled up his fists, and it scared me he would punch me, but he just slapped me. 'Take it back. That's not true.' Like a fool, I said, 'Then why is she here with you now, crying and begging you not to tell me? Did you tell her we had sex last night? I bet you told her I'm never available.'"

I swiped at a tear sliding down my cheek with the back of my hand. "Sorry, I didn't mean to cry."

Some things are too difficult to tell your attorney, I realized with a start. No, I could not tell her about that last, horrible night. Hell, I could tell no one.

Maggie handed me the box of Kleenex, the essential item in every family lawyer's office. "It's okay, you may cry. Go on."

I wiped my nose with the tissue and started again. "Well, Robin's eyes were enormous as soup plates at that, and I knew I nailed it. 'You lied to her, just like you lie to me. Admit it, Jackson.' And then things went to hell in a hand basket, with him yelling at me I was a lying, frigid bitch, her screaming, begging him not to hit me, and him smacking me so hard it knocked me into the wall at the edge of the stairs. Hairy went freaking balls to the wall nuts then and began barking like crazy, snarling and showing his teeth. I grabbed for Hairy and I must have lost my balance, because I tumbled down the stairs as I grabbed for my dog. It terrified me my dog would bite Jack and then Jack would insist I have my 'mad dog' put down. I lost my balance and rolled down the stairs."

"Oh, hell no. I know better than that. Jackson shoved you down the stairs to look like a big man for his lover. Quit making excuses for him, Sara." Maggie looked furious.

I wiped my tears and blew my nose. "Yeah, maybe so. Anyway, I hung on to Hairy. As soon as I caught my breath, I pulled Hairy and myself up and I ran down the rest of the stairs. My knees knocked together so hard I feared I would fall again. Robin looked shocked and stared at me, wordless. I grabbed my purse and keys, threw Hairy in my car, and sat there sobbing for a couple of minutes before I collected myself enough to drive to Liz's club. I knew I would be safe in the apartment. Monday, I drove home after I confirmed Jack went to the Harris County Courthouse to testify in a trial. I retrieved my files, some clothes, and dog supplies. Hairy and I have stayed at the apartment over Liz's bar ever since."

Maggie stared at me, shaking her head before she spoke. "My god, girl, that's when you should have had the locks changed and retaken possession of your house. You know you're an idiot, right?"

I nodded. "Yes, I-I know. I was too scared, Aunt Mags. I didn't want to risk him coming back and breaking in the house. God knows what he would have done then."

Aunt Maggie frowned as her lips narrowed. She crossed her arms and began tapping one foot. "Dammit, you should have left him years ago after that blasted Christmas party. Jackson Talbott is crazy mean. I swear, Jack has a narcissistic personality disorder. The man may be a sociopath. You know, I urged you to leave him back then. Sara, you deserve better than the likes of that sorry man."

I struggled not to cry again, so I nodded. Jack knew Maggie wanted me to leave him and somehow convinced me to quit my job instead of divorcing him. Oh my god, I never meant to hurt you. I love you, babe, he said, and I promise on my mother's grave, I'll never hurt you again.

She pulled the case folder in front of her. "Is everything in the file?"

I nodded. "Oh, yes, except the supplemental social study report. Helen hasn't filed her supplemental report yet. Her original report and the psych evals are here, and all of those reports recommend Robin keep custody of little Mike. He is an adorable little boy, and I love him to the moon and back. The custody evaluator delineated forty-five pages of reasons Sonny Cangelosi and his lovely child bride should not have custody of Mike. She talked to the ten references Robin supplied and the three Sonny provided. One of Sonny's references was his new wife, a second was his parole officer."

Maggie looked up at me. "You must be joking."

I shook my head. "I shit you not, Aunt Mags, and it gets better. His third reference was his brother, Bruno, whose rap sheet is longer than Sonny's."

"Good grief," she muttered as she wrote notes.

I reached over and tried to smile as I squeezed her arm. "The court investigator said Robin appears to have a stable home, stable job, and Mike has a safe and stable home environment with his mother. Sonny can offer Mike none of those things. He paid no child support in over a year since his release from prison. He has not visited Mikey except under supervision, and he endangered Mikey on repeated occasions, which is why the judge ordered his visits to be supervised. It's also why the social study investigator cannot see Sonny with Mikey."

"The Judge won't allow investigators to observe visits at the Safe Center," said Maggie as she jotted down more notes.

"Exactly. Oh, yeah, Helen commended Robin for putting Mike's needs first, not taking Mike to his dad's house for visits, and for putting her social life on hold through all this."

"Ouch." Aunt Maggie winced.

"Yeah, isn't that one amusing? Plus, Cangelosi claims he impregnated Baby Cakes when she paid a conjugal visit to him at the Big House. He figured he could get custody of Mike if he had a half-sibling in the house."

Maggie blinked. "Are you serious?"

I nodded. "As the plague."

I started crying again, you know, that full-blown, ugly crying we gals hate to do. We call it ugly crying because our skin gets red blotches, our noses drip snot, and we just look like a hot messes in action. Aunt Maggie reached over and handed me another Kleenex, and I wiped my cheeks as I struggled to regain my composure. "I'm Mikey's godmother, and I love that little boy to the moon and back. Jackson Talbott may be an ass, but he is still a far sight better than her psychotic, drug pushing ex-husband. The psych evaluation pegged Sonny as schizophrenic. I thought he was bipolar, but he told the forensic psychologist he hears voices tell him what to do. The psychologist did not believe Sonny when he spoke about the voices he hears over his phone. I would have thought the voices emanated from using too much meth or crack, although I thought Sonny was too smart to do either, since most pushers don't use those poisons. Last of all, I believe Sonny Cangelosi is in the Mob. Hell, Jack can be a total Jack Ass, but Sonny Cangelosi can be the Son of Satan. I would never let the man know it, but Sonny Cangelosi scares me shitless."

Her eyes narrowed. "Hmph. I would think after Jackson, nothing would scare you, Sara."

Wordlessly, I shrugged again as I struggled to compose myself.

Maggie reviewed the file and then looked up at me. "Okay, call Robin and tell her I will substitute in as counsel of record for her. Warn her Jack should not live with her and Mike during the pendency of this case and the trial."

"I don't have any idea what they are doing, nor do I care."

Chapter 4
Sara

My cell phone rang as I walked into the apartment from my conference with Maggie. I grabbed it from my handbag before I checked caller ID, and then winced as I realized Jack was on the other end of the call.

"Where have you been all afternoon?"

I rolled my eyes as I bristled at his acerbic tone. "And hello to you, too, Mr. Talbott. I've been out. Why?"

As I smirked, I could almost see Jack grinding his teeth. I flicked imaginary lint off my blouse.

"Cangelosi must have called Robin fifteen times today about seeing Mike. We tried to call you on your cell for advice, but you did not bother to answer or call back."

I sniffed. "Sorry, I did not realize you called. I silenced my phone. However, Robin knows as well as I do Sonny has supervised visits at the Safe Center. He sees Mike on the first and third Saturdays of the month from 9 to 12, under their supervision. This is Sunday and the second weekend of the month. The orders do not entitle Sonny to a visit today. So, what's the problem?"

I could almost see Jack pulling his hair out. Of course, he wouldn't pull it out because he was too vain about his 'glorious locks of gold,' but I could tell this could get to be fun.

"The damned man threatened her. What should she do?" Jack's words were so clipped they could have frosted the nuts off a chipmunk.

"Oh, for the love of… Call the cops, not me. Sounds like a criminal matter. Not my problem." I snapped my words tight and crisp right back at him. "And don't take that tone with me, Mr. Big Shot."

He didn't reply for a few seconds, because I startled him. "What did you say?"

"You heard me, Lover Boy. Do not take that tone with me. I do not live my life for you any longer. This is the weekend. I have my own life, and this is my time. I am not at work today, and I have no obligation to answer work-related calls. If your little sweetie has a problem, call the cops. This is not my problem. Got it?"

It felt fabulous to tell him to leave me alone.

Jack was silent except for some furious, heavy breathing for a couple of minutes. I spoke up again. "If that's all…"

"No, dammit, Sara, that is not all. The man is a psycho. You know he is nuts. He's stalking your client, Robin. You must do something."

"Whoa, hoss. You mentioned nothing about stalking before. What happened that makes you say he is stalking her? Take a breath, slow down, and tell me what happened. There must be more to this than you first told me." I rubbed my forehead. Yeah, I could feel the migraine coming on. As if I wanted to have to deal with Robin, not to mention my blasted soon-to-be ex-husband, too.

Jack's breathing slowed before he spoke. "Sonny called this morning, demanding to see Mike. Robin told him no, but he can see him next Saturday at the Center per the orders. He started cursing her. He told her the social study investigator was coming to his 'crib' today, and he wanted the woman to see Mike with him at the house. Robin told Sonny that was not her problem, and perhaps the social study investigator could see them together next Saturday at the Center, where Sonny visits. She hung up again. He called back again, ranting and raving, and told her if she hung up again, he would come over and kick her ass."

"Did you hear him say that?"

"Yeah, I picked up the extension when the phone rang. We figured it was him." Jack sounded calmer by then.

"You guys didn't bother to tape record that call, did you?" That would have been too much to ask for.

I could hear his palm hit his forehead. "Yes, but the machine did not record. It got part of the conversation, but not everything. Robin, I told you we needed to record him. She didn't want to record those calls. But I heard him, Sara—"

"And you are my husband. Just tell me, Jack, how credible does that make you as a fact witness? Better than nothing, but not much, especially if the judge figures out you are Robin's Sugar Daddy." I snapped the words at him lickety split.

"Drat, I just figured we could say I am her accountant, and I went over to help her."

"With some early Sunday morning accounting emergency? Yes, like that is a credible story. Then what happened?"

The ruse was not too bad as cover stories went. I didn't want to admit it, but they could say they were prepping for trial.

"The last time she answered, Robin told him to come on over, and the cops would await his arrival. Then she hung up. She advised the social study investigator what Sonny wanted to pull, and then she let the phone go to the machine the rest of the day. He must have called fifteen times in all. Each time, he got worse."

"So, there are recordings of the calls?" I perked up at the new information.

"Oh, yeah, at least a dozen. In the last one, he yells something in Italian. You might know what he said. I told Robin we had to call you, because this was serious. I made her leave the house. She is at the Marina Hotel with Mike." He sounded much calmer now.

"Does Mr. Nutcase know where she is?"

"Hell, no. My god, how stupid do you think I am?"

I didn't respond to his question. It was hard, but I bit my tongue.

After a second, he must have realized what he asked. After a long pause, he continued. "Uh, I told her not to call him back."

"But will she mind you?" I could not resist the subtle dig.

"Oh, yeah, she is terrified he will find her. She knows he would beat the crap out of her and take Mike. I tell you, Sara, the man is a total whack job. You gotta do something."

I took a deep breath. "No, Jack, I don't. First, if you report it to the police as a stalking or as a terroristic threat, they can get her a magistrate's protective order. That would help the custody case. This sounds like a terroristic threat, not a stalking. Second, she needs a different attorney. You know, someone who is not married to her lover. This case is way too close for comfort. Don't you understand 'conflict of interest'?"

He did not utter a word.

"Jackson? Did you hear me? Jack?"

"Come on, Sara, do it. She trusts you. Listen, babe, you know little Mike. He's been to our house before. You cannot let this psychopath hurt little Mikey."

I shut my eyes. I hate it when he calls me 'babe.' It always means he wants something.

Jack knows my biggest weaknesses are dogs and children. Children are precious to me. Four years ago, I suffered a tubal pregnancy and one of my Fallopian tubes ruptured. My ob-gyn told me I would never get pregnant afterwards without artificial insemination or fertility drugs. That was fine for Jack. He always swore he never wanted kids, anyway. It upset him when I refused to have my remaining tube tied since 'we' didn't want children. My dogs became so important to me because they fill a void in my life.

Mike is a delightful child, full of energy and life. Jack knows I would kill anyone who tried to hurt Mike. I took a ragged breath before I answered Jack. "You are a sorry bastard."

"Yes, I am."

I blinked, shocked he admitted it. I took a deep breath. "No, I won't let anyone hurt Mike, but when are you going to quit hurting me, Jackson? Why am I in the middle of this family circus? Why?"

My voice broke as a tear slid down my cheek.

As Hairy growled, I looked down and saw the hackles rising around his neck. My dog never likes it when I become upset. I reached down and patted his head, trying to soothe the savage beast in this woman's best friend. After a pause, he made the odd little snort Skye terriers make. Hairy laid his head down on top of my feet, as if he could protect me from whatever mean old bad thing upset me if his head covered my feet. But then, my dog is a big old ball of goof.

"She trusts you, Sara. I trust you."

I replicated Hairy's snort. "Oh, yeah, sure, but I don't trust either of you." I threw the words right back at him.

"She needs you."

"Of course, but she needs your glorious hunk of burning love more than she needs me to be her attorney. She needs a different attorney, Jackson. Hire her one. I will even agree to pay the retainer from our community funds. I will put it in writing. It would be my privilege, my absolute delight, to help pay for another attorney for your lover. Just, please, Jack, go hire her another attorney. I'll tell the court I'm sick, that I've had a nervous breakdown, or I- I've had a heart attack. Something. Anything." My voice broke. I did not tell him I talked to Aunt Mags or that she would take Robin's case and my divorce; I wanted to surprise him with the service of the divorce papers. However, I could not take much more of his needling and cajoling. "Please, Jack."

He still pushed. "Babe, she needs you. Sara, you know the case. Hell, you have worked it for months. You know Sonny, you know all of them. She needs you, Sara."

Damn his sorry cheating ass. The man can be so persuasive when he sets his mind on it. That sweet, easy, persuasive tone always gets juries to eat out of the palm of his hand. I swear the blasted man could sell ice in Antarctica. He sure as hell affected me right then. I did not want to cave into his pleas, but I felt my resolve weakening as the tears threatened to spill over. Dammit, I hated it when he made me cry. "I thought she needed you."

He paused a moment before he responded. "Mike needs you."

I snorted again. "Mikey has a very competent amicus attorney. And don't call me 'babe', Jackson. 'Sara Baby' was a girl you claimed you loved a long time ago, but you don't love me anymore. You haven't loved me for ages, if you ever did. Robin is your love this week. She used to be one of my dearest friends before she stabbed me right through the heart in this whole sordid mess. So, never call me 'babe' again, Jackson Talbott. You gave up that right when you started having an affair with Robin." My tears flowed, with nothing to stop them, dammit, but I somehow resisted the urge to remind him he called Robin 'babe,' now.

"That's not true. I-I loved you..." he stammered.

"Don't think about going there, Jackson, not after all we have been through over the years. Robin needs to call the cops when Sonny calls her, making threats. And do us all a favor. Get the woman another attorney. Do not depend on me. It is unreasonable to ask your wife to represent your lover when you want a divorce to marry her. That's just plain tacky." I slammed the phone down, my hands shaking.

Dara and Liz came up behind me, and Liz slipped an arm around my shoulders. I stood there sobbing with my head on her bosom, hiccuping into the wet spot my tears made in her hair. Liz remained silent as she rubbed my back until I was all cried out. "What are you going to do?"

I kind of waved my hands and shook my head. "I don't know."

She waited a minute to answer, to give me a little time to get my emotions under control. "You need a lawyer, Sara. It's time to file for divorce. Did you hire Maggie?"

After a long pause, I nodded my head. "Yes, she is preparing the paperwork. I'll sign the affidavit tomorrow, and then she will file it."

Dara nodded, her lips grim. "About damn time."

Later, as I slid into my bed, I gasped as Captain Johnny materialized before me. "I tried to keep him from reaching you."

I struggled upright. "What do you mean, Captain Johnny?"

He sighed. Let me tell you: the sound of a ghost sighing is one creepy, scary sound. "I blocked a dozen calls he made to you, but I couldn't catch the last call."

I reached over to stroke his cheek before I realized I could not stroke the cheek of a ghost. I pulled my hand back. "I appreciate you were looking out for me, Captain Johnny. Yes, he upset me. No, I did not expect him to be able to upset me anymore. But, Johnny, why were you blocking his calls?"

"I think he gave up the right to telephone you about problems his woman experiences when he treated you in the abysmal manner in which he gutted you last weekend."

The laugh tickled my throat, but I bit it back. "Gutted me, hmm? You nailed that one. Thanks, Captain Johnny. You could just give me the heads up if he tries to call, to keep me from answering his calls unless I want to talk to him."

"I suppose I could do that, Sara. It's just that-"

"Hmm, hmm…"

We both turned to see Tamsin tapping a foot. "Be careful what you say, darling."

Johnny paled at her words. "Of course, my love, you're quite right. I can do that, Sara. However, you must listen for my warnings."

Tamsin nodded as she gave him a slight smile, and I struggled not to laugh. "Fine, I'll do that, Captain Johnny."

He beamed as I blew him a kiss. Tamsin and he shimmered out of my sight.

I drove back to Maggie's office Monday morning to review my Original Petition for Divorce and the affidavit. When her legal assistant, Linda, and I finished tweaking the affidavit, Maggie signed the Petition. I signed the affidavit and Linda notarized it. I next perused the Motion to Substitute and Aunt Maggie and I signed it before my aunt handed it to her legal assistant. Then I told Aunt Maggie about the calls from Sonny to Robin and Jack's conversation with me.

Her eyes narrowed. "I thought I told you not to talk to him, Sara?"

Nodding, I felt a rush of heat as my cheeks flood with color. "Yes, I know. Before I realized who called, I answered. It won't happen again. I promise I will check caller ID in the future."

She shook her head with a wry frown. "Girl, you are a family lawyer's worst nightmare."

I tried to laugh, but it sounded a lot like the noise a frog makes. I nodded. "Yeah, I know."

Maggie shook her head again. I figured it was time to give her the letter I received from my physician. It stated I suffered from exhaustion, and he recommended I lighten my caseload because it affected my health. She nodded as a smile played upon her lips. "Okay, this almost makes up for you talking to Jackson."

I tried to smile, but I feared I resembled some horror house Jack-o'-lantern.

Linda scanned the documents and e-filed the pleadings in the respective counties.

Maggie smiled. "I should be able to have the process server pick up the service papers late today or in the morning. He will get Jackson served in his offices this evening or sometime tomorrow."

"If he misses Jack at the office, he might catch him at the hotel with Robin. Ask the process server to call me when he serves Jack so I can keep out of sight. Jack will blow a gasket."

She laughed, her pretty green eyes sparkling. "I am counting on Jack showing his proverbial ass. Dan will serve the papers on Jack, and he will call you when he serves him. My bet is Jack will call, too, but do not answer Jack's calls. Let his calls go to voice mail. I want recordings of his anger on your voice mail for the court. If you screw up and answer it, just tell him to call me, then hang up. Do not delete texts or emails, no matter how insulting or demeaning they become. Again, those will make powerful evidence. The nastier he gets, the better for you. When he calls me, I plan to tell him the jig is up, and he needs to put his money where his mouth is. He better hire a well-qualified family attorney and have him call me asap or else we will have a full-blown adversarial hearing before Little Precious's case goes back to trial."

"Ooh, down and dirty, I like that." I tried to smile.

Maggie hugged me. "That's my girl. You stay at the apartment at the bar until we meet with his attorney. Tell Ashley you are not feeling well, and you will work elsewhere."

My heart racing, I gulped. "Ashley knows what is going on. She's telling people that I'm unwell. I have my laptop at the apartment."

She nodded. "Excellent. Ashley should advise Jack to call me if he calls the office. She is not to give him any other information about you. She knows nothing on the record."

With another gulp, I nodded. "That sounds great. I don't want any trouble for Ashley. She's a wonderful legal assistant."

Maggie nodded as she wrote notes. "I agree. God knows I wish she still worked for me. Are you sure you won't come back? You could bring her with you."

I tried to grin. "I'm thinking about it."

Aunt Maggie shrugged. "Okay, I guess that's better than a flat rejection. Ralph Morrissey is going over the financials you emailed to him. He will appraise all the real estate, the boat, the cars, and both businesses."

"Aunt Mags, all I want is my dog, my car, my law practice, and the Morgan Point house. My Nonna left me the house in her will. I moved in it the year after Nonna died. Jack loves the water, and he agreed to live in the Morgan Point house because it's located right on Galveston Bay. We built the pier so he could have his precious sailboat at the house instead of the marina ten miles away. Jack loves the proximity of the house to the lake, and how he can be on the water in minutes. He hates the wildness of the property. Jack struggled for years to tame the land before he threw up his hands in frustration and admitted defeat. I remember he said, 'I give up. The brambles can have the damned land. It's no good for anything but raising your stupid dogs.' That comment should have told me everything I needed to know about Jackson Talbott years before Robin entered his life. I can't remember how many times he confessed he strayed over the years."

Her eyes narrowed. "Bull. You guys own a half dozen rent houses and stock worth millions of dollars. I cannot imagine how much money Jackson made on his Bitcoin investment alone. You have 401k's and pension accounts, and oodles of money in savings. Jack is an ass, but he is a very competent accountant. The man is so frugal his fingers squeak when he rubs them together. You will keep your car, your dog, your legal practice, and the Morgan Point house, which are all your separate property. You will also receive your fair share of the stock, bonds, and real estate holdings. He can have his boat and boat trailer, his accounting practice, his big fancy-schmancy truck, which is so freaking big that I bet he has a teeny little weenie."

I laughed, the sound as dry as autumn leaves crushed beneath your foot. "Nope, sorry to disappoint you. And bless his little old, OCD heart, he always insisted on keeping inventories of all our properties and monetary accounts for insurance. We maintain copies of all those ledger sheets in my office under lock and key. I figured I would need the information in them some day. I already locked down the financial accounts since this mess blew up last week. He cannot sell property, stock, or move sizeable sums of money without my knowledge and written consent."

She smiled as she nodded, pleased with my proactive actions. "Excellent. I will make sure the financial institutions know about the divorce. Jack will learn it is hell to want a divorce from a competent divorce attorney."

I sighed as I relaxed for the first time all week. "Oh, and did you catch the name of his blasted boat?"

"How could I miss it? He named it The Other Woman." She shook her head and rolled her eyes.

"Yes, pretty gutsy, huh? He was always with The Other Woman. God knows his boat is the love of his life."

"Humph. We are going to draw money out of Jack like a tick draws blood out of a dog's bollocks. You are getting at least 65% of the damned community estate or my name is not Margaret Henson."

I reached over and squeezed her hand. She knew more old Southern colloquialisms than you could shake a stick at. "My law practice, my dog, my car, and my house. Just get me out of this hell I'm living in with Jackson Talbott. Anything more will be icing on the cake. I feel so much better now. I felt like Robin's case hung over my head like the Sword of Damocles."

"The Sword of Damocles, hmm? That's how we want Jack to feel when he gets served." Aunt Maggie's eyes twinkled with anticipation.

I left feeling better than I had felt in ages. Hell's bells, I felt better than I had in months if not years. God knew I felt like a whupped pup since I fled my house that fateful afternoon.

When I got back to the apartment, I told Hairy we would ride out this emotional storm until Jack and I completed the divorce. Everyone on the Gulf Coast knows hurricane season lasts until November 1st. By then, we should be out of the storm, in more ways than one. Hairy would be my emotional center, the heart of my personal Storm. I sighed. Even Hairy thinks I am nuts. Sad thing is, he might be right.

We consider hurricanes to be the worst part about living on the Gulf Coast. I have feared hurricanes since I moved to this area. Ike and Harvey were bad enough, but I can never forget Captain Johnny's stories about the devastation the Great Galveston Hurricane of 1900 caused. He may have been dead then, but it still affected him. He says it motivated him to move from the area for ten or twenty years.

The Great Galveston Hurricane of 1900 hit on September 8th. Isaac Cline was the young, ambitious fool of a meteorologist who refused to believe a hurricane could damage Galveston. The town had already survived eleven known hurricanes before the Great Hurricane. Cline knew the storm had developed into a hurricane in the Gulf from about August 30th. Cline became worried and tried to warn the town that a storm was approaching hours before it hit, but the fool never mentioned a hurricane was barreling in on them. People ignored Cline's warning because that weekend was the last opportunity for many people to go to the beach.

The highest point on the island stood a mere 8.7 feet above sea level. By Saturday morning, September 8th, Cline realized he had underestimated the power of the incoming hurricane, and estimated the storm tide would be 15 to 20 feet on landfall. Cline never told the populace a hurricane bore down on the island with an expected storm surge at least ten feet and as much as twenty feet above the highest point. His inadequate warning and a lack of places to take safe refuge on the island doomed many inhabitants of the city, and as a result, many people refused to evacuate to the mainland but remained in Galveston in their homes.

By evening, winds up to 140 miles per hour hit the town. Today, that is considered a Category 4 hurricane. At those speeds, falling and flying debris pose high risks of injury or death to people, pets, and livestock. Many frame homes collapsed. Well-built homes like the Bishop's Palace saw severe damage to their roofs and windows, but those residences survived. Many people took refuge at the Bishop's Palace.

The Category 4 hurricane blew out most windows, uprooted many trees, and demolished 3600 homes. Life-threatening water and food shortages occurred in the aftermath of the Great Hurricane. I heard horror stories from

Galveston old timers about people scavenging for food. The part of the town that survived was uninhabitable for months.

No one knows the actual death count, but Galveston officials estimate one-sixth of the city perished. To venture outdoors was certain death, but staying inside was not much better. Johnny told me people struggled through chest-deep water to climb to upper floors in buildings, only for the buildings to collapse from the force of the water and shattered homes piling up on other homes. The storm carried many victims into the chaos of shattered homes, broken glass, smashed furnishings, as well as the corpses of people and animals. Captain Johnny described horrific sights from the next day as well. He said dead bodies were everywhere. He choked up as he described dead babies in the arms of their deceased mothers.

The Galveston authorities got the brilliant idea to dispose of the unending sea of corpses by loading them onto barges, taking them out onto the Gulf, and dumping them. The bloated and rotting carcasses floated back to shore a week later. After that debacle, the city burned the dead in large pyres onshore. It took six weeks to dispose of all the corpses. The city reeked of the burning corpses. Galveston had become hell on earth.

Johnny told me the sheriffs in nearby counties rounded up able-bodied young men and forced them to go work on the disaster scene. One old guy who was a teenager at the time of the Great Hurricane said his sheriff conscripted him to work in Galveston for weeks. Food was so scarce they ate Fig Newtons, which washed up in watertight tins. The old guy said he could never stand the sight of those cookies after that and never allowed them in his home.

As I thought about the Great Hurricane again, I shivered. I never wanted to live through a hurricane. A hurricane must be the worst thing a person could ever endure. Then I corrected myself. I found myself trapped in a hell of a marriage with Jackson Talbott. Could anything be worse than living in a marriage with someone who neither loves nor respects you?

My thoughts drifted again to the night I left my home. I ran out of the house that fateful Sunday afternoon with my heart pounding and tears streaming down my face as I clutched my beloved dog to my chest. Jack could always intimidate me, but he never scared me as badly as he did that afternoon. He did not just threaten me; he aimed multiple kicks at Hairy. Fortunately, I did not have court the next day since I ran out of the house wearing cut-off shorts, an oversized, 'fifty shades of grey' Skye Terrier t-shirt, and my well-worn Clark's flip flops. I did not take time to grab my hairbrush, much less my toothbrush. Even though I purchased a hairbrush, toothbrush, nightie, and some makeup at a drugstore on the way to the club, my ensemble would not have been a pretty look for court.

Yes, a person could survive worse things than a hurricane. The hell Jack put me through must be the worst thing I would ever endure.

After Aunt Mags e-filed the papers, she somehow worked her magic and got the case set for a temporary orders hearing two weeks later. With some Maggie Magic, she sweet-talked the clerk and got the papers issued that afternoon. I wish I could pull that trick in Harris County because it always takes me at least a week to get papers issued there.

About 9 p.m. that evening, Captain Johnny shimmered before me. "Dan served him, Sara. Be careful and do not answer calls from Jackson."

I gave the ghost a crisp, if insouciant salute. "Aye, aye, Captain!"

I heard Tamsin giggle. "My land, I like that girl."

Johnny frowned and wagged a finger at me. "In my day, I would have had you keelhauled for that act of insubordination, Sara."

I laughed. "No, you'd scowl, but laugh once I left. Anything else?"

I laughed as his ghostly cheeks reddened. It always enchanted me to see his pallid cheeks turn scarlet when I embarrassed him.

Johnny shook his head as he struggled not to laugh. He pointed a thin, bony finger at me. "He will call you any moment now. Remember, don't answer his calls."

I bit back my insubordinate response and smiled. "Thank you, Captain Johnny. I promise not to answer Jack's calls."

Jack started phone bombing me the moment Johnny disappeared. I gulped, squared my shoulders, and ignored the calls from my infuriated husband. At about 10:30, Dara and I went downstairs to the office and locked the door between the office and the bar. Not long after, we saw Jack storm into the bar through the two-way mirror into the office.

"Where is she?" Jack demanded as he slammed both fists on the counter.

Dave finished drawing the beer for a patron and handed the mug to the grateful young med student. "Now, remember, it's a school night. You can purchase two drinks this evening. We agreed not to serve UTMB med students over two drinks on a school night. No more after this one. Boss's rule."

The young first-year med student gave Dave a crisp salute. "Yes, sir, boss man!"

After the customer walked away, Dave turned to Jack. "Who are you looking for?"

Jack rolled his eyes and turned toward the mirror outside the office. He knew it was a two-way mirror, and he figured I was watching him. I snickered as he made the motion with his finger to convey, 'I'm looking at you.' He turned back to Dave. "My wife, you dolt. Where is Sara?"

Dave shrugged. "Beats me, Jackson. Not my week to track her movements. However, she dropped this off for you after court today."

Dave handed Jack an envelope. Liz and I struggled not to laugh as Jack ripped it open. He appeared livid. "Call her attorney?"

Dave acted disinterested. "Heck, I don't know what it says. She left that for you, and I didn't read your mail. I don't violate federal mail tampering laws, which means I don't open other people's mail. You might have noticed the sealed envelope when I handed it to you. She did not tell me what it said. Not my duck."

"Not your—What the hell is that supposed to mean? Never mind, you people are all nuts. Leave it to me to marry into a family of lunatics. Fine, I'll call her effing attorney in the morning, but you tell Little Miss Sara that we will not be having a temporary restraining order hearing in two weeks. Do you understand?"

Dave grinned and shrugged again as he wiped off the barware. "Again, Jackson, not my duck. That is between Sara, her attorney, and you. Now, I am about to post the last drink sign. Unless you want to order a drink, ask me out, or tell me how beautiful my eyes are, you need to mosey on home, wherever that is, cowboy."

Jack turned red in the face as he sputtered under his breath. He whirled around and stormed out of the bar, clutching the letter from me in a tight clenched fist. As the door slammed behind him, Dara and I fell together, laughing.

"Oh, that was worth getting shoved down the stairs," I chortled.

She arched her brow, just like her mom does. "I thought you were clumsy and stumbled?"

"Yeah, sure, like you ever believed I stumbled." We danced together, with the Cohutta Queens, long enough for her to know I don't stumble. We paused and then we both started laughing again. Hairy barked as he chased his tail.

Chapter 5
Sara

The week sped by once the process server delivered the divorce papers to Jack. Robin went to Maggie's office, signed a contract with her, and slunk away like a whupped pup after commenting it embarrassed her when things got so out of control. Mags told the girl not to tell anyone else of her pregnancy, and to keep a low profile with Jack. Maggie also warned Robin to stay out of her house for the time being, since Sonny made threats of violence directed towards Robin. She explained that Robin's attorney of record would be Janice McLaughlin, an associate in the firm, if the case did not settle at mediation. Aunt Maggie would represent me in my divorce. Robin turned beet red, mumbled some unintelligible gibberish, signed a letter allowing Maggie to represent both of us, and then almost ran from the office. I guess she did not notice my car parked in the lot beneath the massive oak tree or think that I might have been in Maggie's office watching it all on the office 'Ring' security system.

I almost felt sorry for Robin. I struggled to tell myself she was a piss poor friend, and she deserved whatever she got. The bottom line was no one deserved Sonny or the hell he would put her through if he realized she was pregnant by Jackson Talbott before the custody case ended.

On Wednesday morning, Anthony Terwinney filed an answer and counterclaim on behalf of Jack. Less than an hour later, Anthony called Maggie. They set up an informal mediation to negotiate a settlement agreement for Friday afternoon.

On Thursday afternoon, Jack called my office. He surprised me. I chewed on my thumbnail until I faced the situation and took the call. Jack sounded shaken but calm. At the end of the conversation, I held the phone for a moment before sitting it back down into its cradle.

"Everything okay, boss?" Ashley frowned at me.

I shook my head as I sat staring at the phone cradled in my hands. "I would swear he was about to ask if I was sure I wanted a divorce."

She gawked at me in disbelief. "Nah. Must be your imagination, boss."

I shook my head again. "It wasn't so much his words as that tonal quality people get sometimes after they served the divorce petition. I tell you; he is equivocating. Big time."

She looked as shocked as I felt. "Well, shit."

"That's what I say. You watch. He'll claim I wanted the divorce because I filed."

Ashley looked panic-stricken. "Well, you want the divorce, right? You don't want him back, do you? Say you don't, Sara. Please, tell me, you don't."

I grinned. "Not just no, but hell, no. You know what I always tell my clients."

She relaxed as she remembered my standard advice. "Once a cheater, always a cheater. Don't take them back once you catch them with their pants down."

"You got it." God knew I put up with Jack's manipulation and cheating far too long. Like Mom said, it was past the time to give the tool named Jackson Talbott to someone else. I deserved better.

I never told Ashley I caught Jack cheating lots of times, but I just looked the other way for years. I could not face being a failure at my marriage. Likewise, I could not admit to Ashley what a goober I had been to stay with the sorry cheating louse, especially considering the domestic violence I endured. I could well understand why a client would reconcile with a cheating spouse or even one who hit like Jack. I always wanted to believe he would not wander again if I let him return. Maybe.

But letting Jack return never worked, and he always cheated again. I damned sure knew it would not this time either. Thank heaven he did not ask for one more chance.

I took a deep breath. Yes, I knew better. Jack loves The Other Woman. The bastard even named his blasted boat for the other women in his life. And now, his other woman would have his baby, the baby I never gave him.

I felt my shoulders slump as I sighed. Time to cut the cord.

***

Friday afternoon arrived.

Johnny and Tamsin gave me a pep talk before I headed to Maggie's office. You have never been on the receiving end of a stern talk until you get it from your guardian angel and her assistant angel in training. Johnny gave stellar advice. "Listen to your attorney and don't let the blasted man upset you. He is not worth it."

I smiled. "Thank you, Captain Johnny. I intend to listen to Maggie, and I shall work hard not to let Jack upset me."

Lord have mercy, I would kiss that ghost if I could.

All week, I practiced meditation to prepare for the Friday conference. I wanted to be as strong as possible for the Friday Ordeal. By Friday, I reckoned I was as ready as possible. As I drove up to Maggie's office, I repeated the mantra I practiced all week: I am a good person; I am healthy and happy; I am financially secure; I am going to be fine. I took another deep breath, in through my nose, out through my mouth. Calm, Sara. Remain calm.

If I just believed the mantra, but I worked hard on believing it. I damned sure would not let Jack rattle me during our negotiations. I continued the mantra: I am a good person; I am healthy and happy; I am financially secure; I am going to be fine. Take another breath. Stay calm, focused, and relaxed. One foot in front of the other. Open the door, walk into the office.

I met with Maggie for an hour before the scheduled meeting with Terwinney and Jack. Dressed in a modest yet form fitting, navy-blue dress with navy-blue and white pumps, I hoped I looked like a slim, trim, fighting machine.

Maggie and I reviewed the accounting from Ralph Morrissey. With a little Maggie Magic, she got certified copies of the deeds to all the real properties we owned. She also got a certified copy of Nonna's Will and the deed which confirmed the Morgan Point house transferred to me. Jack and I never took out a loan for any updates on the house. Dad gave me the money for the remodeling work from my trust fund, fearing the character of the house might change if we ever refinanced it in both our names. Boy, did he peg that one. I guess my dad saw the cad in Jack from the start. Dad provided copies of all the checks he paid to the contractors, as well as copies of the contracts for the work done.

My family tried to warn me about Jack, but I ignored their concerns. Kirk called Jack a 'money-grubbing man whore.' His harsh words pissed me off, big time, and as a result, Jack and I eloped when Jack somehow poured on the sweet talk and convinced me to run off to Vegas to get married. Elopement proved to be a mistake of epic proportions.

Marry in haste, repent at leisure.

Anthony Terwinney, a decent family lawyer from the Clear Lake area, was no match for Aunt Mags. Poor Jack either did not know it or the other top guns refused to take his case. Sometimes, lawyers refuse to take cases against other lawyers they know and respect. Terwinney is young and with the braggadocio that makes jackasses out of young lawyers, especially when up against far more experienced attorneys. Maggie and I smiled at each other when they entered the building. Maggie went to the lobby to bring them into the conference room.

As she stepped out of the conference room, Captain Johnny shimmered into shape before me.

"Why, hello, Captain Johnny. Did you come to wish me luck?"

He looked worried, if not downright flustered. "Sara, be careful this afternoon. Do not lose your temper."

I chuckled and held up my fingers as if I were about to make the Scout's pledge. "I swear."

He frowned. "I'm serious, dear girl, serious as death. And do not go back to Morgan Point tonight."

I laughed and gave him a smart salute. "Aye, aye, Captain!"

He rolled his eyes as he dematerialized. "Insouciant wench."

Jack and Anthony entered the conference room. The sun glared through the windows into their faces. Jack winced as his attorney frowned, especially when he noticed there were no blinds to shut to cut down the glare into their eyes.

Show Time.

There are few things I call 'Show Time.' Those include dog shows, of course, court, and meetings like this one. This was Show Time, and we had the proverbial foot up, with the sun behind us, glaring in Anthony's and Jack's faces. Even small revenges are sweet.

Jack sat glaring at me, his rage controlled just below his surface as the sun's glare in his eyes pushed him to the edge of his self-control. Anthony looked aggravated, with a frown on his face and a foot tapping with nervous energy. I struggled to keep from 'licking the cream from my catty little smirk,' as Jack often described it. Linda brought in a fresh pot of coffee and told everyone where the water and sodas were located.

Anthony cleared his throat. "I drafted a preliminary settlement proposal. As you know, Jackson is a forensic accountant. He keeps the records on their properties and the profits and losses from both businesses. I think our proposed distribution of community assets is fair."

Maggie took the spreadsheet and snorted as she reviewed it. "We realize Jack is a forensic accountant, so Ralph Morrissey helped me prepare our list of community and separate assets. You will note first the Morgan Point house is Sara's separate property. She inherited it from her grandmother."

I noticed the shocked expressions on Anthony's face. Jack huffed up, his face turning redder by the minute. "The nature of the property changed when we refinanced it in both our names."

As I struggled to keep a neutral face, Maggie snorted again. "Nice try, Jackson, but we know you did not refinance the house. Sara's father gifted her the money to remodel the house. I have a copy of all the checks he sent to Sara, as well as the bank records which show the money went into her separate property banking account, which she maintained from before the marriage. If you have a deed of trust for the Morgan Point house, it is a fraud. He filed no deed of trust for refinancing at the courthouse in Harris County."

Jack squirmed in his chair as his face flushed dark red. Anthony glanced at his client and then back at Maggie. He squirmed in his chair like a toddler caught with his hand in the cookie jar.

Aunt Mags smiled and continued. "Anthony, I see you relied on Jack's word and did not confirm the information he gave you. Here is a correct and up-to-date accounting of the various real properties titled in both our clients' names. You will notice there are community-owned real properties here in Galveston, Brazoria, Harris, and Montgomery counties. Jackson also has several properties in Travis and Bexar Counties, which he bought while he was in college before our clients married. Those are his separate property, like the Morgan Point house is Sara's separate property. I attached copies of the real property records, including any relevant deeds of trusts to each property in either of their names."

Jack pulled his glasses out of his pocket and peered at the list with Anthony. He looked up and smirked at me. "Number four and number seven both sold last year."

Maggie smiled again. "Well, that's interesting, Jackson. Sara did not sign any contracts to sell, and the real property records of neither Galveston nor Harris County reflect those two alleged sales."

Jack smirked at me. "They sold on contract for title."

Maggie flashed Jack another amiable smile. "Jackson, if Sara did not sign those contracts, and if you cannot produce a power of attorney where Sara allowed you to contract to sell those properties, then the contracts are invalid."

I grabbed the alleged contract for a three-bedroom townhouse that overlooked Galveston Bay. "No, I did not authorize the sale of the Seabrook property to Robin. I signed a rental contract with her."

Maggie looked over her glasses to glower, first at me and then at Jack. We had rehearsed this little Good Cop–Bad Cop scenario. "Behave, Sara. You know better."

I put on my best shame-faced look and bit my lip as I glanced down at my hands. I allowed my hands to tremble just a little.

Aunt Maggie turned her glare towards Jack. I struggled to hold back the laughter as he squirmed in his chair. "You sold a house overlooking Galveston

Bay to your lover for half the fair market value? With no down payment? That is downright sleazy, even for you."

Jack's face twisted with fury. "Now, listen here, Maggie—"

As he pushed back his chair, Anthony laid a land on Jack's arm. Anthony did not look happy. He had already caught his client in several lies. "Sit down, Jack. Maggie, could you give me a few minutes alone with my client?"

She smiled at Anthony as she gathered up the original documents. "Of course, Anthony. I'm sure you understand why I will not leave the certified copies of the deeds to the properties with Jackson. Knock on my office door when Jackson is ready to negotiate in good faith."

He chewed his lip as he nodded, and we went to her office. A few minutes later, he knocked on the door. "We are ready, if you would like to resume talking."

We walked back into the conference room. Jack sat slumped in the chair, a look of frustrated resignation on his face. Anthony paused for a second as he stared at his client. "May I present your amended offer now?"

Jack sat slumped in the chair, his arms crossed and tight to his body as he pouted. Have you ever seen a thirty-eight-year-old man pout like a little child before? Not a pretty sight. I bit my tongue to keep from laughing. I moved my hand up over my mouth so Jack could not see his catty little wife grin at his discomfort. He glowered at me again. "Yeah, fine."

Maggie kept her poker face until she reviewed the document. "I see you added the two houses you claimed had sold back on the list, besides the Lake Livingston condo, the Surfside Beach house, and the Green Tee property. However, as I stated before, Morgan Point is not a negotiable issue. It is Sara's separate property, just as the Lake Travis condominiums and the San Antonio apartment are Jack's separate property."

"Dammit, I put a lot of work into remodeling that property." Jack's face turned purple with rage.

I rolled my eyes. "Bullshit, Jackson. Dad paid the contractors for all the work. You did not do one damned thing in the house. You supervised them build the pier for your blasted sailboat, to ensure they built it where you wanted it."

Maggie took a deep breath and frowned at me. "No need to argue with him, Sara. We can discuss it all at the hearing on temporary orders. I suspect Judge Graham will be especially interested that Jackson tried to sell the Seabrook house to his paramour for half its worth."

She stood up and started picking up the documents again.

Jack paled and slumped back into his chair, his mouth tight with worry, anger, or perhaps some of both. He looked over at Anthony. "She can't do that, can she, Tony?"

"Oh, yes, she can. Maggie, what does your client want?"

"Yes, what are you proposing?" Jack leaned against the conference table and rubbed his forehead, as if he were getting the Mother of All Headaches. I hoped he was.

Maggie smiled as she pushed our proposed division spreadsheet over to Anthony. "Why, gentlemen, I thought you would never ask."

Jack flinched and Anthony began his posturing again, and I just sat back, enjoying the shit show in progress. After allowing Tony to play at being an experienced lawyer, Maggie spoke. "Listen, Anthony, your client admitted to adultery with one of Sara's family law clients. He impregnated the girl."

Anthony stopped mid-sentence, jaw slack, stunned by that juicy little tidbit of information. "Wh-wh-what did you say?"

Maggie flashed him her most angelic smile. "Oh, didn't Jackson bother to tell you Robin Cangelosi is pregnant? Her ex-husband, who is mob related, has been to the pen three times. Sonny Cangelosi is stalking Ms. Cangelosi. God knows what he has on your client with this sordid affair going on. Ms. Cangelosi agreed to hire my firm, but until the judge signs the substitution, Sara remains ensnared in this matter. Our settlement proposal is contingent upon me taking over as first chair for Sara if the Judge will not let her withdraw. That would absolve Sara of any malpractice issue and ensure Sara still attends proceedings. She knows the case far better than I could ever know it on such short notice. In exchange, Sara wants 70% of the community estate. Not just the community estate Jack claims exists, but all the community estate. We're certain there is more, but this is all we located this week. We want a clause stating she can come back for five years and receive 70% of anything else we turn up which Jack hid, right, Sara?"

"I don't know, Maggie. If he takes the deal today, I'll sign a waiver and walk away from any hidden assets. After today?" I shrugged. "I don't think I'd be so nice. The Texas Family Code says I get 100% if it goes to Court within five years after the trial and the Judge determines he hid assets from me."

Jack paled, and the muscle over his left eye twitched. I knew it scared him shitless if that muscle was twitching. As I continued to repeat my mantra, I relaxed a bit. I am a good person; I am healthy and happy; I am financially secure. I am going to be fine. Breathe. Now, take another breath. Now, another. Everything will be fine. Stay calm and carry on.

I guess all my visualizing and meditating paid off, because Jack caved in after less than an hour. We negotiated the minute details of the agreement for another hour before we signed a binding settlement agreement. We would divide the stocks, bonds, and cryptocurrency 50-50. In addition, Jack would keep his accounting practice and all revenues, his truck, 40-foot sailboat and boat trailer, the two houses he tried to short sell, and several other properties besides his separate properties for about 30% of the community estate. I would keep the Morgan Point house and all the improvements thereon, my Lexus SUV, which was a community asset, the BMW convertible Dad gave me when I graduated from Rice, my legal practice and all revenues, my beloved dogs, and other real properties. Jack made a big show of saying he wanted nothing to do with the dogs. My part of the community estate totaled to an impressive 70%. Maggie promised she would get me at least 65% of the community estate, and she got more without ever having to go to court and air our sordid family business. I agreed to let him dock his precious sailboat on my pier for ninety days. Maggie would represent Robin in the custody case. No mention of his adulterous behavior with Robin would come out in the divorce court, and I could divorce him in sixty days. He could move in with Robin, and I could return to my house later that evening.

As we signed the documents, I looked at him and smiled. "You need to revise your will."

Jack looked surprised. "Why? I figured you wanted me dead."

I blinked before I answered. "No, I do not want you dead. Why would you think that? Jackson, you have a baby coming. God forbid if something happens before your baby arrives. You need to make plans."

He laughed, as if embarrassed. "Okay, I guess you're right. I will take care of that."

"Listen, I want only what I deserve, Jack. We just worked out what we each receive. Understand?"

He stared at me like he could not understand me and shook his head. "You were always such an enigma."

That was better than what he called me before I ran out of the house that last evening. 'Enigma' is so much nicer than 'fucking frigid bitch.'

As we finished signing the Marital Settlement Agreement, Linda took the original to make copies. I stood in a corner, whispering to Maggie as Jack's phone rang. Maggie and I quit talking as he answered the phone.

"Hello, darling. How is my little fluffy puppy tonight?"

I went numb at his words.

Maggie arched her brows as I paled at his words. "Are you okay?"

I shook my head as I pinched my lips together in anger. I pushed back from the conference table and started towards the door.

She frowned as she stopped me before I could leave. "What was that all about?"

"Nothing," I snapped. "Nothing is wrong. Right, Jackson?"

Jack looked surprised to realize anyone might have heard what he said or took an interest in his comment when he realized what he said. His face turned red. "Oh, shit."

"Yeah. Oh shit, Jack. May I ask why you felt it necessary to even give her my nickname? Or have you shared it with all your whores?"

You could have cut butter with the subtle softness of my voice right then.

Jack flinched again. "Now, listen, Sara…"

"Oh, don't give me that 'Now, Sara,' patronizing bullshit. You called me your little fluffy puppy before we married. Maggie, do you want to know what it means? 'Are you fluffy, puppy?' It means, 'are you horny, babe?' It's Jack's special code. Well, so tell us, Jack. Is your little whore feeling horny tonight? You make me sick. I remained faithful for all these freaking years, four years before marriage, and six after. I never once cheated on you. Believe me, I thought about cheating a few times when I caught you, but I never once indulged in payback fuckery. I never cheated. Oh, I thought about it, and I damned sure had some fabulous opportunities, but I never once cheated. How long have you been cheating with my client? You swore for years you didn't want a baby. Now, your little fluffy puppy and you expect a baby. And the one phrase you swore was special to us, our special code. You even gave that to her. Dammit, Jack, you sorry bastard, you wouldn't know special if it jumped up and bit you on your hairy ass." I stood and threw the settlement papers in his face before I wheeled around to leave.

He was at the door before me and grabbed my arm. "Sara, will you be at court on Monday?"

"Of course I will, you blithering jackass. I am her attorney of record. Now, get your hands off me this minute, or I shall file criminal charges against you for assault this time."

I stormed from the conference room. Maggie followed me into the one place Jackson would not follow: the ladies' restroom. She put her arms around my shoulders as I sobbed into the sink. "Okay, what was that all about?"

"He called her... his... fluffy puppy."

Maggie frowned, and I could see the impatience in her eyes. "Yeah, I caught that part. So what?"

I struggled to get the words out. "You don't understand. He called me his little fluffy puppy. Jackson even gave that woman my nickname. He gave her his love. He gave her the baby he never wanted me to have. The bastard even gave her the blasted pet name he called me."

Maggie pulled me around so she could peer into my eyes. "Sara, don't you understand why?"

I struggled to stop crying. I hiccuped as I shook my head. "No, why?"

She snickered. "You big ball of goof, you should know a man calls the new woman the same thing you called the last one, so you don't eff up and call out the wrong name while you're having sex. That's why so many second wives have the same or nickname as wife number one."

I stared at her for a minute until we both started laughing. "I should have thought of that."

She hugged me. "You are under a lot of stress, although I loved it when you told him you never engaged in payback fuckery. Is that even a word?"

I nodded. "It's old-fashioned, but it's a word."

She chuckled. "I forgot your stepmom writes historical novels. Leave through the back door. I am gonna tear him a new one, but I will allow the agreement to remain in place."

I struggled to quit laughing. "I'm fine with the blasted agreement. When he called her his little fluffy puppy, I didn't dream it would hurt so much."

"I understand. Now, wash your face and fix your lipstick. Linda, help her slip out the back door. I want Sara long gone before Lover Boy goes to his big ol' macho man truck. He will be out of the house within the next hour. Get some dinner and then go home."

I nodded, ran a brush through my hair, and fixed my lipstick before I headed to my car. I was still in Maggie's parking lot when my phone rang. "Yeah, I'm leaving now."

The caller paused for a minute before she replied. "Are you okay?"

"Hell, no, I'm not okay," I snapped.

She paused before she spoke again. "Get some supper and then go home."

"Yeah, sure." I disconnected the call, pulled out onto the road, and headed toward the house.

Dinner what not what I craved. I wanted a margarita badly, and I intended to have me a pitcher or two.

Hell, I intended to celebrate.

Chapter 6
Sara

A half hour later, I pulled up to a little bar a half mile from the Morgan Point house. It made sense to wait until Jack drove by as he left before I went home since he would have to leave down this road from our cul-de-sac. I went inside my old stomping grounds and slid onto a barstool. I had one helluva a migraine and rubbed my hands across my face. The headache promised to become the Mother of All Migraines. Dad gets them, too. It seems I inherited both my amber-colored eyes and my tendency to suffer migraines from my dad.

I had not been in The Office for three years, and yet, as soon as I slid onto the stool, it felt like I had never left. I always chuckled at the name. Jack could be out sailing on The Other Woman while I sat at The Office. Little more than a beer joint, but the bartender in this dive made the best margaritas in Texas.

My hands shook I pulled the fresh pack of cigarettes out of my purse. I stopped two blocks down the street from the bar to buy the pack, and I intended to smoke my little death sticks. On the third try, I quit trying to get the lighter to work and frowned.

As the bartender came up, he grinned at me. "Hey, girl, I haven't seen you in ages."

"Hey, Sandy. Give me a margarita. Rocks. Salt."

He looked kind of funny. "Uh, Sara, you don't handle rita's very well. Are you sure?"

I nodded and glared at him. "Yeah, Sandy baby, never surer. Rita, rocks, salt. And Sandy, if I want a lecture, I'll call my mother. Since you are not my mom, keep the sidebar comments to yourself. Once again, I want a margarita on the rocks, made with Patron, *por favor*. Lots of salt, and give me a sidecar of Amaretto."

The bartender looked even more surprised by my selection. He bent over to light my cigarette. "Italian margarita? Hell, Sara, I thought you gave those up. What gives?"

I closed my eyes as I inhaled the cigarette fumes for the first time in years, loving and hating the burn as it hit my lungs. Sandy waited as I coughed. "The ciggies or the 'rita?"

He shrugged. "Both will kill you. Are you sure you want the margarita? I haven't seen you drink one in years."

"You haven't seen me in years, and I want them right now tonight, by damn. Come on, quit stalling, make me a margarita on the rocks, with salt and a sidecar of Amaretto." I flicked the ash into the ashtray and glared at him. "And keep 'em coming, sweetie. I'm celebrating."

He gave me another odd look and then nodded. "Okay, it's your life, not mine. Coming right up."

Sandy always made the sweetest ritas on the Texas Gulf Coast. I closed my eyes as the smooth, seductive concoction slid down my throat. I almost convulsed from the painful knowledge that I gave up these wonderful creations I love for so long. How could I stand to give them up? Why did I do it? I no longer remembered why I abandoned the salty rim of the glass, the sweetness of agave, the bitterness of the tequila, and the sourness of the limes, which all combine to form the perfect cocktail. The ice helps cool down the spiciness, the acidity compliments fatty foods like meat and cheese, and the salty rim adds depth to the salt in your food. That salt also helps neutralize bitter tastes on the tongue. Yes, margaritas taste like a little bit of heaven to me, perfect in every way.

I picked up my half-empty glass and moved over to a table by the window where I could keep an eye out to see when Jackson left my house. As I relaxed for the first time in two weeks, I slipped my feet out of my sling back Manolos. I winced as I slipped an earring off. God only knew why I wore clip earrings that morning. I sighed as I slipped the other one off and laid them beside my drink. I leaned back in the club chair, to alternate between sipping my rita, watching for Jack's truck, and eying the dancers. Soon, my glass was empty, and I motioned for another.

By the third drink, I sang the words to the tunes on the jukebox. Tequila makes her clothes fall off, said the song, and I laughed as I pulled off my headband and shook my hair loose. I slipped off my jacket and swung it over my head to toss it to the men watching nearby.

Sandy shook his head. "Watch out, Sara. Don't go crazy."

I wagged my finger at him. "Don't you worry about me, sugar. We're getting a divorce, and we just worked out the settlement agreement, so I'll be crazy tonight if I want to be crazy."

He rolled his eyes again, slung his bar towel over his shoulder, and walked back to the bar counter.

Two more margaritas, and I sang the words to the song about the guy who drank tequila shots. The boys in the bar hollered and clapped when I tossed my pumps across the room. One fellow picked up one of the pricey Manolo's, kissed the insole and yelled, "I'll keep it forever, darlin'."

"You do that, sugar. Those pumps cost my ex-husband a fortune. In fact, drink a margarita out of that pricey little slipper." I winked back at him.

First thing I knew, someone put on that Luke Bryan song I love. I got up and started dancing around the dance floor singing the refrain, 'one margarita, two margarita, three margarita, shot!'

Sandy stuck an order of nachos in front of me. "Eat."

I wrinkled my nose, but I nibbled at the nachos along with what I think was my sixth margarita.

As I finished my nachos and number six, I stumbled over to the bar. "Gimme another one, Sandy."

"No more of those for you, lady. You are way over your limit." Sandy glowered at me as he wiped a glass dry with a clean bar towel.

I frowned and handed him my credit card. "That's enough, Sandy. I did not come in here for a lecture. Serve me the freakin' margarita. Make it with Patron. Now."

He shrugged. "Nope. *No mas.* You'll be sick to—"

"Not your problem. Tomorrow is not a workday. Besides, it would make Jack way too happy if I got sick on ritas."

Sandy frowned as I danced up close to him. "Sorry, Sara, no more for you tonight. You are way over your limit. You know I'm never supposed to give you over three, and you have had twice that many tonight."

I pouted as I fingered the fabric of his western-cut shirt. "You are no fun tonight, Sandy. Don't worry about tomorrow. It's going to be Saturday. I don't have to be at court. Come on, man. Just one shot of Patron, for old times. Then I will go home."

He shook his head as he pulled my fingers off his shirt. "Heck, girl, you can't walk straight now. It's all you can do to remain vertical. Hate to tell you, but I cannot allow you to drive, even if you live less than a half mile down the road from here."

I pouted again and tucked my hair behind my ears. "Fine, I'll walk."

He struggled not to laugh. "What will Jack say if you go home drunk?"

Indignant at the allegation, I sniffed in disdain. "Jack left. Besides, I'm not drunk. Just a little intoxicated. Just one shot, and I promise I'll go home."

He burst into laughter. "Where is Jack tonight?"

Shrugging, I took the shot glass from him. "*Yo no se.* The Jack Ass has left the building."

"The tomcat is away, so the little kitty cat plays, huh?" He laughed again.

I shook my head. "Nope. He left for good. We negoriatered… uh… we negotificated… uh… we worked out a divorce agreement today. He gets his boat, his truck, and his floozy, and I get everything else. Well, just about everything else."

Sandy looked surprised. "You kicked him out, hmm? About time, Sara. Tell you what, I can call Uber, or I can drive you home."

"Then can I have another margarita?" As I batted my eyelashes, one of my false eyelashes fell off.

He chuckled as he picked up the eyelash and handed it to me. Apparently, my attempt to look sexy failed. "Nope. Your mama called and said, '*no mas tequila para ella*'."

"Dammit, man, you know my mama don' speak no Spanish. She's a Georgia peach."

He burst into laughter as he took off his apron. "Missy, watch the bar. I'm taking Miss Sara home. I will be back in ten minutes."

He poured me into my car and drove me to the house, where I slid out of the front seat, slithered to the front door, unlocked it and sat my purse down in the foyer. As I did, I realized to my dismay I left my shoes, my earrings and jacket in the bar. "Looks like Jack was right."

He tilted his head at me. "About what?"

"Damned tequila must'a made my clothes fall off."

Sandy burst out laughing again. "You crack me up, Sara Talbott. Tequila always did that to you, as I recall. Listen, I'll put your things behind the bar. You can pick them up tomorrow. Now, go inside, lock the door, and go to bed."

I wobbled into the house in my stocking feet. "How will you get back to the bar?"

He blew me a kiss. "I can walk. After all, I wore my shoes. Now, lock the door and I will leave."

I did as instructed and somehow set the burglar alarm before I wobbled upstairs to my bedroom. Jack and I added the enormous master bedroom and spa bathroom on to the back of the house when we remodeled it. The master suite overlooked the bay and had expansive views through the floor to ceiling windows over Galveston Bay. You could lie in bed and all you could see was sky and water.

I bit back tears as I watched Jack's boat sail past the house. It was unnecessary to see the name on the side of it for me to know the boat was The Other Woman. The custom sails Jack just had to have for his beloved ketch were discernible from my bedroom window. To add insult to injury, Jack stood hugging that blasted woman in the bow. Dammit, I knew to expect them to sail by the house. My throat tightened in heartfelt longing that both annoyed and aggravated me. How dare my body betray me like this? Dammit, I did not want to love him anymore.

And then it happened. As the boat flew by, Jack bent down to kiss the woman. I shook my head and took a deep breath. He sure did not slow down going out on the water by worrying about me or my reaction to our settlement agreement. Seeing him with her should not hurt so much. If I had not known it before, I realized Jack was not the man I wanted in my life anymore as his boat sailed past my house. Like my family tried to tell me for all these years, I deserved better than sorry Jackson Talbott.

I glanced at my watch and saw it was 9 p.m. They must be headed to Red Fish Island.

Yeah, Jack Ass Talbott and tequila both made me crazy. They ran like poison in my blood. Hell, one more night with that damned man might kill me. God knew the last one damned near did. Like with margaritas, one was too many, and yet one night with Jackson Talbott had never been enough until that last hideous night.

If only I did not get seasick. Maybe we could have made it.

No, I refused to lie to myself any longer. There would always have been The Other Woman for Jack, and as long as The Other Woman existed for him, tequila would be there for me. Talbott and tequila: the ultimate Sara Winslow Talbott poisons.

Dammit, when I taste tequila, I remember how happy I felt when we fell in love back in college. I drank my first margarita with Jackson on the Paradise Pier in Galveston when I was all of nineteen years old. Tequila transports me back to the day when Jack squeezed into my sorority t-shirt, swearing on the Bible that he would love me forever and would never leave me. And then, dammit, I remember how much I loved the blasted man back then, how much I thought I needed him. He always made me feel like I could never succeed without him by my side. It did not help to remember how good the sex always was for ages, even when we no longer talked anymore. Well, good until that last night, I thought, as I ran my hands up and down my arms.

And that evening when I tasted the tequila, I realized how much I still love you, Jackson Talbott. How much I still want you, how damned much I need you.

No, I was wrong. I don't need you anymore. Maybe I still love you. Maybe I will always want you, but I damn sure do not need your sorry, cheating ass.

Thank God Jack didn't figure out years ago how tequila transported me back to our glory days. He would have insisted I drink margaritas all the time instead of insisting I quit drinking them because 'they make you crazy, Sara.'

I would be a full-blown alcoholic by now if I had not quit drinking margaritas when he insisted, but maybe I would still have Jackson Talbott.

Don't do this to yourself, Sara. You don't need the sorry, philandering man anymore.

I wiped another tear from my face and collapsed across the bed. The whispers from the ghostly voices as they flitted around my room went unheeded as I succumbed to the tequila-induced sleep.

Chapter 7
Sara

I crawled out of bed at the ass crack of noon the next morning. My head pounded with a God-awful hangover headache, the first one I experienced in years. I felt nauseated and more than a little dizzy as I pulled myself out of the bed.

Once I maneuvered my way to the kitchen, I made a fresh pot of coffee and nibbled on a slice of dry toast before I swallowed a couple of ibuprofens. The toast helped settle my rolling stomach. As my hangover headache lessened, I took a quick shower. Once bathed, I pulled on my cut-off shorts, a t-shirt, my ever-faithful flip-flops, and drove back to Nefertiti's in Galveston. My dog ran to me in joyful abandon, thrilled I returned to him. After Hairy quit washing my face and hands with doggy kisses, I chatted with my family for an hour. We loaded my things into the SUV and headed back to Morgan Point with my dog and my two dads in tow.

I bit back laughter as Dad insisted he needed to scope out the house and make sure the Jack Ass had not sabotaged it. I tried to tell him I slept there last night with no problems. Kirk tagged along with Daddy to search the house with the hope they might still bite Jack's ears off. They both longed for an opportunity to confront Jackson.

Kirk frowned when he discovered the bookcase under the back staircase standing ajar. The Murphy bookcase covered a heavy steel door, neither of which was there the last time they visited. "What's this?"

I chuckled as I punched in the combination to the safe door, unlocked it, and swung it open. "It's my hidden safe room. It surprises me Jack left the bookcase open to reveal the steel door when he left. Hmm, I wonder what he took. The safe room is supposed to withstand the heat from a fire for up to four hours. It is also supposed to be a place to hide in case of a home invasion. We liked the way the entrance to Liz's apartment at the Bone Yard—oops, at Nefertiti's—is hidden by a Murphy bookcase. I always loved how it protects her apartment, since access to the apartment is hidden from view by the secret door. If someone tried to break into this house, I could hide in here. I can open the door from inside the room, so I cannot get stuck inside it. Come on, let me show you."

Kirk sniffed in disdain as we entered what we used as a storeroom for my closed cases. His eyes lit up as he spotted the gun safe, but his excitement turned to disgust as I opened it.

I stared into the empty gun safe, feeling a little more than a tad unsettled. "Hmm, I guess this explains why he left the bookcase open. Jack Ass took his guns and ammo."

Dad's eyes narrowed. "How many guns did he have?"

I shrugged. "Three, I think. The handgun he carried with him unless he went to court to testify. He also had a 30-06 hunting rifle and a twelve-gauge shotgun. He had a couple of boxes of ammo for each, and a nice gun case to transport each of them."

Kirk looked horrified. "Jack left you way out here on Morgan Point with no way to protect yourself?"

Dad rolled his eyes. "We better make a trip to Cabela's and buy you some protection."

Frowning, I shook my head. They both took me to the range when I was younger in futile attempts to teach me how to handle a firearm. "I have a state-of-the-art burglar alarm system and a hidden, safe room. My Skye terrier would bark his head off if anyone tried to break in here. You both know first hand that guns scare the fire out of me. I don't want a gun. With my luck, I would shoot myself instead of the intruder. Buy me some pepper spray."

Both men looked frustrated, if not downright disgusted, but they let the subject go with some grumbling. I turned to go back to the kitchen where I had been cleaning my refrigerator. Jack left it in a horrible condition to pay me back for him losing the house. I gasped as I ran into the semi-solid form of Captain Johnny. Hands on his translucent hips, he glowered at me. I tried to stifle a giggle. "What's the matter, Captain Johnny?" I asked.

He shook his head. "I told you not to stay here last night. You should not stay way out here alone. This house provides no safety for you, Sara."

The ghost appeared deadly serious. I snickered at my mental pun. Deadly serious, from a ghost. Yeah, Sara. I struggled to wipe the grin off my face. "Why not, Captain Johnny? Think something might jump out at me in the night and yell, 'boo!'?"

To my amazement, he rolled his eyes and shook his head. I did not know a ghost could roll his eyes. "I am quite serious, Sara. Ari did not heed my warning in Cairo, and terrible evil befell Elizabeth. You should not stay out here alone. I told you not to come out here last night."

A chill ran down my spine, causing me to frown. "You did?"

"Yes, my dear, I did. It is not safe for you to be here alone. Something evil shall happen in this house. I feel the danger in my bones."

I could feel my forehead wrinkle as I considered his words. I did not remember any dire warnings from Captain Johnny. "You don't have any bones, Captain Johnny. You are a ghost. This is my home. It has not been safe for me for a couple of years, but it is my home. I do not intend to let Jackson Talbott or anyone else run me off from my house ever again."

He frowned as he dematerialized. "It is not Jackson you should fear…"

About then, the doorbell rang. I shook my head and threw my hands up in the air as I went to open the door. I stood there, stunned at the sight of two Harris County sheriff's deputies standing outside my door. "Uh, how may I help you, officers?"

One big, burly looking, ruddy-cheeked deputy put his hands on his hips. I knew he had easy access to his handgun in that position. "Are you Mrs. Sara Talbott?"

Heart pounding, I ran my hands up and down my arms as I nodded. "Yes, I'm Sara Talbott. What's wrong? Why are you officers here?"

The second deputy was tall, thin, and with a dark complexion. She frowned at her partner, shook her head, and smiled at me. "Mrs. Talbott, could we come in? This is not something to be discussed at the front door."

I glanced down the street, and I thought my eyes might bulge out of my head when I saw one of my neighbors standing outside gawking as he watched the encounter between the police and me. I nodded and pushed the door open wide. "Yes, of course, officers. Please, come in."

As we started into the living room, Dad looked down from the loft. He frowned at the sight of the two uniformed peace officers. "What's wrong, Sara?"

I shrugged. "I don't know, Daddy. The officers asked to come in."

Dad frowned and headed down the stairs as Kirk stuck his head out of the kitchen. "My god, the man left this refrigerator in a mess. Oh, excuse me, I didn't realize you had company, darlin'."

Heart pounding, I struggled to smile. "Not a problem. Uh, deputies, this is my dad, Dr. Richard Winslow, and my stepdad, Mr. Kirk O'Malley. I didn't catch your names, officers. What's going on?"

The big burly guy looked a bit rattled to discover the two men in the house with me. I figured he hoped to encounter me alone. It is so much easier to intimidate women, especially petite women, when we are alone. "My name's O'Connor, ma'am. When did you last see your husband, Mrs. Talbott?"

My heart clamored in my chest as I frowned again. "Yesterday afternoon. Why?"

He frowned right back at me. "And you're not worried about him?"

I shook my head. "No, we're separated, and he's a big boy. He can watch out for himself. Why? Should I be worried about him?"

He started to say something, and appeared frustrated when the tall, thin deputy spoke first. "Mrs. Talbott, forgive our tenseness this afternoon. I'm Deputy Alexander. The Galveston County Sheriff's Office found your husband's body this morning. They requested we come out to notify you."

As I felt the color drain from my face, I reached out to grab a chair to steady myself. "Whoa, hold on just a minute. Did you say…"

"Have a seat, ma'am. The Galveston County Sheriff's Office found his body, Mrs. Talbott. You said you saw him yesterday?"

I nodded and sat down with a thud before I answered. "Uh, yes, we met for a settlement conference at my attorney's office. I left around 5, after we entered a property settlement agreement. He left after I did. I can't believe he's dead."

"Where was he staying, Mrs. Talbott?"

As Jack's surviving spouse, I realized was the top suspect in any murder investigation. I blinked back tears as I struggled not to cry. Oh, heck, maybe I should cry. With a deep breath, I rubbed my trembling hand across my forehead. "Officer, I don't know. I thought he was staying on his sailboat. When I came home about 9 last night, I saw his boat sail by the house a little later. I figured he headed out to Red Fish Island."

The big guy's eyes narrowed at that. "Why did you think he went out there, ma'am?"

"He liked to sail out there and fish. Why?" I felt my brow crinkle as I frowned at the big lug.

Deputy O'Connor ignored my question. "When was the last time you went out there?"

I lifted my hands as I shrugged. "Gosh, I don't know, maybe a year ago. We bought the boat he always wanted, only to discover that I got seasick whenever we went sailing. Jack loved to sail out to Red Fish Island. Jackson would anchor offshore and swim to the beach along the sandbar. He loved to hike for a couple of hours and observe the birds nesting in the thick brush and vegetation, and he found it very calming after a stressful day at the office. Later, when he was back on his boat, he would throw out a line and catch some trout for dinner. However, after three or four unpleasant experiences, I refused to go out on the bay on the boat with him again. I tired of puking up my toenails out there."

"Any guns in the house, Mrs. Talbott?" the tall, thin deputy asked.

I shook my head. "No, deputy." I realized I would be well-advised to not to mention Jack owned guns, but they were missing. My eyes narrowed. "Why? Was he shot?"

Deputy O'Connor smirked at me. "Why would you ask that?"

"Really, dude? That is some way to show empathy with a person. You came in here and announced my husband is dead, and you stand there smirking at me. As I told you, Jack and I were getting a divorce, but I would not wish death on anyone. You asked if there were any guns in the house. As an attorney, my logical next question must be, 'was he shot?' I would think any intelligent, experienced peace officer would comprehend that."

Deputy O'Connor huffed up at my not-so-veiled insult to his intellect and then turned a sickly shade of green. "Uh… did you say you are an attorney?"

I nodded as I stood up. "Yes, sir, I said I'm an attorney. I practice using my maiden name, Sara Winslow."

"Holy shit fire," he muttered with a nervous glance at his partner.

"You know, I could not have said it better, Deputy O'Connor. Considering your officious demeanor here today, I must end this interview. If you have additional questions, please call my attorney, Margaret Henson. Her office is in Clear Lake City. She can arrange any additional questioning of me when she can be present."

Officer O'Connor's cheeks flushed bright red as he stammered. Deputy Alexander stood up and started towards the door. "May I inquire why you have an attorney, Mrs. Talbott?"

Jeez Louise, how many times would I have to tell them? I knew my smile was thin as a pencil lead as my eyes shot daggers at both officers. "As I stated, my husband and I are—well, I mean we were—getting a divorce. Like myself, Ms. Henson has a general practice and handles criminal and family matters. You have more questions? Call Ms. Henson."

I escorted the deputies to the door. After they left, I stood trembling with rage as I watched them go to their patrol car.

Dad cleared his throat. "Baby girl, what just happened? Why did you get snippy with the deputies? I thought everything was going well."

Kirk stood listening to us in silence. I noticed he nibbled on his lip. I never saw him do that before in the sixteen years I had known him.

I took a deep breath. "Jack must have died from a gunshot wound. As his surviving spouse, I am their prime suspect. Tubby O'Connor made that clear when he asked if there were any guns in the house, and when the officer looked like the cat caught slurping down that saucer of cream when I asked if someone shot Jack. That fat turd thinks I killed Jackson."

Dad looked horrified. Kirk nodded, grim-faced. "That was my take on him, too. You're the easy target."

"But Sara didn't kill him," Dad protested.

"Of course, she didn't kill him, Rick. She doesn't have it in her to kill anyone. She cried when she caught a mouse in a trap once," snapped Kirk.

"But I am the logical suspect. A significant other, spouse, or family member commits sixty-two percent of all murders."

"That group would include Robin." Dad sounded pensive. "Or at least a dozen other women. However, significant others, spouses or family members commit only about 5% of all men murdered. That means someone besides a significant other or spouse kills the remaining 95% of all men murdered. I bet the statistic is much higher for women killed by men."

I nodded, excited and more than a little startled Dad knew the stats on this issue. "Yes, the significant other group includes Robin or any of his jilted lovers. It could even include clients who had a grudge against him for some unknown reason. However, Jack left me for his pregnant lover, which gave me a damned powerful motive to kill him. Most women who murder their significant other either kill because their spouse abused them, or in retaliation for something their spouse did to them. Jack hit me more than once, as we all know. Thank God I have on makeup today or they could still see my fading bruises. I also would have a damned good reason to retaliate against him because of Robin, not to mention all the other affairs he had over the years. I had a motive. When I realized they were checking me out as a murder suspect, I did not intend to say anything else without my attorney present. I said too much as it was."

Dad winced. "Ouch."

Nodding, I echoed his wince. "Yeah, double ouch. Now, they must decide if I had the opportunity and intent to kill him. I was here alone from about 9 through the rest of the night. I might have had the opportunity, depending on the time when someone murdered him. However, I did not know he would go out to Red Fish Island alone. Or was he alone? I thought someone was on the sailboat with him when he sailed past around 9. I figured Robin accompanied him. Lord knows I never said, 'I want to kill Jackson,' but He knows I had plenty of reasons to say it. And people in Maggie's office saw me fighting mad at him yesterday."

Kirk frowned. "Why? I thought you guys worked out a marital settlement agreement."

I nodded. "We did. Then, he got a phone call from Robin, and he called her... well, he called her an old pet name he used to call me, and I went all Irish – Italian on him. Dammit, it upset me. Maggie calmed me down, but some people could say my anger showed intent."

"Triple ouch. So, now what, kiddo?" Dad looked worried.

I reached up to give my dad a hug. As I felt the tension ease from his shoulders, I gave him a quick peck on his cheek. "Now, we all keep our mouths shut. No one says anything about Robin or Jack's cheating ways, and let's see what the officers say to us. Don't volunteer information. If they talk to you and ask if you know why they are questioning you guys, tell them, 'No, I don't have a clue.' Remember, loose lips—"

"Sink ships," Kirk concluded. "Aye, aye, captain!"

Kirk winked as he gave me a crisp salute.

As I glanced across the room, I saw Captain Johnny nod his head at us. "Well said, Sara. Now, remember what I told you. It is not safe for you to stay way out here alone right now."

I smiled at him and blew him a kiss. "I understand, Captain Johnny."

Kirk's eyes narrowed. "Did ye ken someone murdered the man, Captain?"

Captain Johnny's pale cheeks flushed with embarrassment. "Yes, Kirk, I knew."

I blinked as the specter disappeared. "Why won't he talk about it? Do you think Johnny knows who killed Jack?"

Kirk nodded. "Aye, he probably does, but he has a problem."

My eyes narrowed as I studied Kirk. "What would that be?"

"I dinna think the Lord will permit him to reveal the identity of the killer."

His words startled me. "Why not?"

Kirk shrugged. "Who knows? The Lord works in mysterious ways. However, Johnny trains to become an angel, so he is bound by certain angelic rules not to identify the killer. It would comprise manipulation of the facts surrounding Jack's death. Johnny can warn you, he can give clues, but he cannot tell you who committed the murder... or why."

I rubbed my arms as an unexpected icy chill crept down my spine.

Dad and Kirk helped me clean the house for another couple of hours. Around six, we cleaned up to go meet Mom, my stepmom, Fancy, Liz, Ari, and the kids for dinner at the Isle of Capri Restaurant, which overlooks Clear Lake. Bella and Miguel would have dinner with some of his med school classmates in Houston.

I have loved the Isle of Capri since I discovered it while I attended Rice University. A guy I dated with a wad of cash burning his fingers used to bring me out here for dinner. The couple who own the restaurant immigrated from the Isle of Capri in Italy decades ago. Their cuisine is *molto authentico*, as Nonna used to say. It is about halfway between my Morgan Point house and Liz's bar—oops, fine eatery—in Galveston. The food and ambiance are fabulous. It sits right on Clear Lake, and people often hold weddings and other special events there. It surprised me Liz and Ari did not get married there. Instead, they married on the beach at Galveston Island State Park.

That night, we convinced the staff to allow us to eat *alfresco* on the patio, where they allowed Hairy to sit beside me. We feasted on calamari, fried shrimp, fresh grilled fish, salads, and, of course, vino. Everything tasted excellent, as usual. We had a lovely Santa Margherita pinot grigio, which paired well with the seafood. How can you eat at Clear Lake and not eat seafood? How can you eat Italian and not have a glass of wine? I had one glass of wine and then switched to water.

It always struck me as odd that wine never tempted me like margaritas do. There is something about the delectable concoction of icy cold lime juice, Cointreau, and Patron that is irresistible to me, especially if you add a sidecar of Amaretto. Once I start drinking them, I find it damned near impossible to stop.

Mom swears I am an alcoholic. She hurts my feelings when she throws the label at me. I contend I would only be an alcoholic if I could not control my urge drinking any other alcohol, and I went without a margarita for three years until last night. Okay, I would have had more last night if Sandy had not cut me off, but I did not drink until I blacked out. I have never done that.

From my criminal defense work, I understand alcoholism, or alcohol use disorder as it is now termed, is a chronic disease characterized by uncontrolled drinking and a preoccupation with alcohol. An alcoholic has a physical and mental dependence on alcoholic beverages. An alcoholic can go into withdrawal symptoms if they stop drinking alcoholic beverages. The alcoholic lacks the ability to stop or cut down their drinking on their own. Yes, I craved a margarita for a couple of weeks after I quit drinking them, but I quit drinking them on my own, and I never went into anything I would call 'withdrawal.' I did not have the shakes, and I did not need to be hospitalized to quit drinking margaritas. And yes, I wanted one from time to time since then, but I abstained from the delectable concoctions until last night when I celebrated my win at the settlement conference. Of course, neither Kirk, Liz nor Dave would give me a margarita if I went down on both knees begging for one.

Alcoholics lack control and have abnormal cravings or feelings of irritability in the absence of alcohol. Drinking contributes to problems with relationships, jobs, and finances. I had relationship problems with Jack, but our problems were asshole related, not alcohol related.

Alcoholics are dishonest with themselves and others about how much and how often they drink as well. Okay, I probably was not honest with myself years ago about how often I drank margaritas. I would drink a couple of them every day when I got home for a year before I forced myself to quit drinking them. Hell, I still want one, and I drank a passel of them last night, but I can control the urge. I controlled the urge for years now.

When a drinking problem becomes severe, professionals call it alcohol use disorder. Psychologists define five types of alcoholics: 1. the young adult subtype, 2. the young antisocial subtype, 3. functional subtype, 4. the intermediate familial subtype, and 5. the chronic severe subtype. The National Institute on Alcohol Abuse and Alcoholism (the NIAAA) also defines several types of drinkers: 1. the border dependent, 2. the bored drinker, 3. the community drinker, 4. the conformist drinker, 5. the depressed drinker, 6. the de-stressed drinker, 7. the hedonistic drinker, 8. the macho drinker, and 9. the re-bonding drinker. Okay, I admit I have used a margarita to de-stress in the past, but I do not think that makes me an alcoholic. Maybe there is a touch of hedonist in me, too. As Jack used to say, and like happened last night, margaritas make my clothes fall off. If I had a combination of those two, I would have been a border dependent drinker, but I am not not an alcoholic. I was not an alcoholic back then and I am not an alcoholic now.

That is why I quit drinking margaritas for years until yesterday. I do not want to become an alcoholic. Nowadays, I walk, meditate, take a bubble bath, or read if I want to de-stress. Sometimes I have a glass of wine or two fingers of single malt whiskey. I usually drink only one or two drinks a month at most. I realize I have been drinking more while I stayed at the bar. Of course, I endured a mammoth-sized amount of stress for the past couple of weeks, too.

Okay, I admit it will be better for me to be back in my home and away from the constant temptations of the bar.

Johnny says it is not safe for me to be at the house alone, but I think it is less safe for me to live in the apartment over the bar where that bottle of Patron tequila downstairs calls my name. Thus far, I resisted the lure of the Patron, but would I be able to continue to not binge on 'ritas if I moved back over there? And would I be safer from Jack's killer if I were there instead of at my house?

What a conundrum.

Liz was the one who convinced me to quit drinking 'ritas. She got through to me where Mom could not. I still do not think I am an alcoholic, but I might have headed down that slippery path if I had not stopped drinking those sweet, seductive concoctions.

Hmm, I wonder if there is such a thing as a margarita-holic?

Anyway, I am determined to stay away from the delectable demon drinks now. If I want something alcoholic, I will allow myself to have a glass of wine. It has less alcohol content than tequila or scotch. I do not think I ever had over one glass of wine in an evening in my life. I hate the taste of beer, and I learned I am allergic to rye while in college. That was the sickest I ever became in my life unless I was on a sailboat. I will drink scotch, and high-quality single malt scotch like Glenfiddich or Talisker. I never drink blended scotch which I think is an abomination. Jack toked a little weed now and then, but I never wanted to try it. He offered it to me from time to time, but the smell alone made my head hurt and my stomach roll. I hated to think how badly I would feel if I toked a joint or two.

No, my Waterloo has always been a margarita on the rocks, made with Patron tequila and Cointreau, with salt on the rim of the glass. It is damned hard for me to say no to a well-made 'rita.

Now, I must avoid drinking any alcohol while the authorities investigated Jack's murder. My life, liberty and pursuit of happiness might well depend on my sobriety. God only knew I did not need to mouth off while 'under the influence,' and have anyone say I might have offed the Jack Ass, even if he was a Jack Ass.

Captain Johnny, Tamsin and I talked until late that night when I stayed at the apartment over the bar. Johnny agreed I needed to keep my wits about me and to strive not to give the 'coppers' any reason to think I killed Jack. "Because you did not kill him."

I tilted my head. "No, I didn't kill him, but how do you know I am not guilty of murdering him, Johnny?"

He smiled. "Tamsin and I kept watch over you from the time you landed in that disreputable establishment down the street until this morning. We knew something horrid would happen last night or tonight, and we feared it would happen to you."

I blinked as his words sank in. "You mean my guardian angel and guardian angel in training watched over me last night?"

Tamsin nodded as Johnny blushed. "Yes, my dear, you had angels watching over you all night long."

I beamed at them both. "In that case, I know everything will work out fine."

Johnny shook his head as a look of impatience crossed his translucent, ghostly features. "You must promise to be careful, Sara. Not only to prevent the police from arresting you, but to remain on alert against whoever killed Jack. We do not know why they killed him. His killer might come after you next."

Cold chills ran down my spine as I took in his words.

Could someone really come after me next? And why would they?

Chapter 8
Sara

The next day, I still shook with nervous tension and found myself in tears with little to no effort. I let Aunt Mags know someone murdered Jackson out at Red Fish Island, and the police might want to arrange another talk with me, with her present. She sounded horrified to learn I said anything to them other than 'call my attorney.' She told me she would file a Notice of Death with the Harris County divorce court.

I then called Robin to tell her someone had murdered Jackson. I could not calm her as she became hysterical. As she sobbed, I told her we could talk more at court the next day.

"No, wait." She struggled to control her sobs. "Will you let me attend his funeral?"

The question startled me. "What?"

She sniffed again as she tried to talk. "Jack's funeral. Will you tell me when it is? Can I attend it? Oh my god, Sara, I loved him so much."

I rolled my eyes as I stifled the urge to make gagging sounds, more than a little tempted to tell her 'no.' I sighed. "Yeah, sure. Whatever."

She took the hint and dropped the subject.

What did I care if Jack's lover attended a service for him? Of course, I could be cruel and refuse her request, but it would accomplish nothing and cause additional friction I did not need in my life. Jack was dead. Whatever.

With some not-so-subtle encouragement from my family, I spent Sunday night in Galveston at the apartment over the bar with Liz, Ari, and their kids. Monday morning, I donned a severe black suit and a demure white blouse for court. I pulled my hair back into a sleek, low chignon like I used to wear my hair when I competed in dance competitions. I wore a minimum of makeup and demure pearls in my pierced ears. With my legs covered in the antiquated pantyhose I hate, and my feet slipped into my black patent leather Louboutin pumps, I arrived at the courthouse fifteen minutes before docket call, looking every bit like the grieving widow. Dad and Kirk accompanied me. They went to the law library, where they would wait for me.

I held a lace trimmed hankie to my nose and made frequent sniffing noises. I sought the solitude of a corner in the jury room as I waited for docket/ call.

As the judge began calling the docket, I slipped back into the room where I stood by the door with a hankie pressed to my nose. When the judge called the Cangelosi case, the judge called the attorneys to the front. In a muffled voice, he asked how I was doing. I sniffed again, took a deep, ragged breath. "I have been better, your Honor."

And damned if my voice cracked then. The judge frowned.

"You have no business even attempting to be in court today, Sara. Someone murdered your husband Friday night." Judge Henderson's voice was firm but kind. "Are you even able to proceed?"

I shook my head, overwhelmed by unexpected emotions, which rendered me unable to speak.

Maggie shook her head. "She is not, your honor. Sara is loath to admit it, but she has undergone a horrible shock. Someone murdered her husband less than 72 hours ago, and his murderer remains still loose on the streets. The poor girl slept little since she learned of his death."

The judge nodded, his demeanor serious and concerned. "Yes, I imagine you have been most upset by this tragedy. Sara, we all call you Ms. Winslow, but most of us know you are Mrs. Talbott. I extend my sincere condolences over your husband's untimely death. You asked this Court to allow Ms. Henson to take over your case. Mr. Jacobs, do you oppose her motion?"

John Jacobs cleared his throat as he glanced at his client. "No, your honor. Last week, I might have opposed it. Today, I would be a heel if I failed to agree to it."

"Ms. Cangelosi, I see you signed the Motion to Substitute. I take it you have no opposition?"

Robin gulped and cut her eyes at me. "No, your Honor. I think this would be the best thing right now. Poor Sara has been ill and now, with her husband's death, it would be cruel to make her continue to try a case in a couple of weeks. Ms. Henson agreed to take the case, and I am confident she will be ready to try it."

Maggie cleared her throat. "May I make a suggestion, your honor?"

The judge nodded. "Of course, Ms. Henson. And thank you for stepping up to the bat to help Sara on this matter."

Maggie bowed her head. "You're welcome, your honor. My pleasure. Sara is a fine attorney, my niece, and a dear friend. This is a horrible ordeal for her. As you mentioned, I moved to substitute as counsel for Ms. Cangelosi last week. Like Ms. Cangelosi stated, Sara has had some health issues, and her physician recommended she take a leave of absence. Then, this horrible situation arose with poor Jackson. Anyway, this matter has not mediated yet. Given the current situation, and that the court investigator supplemented her social study this past weekend, I suggest we pass the case one month, and the parties mediate the case in the interim period."

The judge nodded like a bobble-headed doll in the back of a station wagon. "Fine idea, Ms. Henson, fine idea. Mr. Cooper, don't you think that's a fine idea?"

The attorney for Sonny Cangelosi looked relieved the judge would not force him to proceed in the trial against the grieving widow and Maggie Henson, and their client, Saint Robin of Clear Lake. Oh, let me be honest: he looked tickled pinker than pink. Of course, little did he know that Saint Robin was a conniving little whore, I thought. Or that I could be the key suspect in a murder investigation."That sounds like a wonderful idea, your honor. Who would you suggest as a mediator?"

Judge Henderson smiled. "How about Abel Hernandez? I hear he has some free time coming up in the next few weeks."

"I guess I should have mentioned we already set Abel up to mediate the case for us. It's set for November 1," I said.

Judge Henderson smiled. "Excellent. Let me make a call to Abel and see if he can move it up from the November mediation date."

I groaned. The National Specialty was in two weeks, and my vacation letter had been on file since January to cover my two weeks off to drive to Pennsylvania and back. Hairy and Boze were both entered all four days of the shows in Pennsylvania, and we would attend shows in Louisiana on our way to Philadelphia. Hairy was the top winning Skye terrier in the country, and I knew he could win the National Specialty. Okay, I guess it is a little off (uh, did I say, 'a little'??) to fret about dog shows when someone just murdered your husband, but I damned sure was not planning to do anything with Jack during the next two weeks. We planned to go to these shows for the past year, and I set the mediation for November 1 to give plenty of time for the reports to be supplemented and to allow me to go to the Specialty. Fancy, Dara, and I attended the Pennsylvania shows every year for the past fourteen years. Our dogs placed at four shows, took Winner's Dog at two, Winner's Bitch at one, and the judge named Hairy the Select Dog last year. I intended to take Best of Breed if not Best in Specialty Show at this one, if I could get there with my Hairy Potter.

Maggie noticed the look on my face and leaned over to me. "What is the matter?"

"The Skye terrier national specialty is the first week in October. My vacation letter is on file, and I plan to show my dog at it," I answered through gritted teeth as she rolled her eyes.

"Where is it?" she asked under her breath.

"Pennsylvania, near where Jack grew up."

She smiled and patted me on my shoulder. "Your honor, Sara tells me she planned to take Mr. Talbott's cremains back home to Pennsylvania around the first of October for interment. She hoped this matter would be resolved by then. She hoped to be gone about a week." I cut my eyes at her and held up two fingers. "Uh, two weeks. I understand she already had a vacation letter on file for the first two weeks of October. They planned a vacation to visit his family then."

My god, she lies as well as Jack did, I thought with stunned surprise.

"Oh, I am sorry, I had not thought about when you might hold the interment of your husband's remains. Well, let's see if you can coordinate something, and get back here by mid-October. That should give Sara time to wind things up. I am granting your Motion, Sara, but it would be helpful if you could assist Ms. Henson in the mediation. If you need more time, let me know. If Abel can't settle it, no one can. I suppose that means you would both like a short reset to get it settled?"

Both Maggie and John Cooper nodded. "Yes, your Honor."

The judge scribbled some notes onto the docket control sheet. "Okay, I reset this case until November 5, but I encourage you to get this case settled. Mr. Cooper, has your client reviewed the updated reports from the custody evaluator, the amicus attorney, and the psychologist?"

John Cooper blushed as he stammered his answer. He ran a nervous finger around the collar of his starched shirt. "Uh... yes, your Honor. We reviewed them this morning before court."

The judge smiled. "Very good. Mr. Cangelosi, I urge you to follow your attorney's recommendations. Let's get this case settled in a manner befitting Michael's best interest."

Sonny Cangelosi turned scarlet with embarrassment or anger. I could not tell which caused his red face, but I would swear I saw steam arising around his collar. He gave a sharp nod of his head.

I would have sworn the Judge wanted out of the courtroom as badly as I did from the speed with which he rushed us out of there that morning. I had seen nothing like it before.

As we exited the courtroom, Robin grabbed my sleeve. "You're not planning to take him off somewhere else to bury him, are you?"

I looked at her in surprise, as I realized we upset her with my cover story to the Judge. "What? Oh, for God's sake, Robin, let's discuss it outside. This is not the right time or place to discuss it."

"No, I want to know now. Where do you plan to bury him? When? Will you allow me to attend the services?" Her voice broke.

Maggie placed her hand on Robin's back. "Robin, you need to come outside with us. Your ex-husband is listening to us."

Robin's eyes flew open as she looked around, as if terrified Sonny heard her. She paled as she spotted Sonny watching us from across the hallway and nodded. "Yes, ma'am. It's just..."

"Not now, dammit. We can talk outside."

Robin swallowed hard and nodded again, before following Maggie out the door. I stood a moment, staring at Cangelosi, before I turned to leave, as well. As I turned, he nodded as he reached out to touch my arm.

"My condolences at your loss, Mrs. Talbott."

I blinked, unsure Sonny Cangelosi's words rang true. If anyone other than me had a motive to kill Jack, it was Sonny. "Thank you, Mr. Cangelosi."

I turned to walk away and realized he had not released my arm. He reached over and slipped a folded piece of paper into my hand. "Mrs. Talbott, I want you to know I didn't have nothin' to do wit' his death."

My heart raced. "Wh-what do you mean, Mr. Cangelosi?"

Sonny gulped and looked around. He ran a finger around the neckline of his shirt as he glanced down the crowded hallway. "Look, I know. About your husband and Robin. I know, but I swear on God's head, I didn't have nothin' to do with his death. So help me God, I swear."

I blinked, stunned, as I realized what he meant. No one could accuse Cagey Cangelosi of beating around the bush this time. "Uh, Mr. Cangelosi..."

"Yeah, yeah, I know I could fight dis, but I reckon enough is enough. It's time to quit kicking a dead horse, as they say, and to move on. I heard the judge use that 'dead horse' line twice during docket call, and it seems appropriate right now. Oh, dammit, I don't mean to compare Mr. Talbott to a dead horse."

His cheeks burned bright red with embarrassment as he shuffled from foot to foot, but he still kept a tight hold on my sleeve.

"Well, they are both dead. The proverbial dead horse and my husband, I mean," I replied.

He nodded as the red color to his cheeks subsided. "Yeah, yeah. But I need to tell you, I know all about it. Robin and your husband, I mean."

My mouth was dry, and my heart pounded hard in my chest. I did not know what to expect next. "So, anything else you need to say, Mr. Cangelosi?"

He nodded. "Yeah. Da police, dey done come by to see me. I swear, Mrs. Talbott, I didn't kill him. Might have wanted to, but I didn't. I don't wanna ever go back to da joint again. I got a sweet wife and two great kids. I got good reasons not to go back to da joint. Been there, done dat, got the tattoos, like they always say."

"Okay." I nodded, unable to think of anything to say in reply which would comprise even a halfway intelligent response.

Sonny cleared his throat as he glanced down the hall again. "Anyway, I wanted you to know you gotta be careful."

I blinked again. "Why do you say that?"

He laughed as he looked around the hallway again. "Look, I didn't kill him. I'd bet my bottom dollar you didn't kill him. You're a classy lady, Mrs. T. You might have had reason to kill the bastard, but you got way more class than to stoop to dat level. Anyway, I figure, if I didn't kill him, and you didn't kill him, and we both damned sure know Robin didn't kill him, then who did?"

I nodded. He made sense. If I assumed he was telling me the truth, and he did not kill Jack, or have anything to do with it, then the essential question was: who killed Jackson? "Okay. I don't know. Who do you think killed him, Sonny?"

Sonny shrugged. "All I can say is Mr. Talbott wasn't squeaky clean like he wanted everyone to think. He had enemies. Not just you or me, mind you. I talked to people who know."

With a start, I realized what he meant. "Now, wait a minute. Are you trying to tell me that Jack was involved in something illegal?"

He shrugged again. "I ain't sayin' nothin' disrespectful about the dead, Mrs. Talbott, but just remember, Jackson Talbott wasn't squeaky clean. There were other folks who wanted him dead, too. Lots of other folks."

"I never said I wanted Jack dead. Do not put words in my mouth." I snapped out the words in anger.

The big palooka hung his head. "I'm sorry, no disrespect intended. It's just, you're a classy lady, Mrs. T. My friends say you need to be careful. Whoever did this to Mr. Talbott is still out there loose, and you could be in danger, too."

Cold tremors ran down my spine again, despite the warmth of the late September afternoon. "Why do you say that?"

He shrugged as he glanced furtively down the hall again. "Like I said, you didn't kill him. I didn't kill him. Who did? You be careful. And, if you need anything, you call dis man."

He pointed to the piece of paper I clutched in my hand. I glanced down at it only a second before I tried to give it back. "Look, I don't think I need this..."

"My friends say I'm supposed to give you dis, Mrs. Talbott. Look, I know you're going out of town next week. I heard you tell the Judge that you're going to Pennsylvania. I hear tell that there's some wise guys in Phillie who could be a problem for you. You have any problem, any problem at all, and you call my friend Ray La Rosa. He'll take care of it."

I felt the color drain from my face and glanced around to make sure no one could overhear us, too. I leaned closer to him to whisper my response. "He's Mafioso?"

He glanced around before he answered. "'*Ndrangheta.*"

I did not know you could feel so cold in 98-degree Texas heat, even if we were inside. I ran my hands up my arms as I shivered while his words sank in. "Mr. Cangelosi, I don't think I'm going to need some Mob wise guy to help me."

He pushed the paper back into my hand, curling my fingers around the scrap. "Trust me, lady, better safe than sorry. You need anything, anything at all, then you call my friend." He glanced around, as if he worried they might catch him talking to me. He ran a finger around the neck of his shirt again. "It's Ray's number. I mean, if you know what I mean, he has connections. He's *la famiglia.* He's got connections. *Capisce?*"

I hesitated a moment, and then nodded. Without thought, I answered in the same language. "*Si, io capisco.* Yeah, I understand. Better safe than sorry. I'll call if I have a problem."

He looked surprised I answered him in Italian. "Look, you got any problems, you call Ray. He'll take good care of you. You're Camila de Rosini's granddaughter, and that means you're *la Principessa della Rossini y Franchetti famiglias* now, and you could be in danger, a lot of danger, unless I miss my bet." He tugged his bottom eyelid with his index finger. "*Tua capisce?*"

My heart lurched. His eyelid tug warned me to be careful. "*Si, como no. Grazie, signore.*"

Honest to God, I felt like I might faint. How did he know my Nonna's maiden name? Mother mentioned that I was *la principessa* when Nonna died, but I blew it off. How could I be a princess? My Nonna's family were olive and grape farmers from Calabria. I felt confident my family had no nobles in its midst. It meant nothing to me when Mother told me I was *la principessa* after Nonna died. Besides, Nonna always called me her little *principessa*. I reached out to grab his hand. "How do you know that *mi famiglia* calls me *la principessa?*"

He shrugged again as he kind of smiled. "I know lots of stuff, Mrs. T. I ain't half as *stupido* as people think I am. I'm just a *paisano*. My parents came here from Sicily when I was a kid. But I ain't *stupido*. You be careful. *Usa la testa. Capisce?*"

He made a motion with a finger to his temple. People might think that motion symbolized shooting, but Nonna used the expression '*usa la testa*' often. I learned many years ago it meant 'use your head. Don't be stupid.'

I nodded. "*Si, ho capito, signore, y grazie molto.*" I folded the little slip of paper and slid it into the zippered section of my handbag.

"*Bene*. And keep your doors locked. I got some ideas about what's going on, Mrs. T, but I know nothing for sure yet. I just know if I am right, it could be bad, *davvero pessimo*. You be careful."

He wheeled around, nodded to his attorney, and strode to his car on the other side of the parking lot.

Maggie stood watching me, with curiosity obvious across her face. "Are you okay?"

I nodded. "Yeah. I'm fine. Come on, let's get out of here."

Maggie grabbed Robin by the arm, and we hurried out of the building. Once outside, Robin could hold back her anger no longer. "What the hell did Sonny say to you?"

"He expressed his condolences over my husband's death. Maggie, he said he knew about Jack and Robin, but he swears he didn't kill Jack."

"Dammit, I hoped he was the killer. Oops, that sounded horrible." Maggie looked shamefaced by her ill-timed faux pas.

"Yes, it did," snapped Robin, as angry color tinged her cheeks.

Maggie looked embarrassed. "Look, Robin, I didn't mean I'm glad Jack died. I meant it would have resolved this custody case right now and would have solved Jack's murder. Robin, you didn't go out to Red Fish Island with him Friday night, did you?"

"Oh, thank god, no. Why? Do you think I killed Jack?" Tears welled up in her eyes.

"Of course not, but I thought you might be in danger, too. Did he call you that evening?"

She sniffed. "Yeah, he called a little before 9. Mikey was running a fever, so I didn't go out there with Jack. He called to check on us before he headed out to Red Fish Island. Jack said he would stay out there overnight to fish. He planned to come back sometime on Saturday." She turned towards me. "Come on, Sara, level with me. What did Sonny say to you?"

"Just that. Sonny expressed his condolences, and he gave me a piece of paper with the phone number for some guy named Ray La Rosa. He said, 'he got connections,' and could help me if things got bad for me."

She looked horrified and shook her head. "His friend, Ray La Rosa? That guy is in the mob. Hell, he's a mob boss in Jersey. You stay away from that man. I bet the mob killed my Jack."

My heart lurched as she referred to my dead husband as 'her' Jack. I bit my tongue to keep from snapping at her that 'her' Jack was my husband. "Yeah. Well, someone killed him, and I didn't do it. If Sonny is lying, then you be careful. He said to be sure to keep your doors locked. Like he said, *usa la testa*. Use your head. Don't be stupid. He swore he knew about Jack and you. He could still try to pull something."

She paled at my words and cut her eyes to make sure Sonny had left.

I stood watching Sonny Cangelosi as he drove off, my mind filled with confused thoughts. Mr. Talbott wasn't squeaky clean, Sonny said. He had enemies. And Sonny gave me the name and number of some uppity-up mob wise guy to call In Case of Emergency next week. And then it hit me.

Shit. Sonny Cangelosi told me the mob killed Jack. But why did he think they would kill Jackson?

Nonna was Italian, and Jack used to call me his little Italian Dish. We honeymooned in Rome and made a trip a few years ago to Southern Italy so he could meet some of my relatives. But was he involved with the mob? Of all the scenarios that ran through my head since Jack's murder, this one never once passed through my noggin.

How could certified public accountant Jackson Talbott, as white bread as they came, have become involved with the Mafia? Jeez Louise, why would he have become involved with *'Ndrangheta*?

It was a conundrum.

About then, Sonny's attorney approached us. He appeared rattled. Maggie smiled as she turned to him. "Did you want to discuss the case, John?"

He gave a curt nod. "Yeah."

He motioned for Maggie to come across the sidewalk underneath a little gazebo to talk with him. He whispered something to her. Her look of surprise startled me. She nodded, and they talked a few more minutes before she came back to us.

"Well, I'll be damned. Sonny told John to non-suit his Motion to Modify."

Robin looked confused. "What do you mean?"

"He gave up, Robin. He's letting you keep custody of Mike," I whispered.

She turned and stared across the street at Sonny, who had circled around the block and sat watching us from his car. He nodded to her and then drove away slowly. "Well, I'll be damned. Maybe this lawsuit was about Jack all along."

I bit back the provocative question I longed to ask. Just how long had you been effing my husband, anyway? I took a deep breath and tried to calm myself. My heart pounded like crazy in my chest, and I knew my blood pressure soared far above my normal rate. Keep your mouth shut, Sara. It's not worth it, especially here outside the courthouse. Just keep your mouth shut.

Instead, I went back inside the courthouse to the law library where I found Dad cruising the internet as Kirk peered into a law book. "Find something interesting?"

Kirk looked up, startled by my voice. "I didn't expect you back so soon. You enjoy this stuff? It seems dry and boring to me."

I chuckled. "It can be boring or quite fascinating. What are you reading?" I eased the case law from his hands and scanned the case summary before I shut the book and put it back on the shelf where it belonged. "It's a bankruptcy case. No wonder you find it dry and boring. Come on, let's go. Anyone besides me need a cup of coffee? We could go to Starbucks on the way back to the club."

Dad looked up and grinned. "Let me sign off this computer. There, I'm done. You know me. I'm always in the mood for coffee. Let's go."

Once we got to the car, Dad turned towards me. "What happened?"

I rubbed my hands across my aching neck. "The judge cut me out of the case and continued the trial setting, but then Sonny threw in the towel. He conceded custody to Robin."

Both men looked stunned.

"You're kidding," Dad said.

I shook my head and crossed my fingers in front of me. "Nope, cross my heart. I swear he threw in the towel. I do not know if he did it based on the custody evaluation update, which was filed yesterday, the psych evaluation update, or what might have motivated him. He told me he knew about Robin and Jack. And then to make matters even stranger, Robin said, 'maybe it was about Jack all along.' Honest to God, I thought I would vomit right there."

"I understand your reaction, Sara, but it appears she may have been right," Dad answered, as his eyes narrowed in speculation.

"Well, let's hope that's the answer. If it is, then it means you're not in any danger." Kirk looked thoughtful.

I frowned and shook my head. "Captain Johnny swears I'm still in danger. Sonny Cangelosi seemed to think so, too."

Dad gave me a sharp look. "Why? What did Cangelosi say?"

"He told me to be careful. He also knew Nonna's birth name, and he called me '*la Principessa della Rossini y Franchetti famiglias*,' like it is a big deal.

No one ever called me '*principessa*' before except *Zio Roberto*. Well, Nonna called me that, too."

Kirk paled. "Did you tell Maggie this?"

I shook my head. "Not just no, but hell, no, especially after Sonny mentioned the '*Ndrangheta*."

"Holy Jesus," muttered Kirk.

"My thought, too." Dad looked freaked out as he nibbled on a thumbnail.

We drove to the Starbucks in silence. As we pulled into a parking place, I spoke. "I think I should call *Zio Roberto* when we get to the apartment. What do you think, Daddy?"

"I think that might be the wisest thing to do, baby girl." He looked grim.

Kirk nodded. "Aye, it's time to call your Uncle Roberto. Maybe he will know what is going on."

Less than a half hour later, we arrived at the bar and hurried upstairs. Once there, I located the phone number for my Uncle Roberto and placed the international call. A few minutes later, he answered. "*Pronto.*"

I could not help it. I grinned. The colloquialism always strikes me as funny. '*Pronto*' means 'ready' in Italian. Foreigners might say '*ciao*,' which means 'hi,' but Italians answer the phone with 'pronto' to let the caller know 'I'm ready for you to talk.' In Texas, we use the Spanish word '*pronto*' to mean 'fast.' Using '*pronto*' at the beginning of a phone call in Italy always amuses me. "*Zio Roberto*? This is Sara. I have a problem."

I explained the situation, beginning with Jack's death, and then asked if I should be worried, or if he felt Jack's murder related to Jack's affair with Robin.

"It is possible, *mi principessa*, but I suspect there is more involved than adultery. I fear there is far more involved here than Jack's affair with this woman, Robin. I will make discrete inquiries, but I think you must remain on guard. Give me a few days and I will call you back. In the meantime, *usa la testa.*"

I bit the corner of my lip as I nodded. "*Si, como no, mi zio. Per favore,* let me know as soon as you learn anything."

"Of course, my darling girl. I will call as soon as I have information which I know is relevant and true."

I hung up the phone, feeling unsettled. There was something else going on, but I could not discern what it was. Yet. However, I would figure it out.

Jackson, what the hell did you get us involved in?

Chapter 9
Sara

It was a rough week. God knows I will never forget the autopsy. Philip Martino, the Senior Assistant District Attorney, insisted the autopsy must take place because some asshat murdered Jack. I agreed, not understanding he meant I must attend it. It appalled me to see the condition of Jack's body. His ravaged body sustained a severe sunburn, with deep second-degree burns over most of his torso. The ravaged condition of his face and extremities horrified me. Crabs ate away much of his chiseled, handsome face, of which he was so proud before other fishermen discovered his corpse. The gunshot wound was stark and brutal. I never saw anything like it before, and I prayed I would see nothing like it again. It shocked me to see Jack's shattered skull and to know someone destroyed his genius intellect in such a brutal manner. He may have been a lousy husband, but he was renowned as a brilliant forensic accountant. Knowing a gunshot killed him was one thing; to see the trauma caused by the gunshot was a different matter. I rushed over to the trash can, vomited, and then sobbed at the appalling sight lying cold and still before me. Philip attempted to comfort me, but I was inconsolable. Poor Philip stood there shuffling from foot to foot as he tried to comfort me, unsure what to do with his hands, while I wept over the sight of my dead husband's shattered skull.

I would bet anything they made me attend the autopsy to see my reaction.

The funeral home cremated Jack after his autopsy. Robin sobbed in hysterics when I told her I had him cremated. I figured she wanted a big, fancy funeral where she could cry and carry on. That would not happen on my dollar. I promise you; the girl did not want to see Jack after they shot him in the head and the crabs dined on his face. It would have traumatized her for life.

The autopsy damn sure traumatized me.

We held a small, private memorial ceremony on Friday morning. I wore my black suit again. Robin wore widow's weeds, black from head to toe, replete with a veil attached to a small, black pillbox hat. At the end of the brief service, I gave the grieving lover half of Jack's ashes. I would spread the other half on the Gulf he loved so much, even if it meant I would be sick out on the bay one last time.

I rolled my eyes when Robin thanked me for giving her half of Jack's ashes. I almost told her she could have them all if she would spread part of the ashes on Red Fish Island, but I decided I needed to do that myself. It would be hard for Robin to go to the place of Jack's murder, even if it had been his favorite place. It would not be a piece of cake for me either.

Robin told me again she felt guilty because she did not accompany Jack out to Redfish Island the fateful night when he last sailed on the bay. She blanched as I pointed out the murderer might have killed her, too, if she had gone with him and then Mikey would have gone to live with Sonny. Somehow, I managed not to tell her I saw a woman on the boat when he sailed past my house that night. She did not need to know at that point that Jack was a philandering son of a bitch. I wondered again for the umpteenth time who accompanied him that fateful night when he died. I figured the horny fool picked up some pretty young thing who turned out to be a hit woman. The authorities located his sailboat at the Hilton on the Lake, moored overlooking Clear Lake. They dusted it for prints, but the murderer had wiped it clean. Someone parked his truck in the Hilton parking lot. The police did not think Jack parked it there, because the murderer wiped it clean of fingerprints, too. Jack reserved a room at the Hilton, and he dropped off some of his belongings in the room before he took the boat out. His guns were nowhere to be found. No one knew who left the boat at the hotel or when they tied up the forty-foot sailboat at the Hilton dock. It sounded more than a little fishy to me that not one employee working in a hotel the size of the Hilton on the Lake saw a forty-foot sailboat come up to the dock. That made me even more curious about who accompanied Jack to the island the night of his murder.

There have long been rumors members of the mob or drug cartels frequented the Hilton. It is the nicest hotel on the lake and lots of people choose to stay there. I always doubted the stories until Jack's boat turned up there. What else could be the connection?

And why on earth was my squeaky-clean husband involved with the mob? How did he become entangled with drug pushers and whoremongers?

Chapter 10
Sara

I felt sapped of energy after the memorial service on Friday morning, but I knew I had too much to do to sit and fret over Jackson. I went into the office and briefed Ashley, my legal assistant, on which cases she should work while I would be gone.

Remember Thelma, from Scooby Doo? Ashley could be Thelma, with her brown pageboy haircut, tortoise-shell glasses, serious demeanor, and a heart of gold. She had worked for me since she was a sophomore in college, before she ever thought about going to law school. With luck, she will still work with me when I retire. She is a gem, and I am lucky to have her. I hear from some attorneys who say they would never let a legal assistant do research, but you would never hear that crap from me. The girl is a legal genius. I let her try her hand at anything she wants, especially now that she has her third-year bar card.

"Did you hold his memorial service?" She looked up at me with expectation written across her face. "Oh, and thanks for letting me skip it."

I nodded. "No problem. Believe me, I would have skipped it if I could. The funeral home cremated him, and we held his blasted memorial service. I gave Robin half of his ashes. I swear, you would have thought she was the grieving widow."

She shrugged. "Well, I bet she perceives herself as his widow."

I sniffed. "Figures. She may be the grieving lover, but the bitch is not his widow. Let's go over the stuff you need to handle over the next few weeks."

Just then, the phone rang. With her usual professional demeanor, Ashley answered the phone. "Law Offices of Sara Winslow. May I help you?" A look of stunned surprise crossed her face. "No, Mr. Talbott is not in this office, Mr. Nasema. However, Ms. Winslow is here, and I am sure she would be happy to talk to you..." She looked up at me, distress written across her face. "He hung up."

I grabbed the caller ID box. "Hmm. He blocked his number. What did he sound like?"

She shrugged, as if she did not know why he called. "Foreign. Heavy accent. He called a time or two before, but he never left a name before this morning. I recognized his voice this time. I wonder what Jack got himself into this time?"

"Well, whatever it was, it got him killed. Look, if that guy calls again, tell him Mr. Talbott does not have an office here, and give him the number to Jack's office. Let Jack's assistant handle those calls. You can even tell him Jack is ..."

"Dead?"

I tried to laugh, but the sound caught in my throat with an unexpected ache of longing. How dare my body and emotions betray me like this? Swallowing hard, I shook off the unwanted feelings for Jackson. "As tempting as that is, I am a little nervous telling just anyone he died, but, yeah, go ahead. This guy may be someone with whom we want to connect. Maybe he knows what got Jack killed. Who knows? Maybe he is the angry husband of one of Jack's many conquests. Wouldn't Robin love to learn about his other conquests? I guess you should give him Maggie's number and have him call her, if he will. Of course, he may not want to talk to a woman since he did not seem eager to talk to you or me. Like I said, who knows?"

Ashley nodded. "Yeah, who knows? He's not from around here."

I nodded, too, as her words sank in. "Hmm, it's odd that so many of Jack's contacts were foreigners, wasn't it?"

Yes, I always thought it seemed odd," she answered, as her eyes narrowed in speculation.

I decided there was no reason to stay home and not go to the Louisiana shows that weekend or the Pennsylvania dog shows, which would begin the following Thursday. The four-day weekend of shows in Pennsylvania would culminate at the biggest United States dog show of the year, the all-terrier show held each year at Montgomery County Junior College in Blue Bell, Pennsylvania.

Dara and I have been close friends since we learned each other existed. Dad's family did not know about me until Fancy and Richard spotted me at a dance competition when I was twelve. Since my half-sister, Dara, and I look enough alike to be twins, it came as a rude awakening for Dad to realize he fathered a child he did not know existed until I was a pre-teen. At that point, he legitimated me and changed my surname to Winslow. Mom raised hell about changing my surname until her mother gave her a hard shove to do it. Oh well, that is a whole other story.

Remember the gorgeous gal named Samantha on Sex in the City? Our friends used to bet they modeled Samantha after Dara, except Dara has red hair like Miranda's hair. I always insisted the show aired when Dara toddled around, and little kids do not inspire femme fatales. Besides, adult Dara made Sex in the City Sam look like chopped liver. I have seen many a man, including my now-dead husband, grow glassy eyed and weep when confronted with Dara Winslow's lovely 38C delights, tiny waist, and curvy hips. Our sister, Elizabeth, says Dara makes her look like a sack of potatoes. Liz has a fabulous figure, and I would never compare her to a lumpy sack of taters. Dara has scrumptious true Irish auburn hair, which she contends is natural only to the Irish. She wears her Irish red hair like a badge of honor. I would bet she got the hair color from her mother, because Fancy's hair and Bella's hair is the same color and has been this color as long as I have known them. God only knows where my red hair originated, although my Grampa Winslow was Irish. Dara had tawny eyes like Dad and me. It always irritated me that Jack never said Dara's red hair and amber eyes looked odd.

My hair was that Irish auburn, too, until my husband complained too many times that hair the color of mine did not belong on an Italian girl. Go figure. People still say Dara and I look enough alike to be twins. Dad says we are his Irish twins. Dara and I say we are sisters with different mothers, which is true.

Dara brought her drop eared, platinum-colored Skye terrier, Boze. She hoped to finish Boze at the Louisiana show on the way to Pennsylvania or in Pennsylvania. I thought it would be fabulous if Boze finished his championship at one of the biggest shows of the year in Pennsylvania, but Dara wanted to bump Boze up to the Best of Breed competition at those shows. A dog enters the Best of Breed class once the dog is a champion, but if the dog earns its championship while on the circuit, the owner can ask the show chair to bump the dog up to Best of Breed competition. Dara bubbled over with excitement at the prospect.

"Hairy better watch out, because Boze could beat him at Montgomery," she said, her eyes shining and her voice filled with excitement and pride for her dog.

I bit back my grin and my smart retort. I did not have the heart or the courage to tell my sister Boze could not beat Hairy that year. She might smack me hard if I dared to tell her again that Hairy was better than his son right then. Dara has a nasty temper and punches a mean left hook. Give Boze a couple of years to mature and he will beat his sire.

When we left Texas, Boze needed one show to complete his championship. We both wanted Boze to finish his championship on the trip. Dara planned to hit a show in Louisiana on the way to Pennsylvania before we would arrive at Lansdale, Pennsylvania on Tuesday.

I pulled the SUV into the hotel in Lake Charles about 8 p.m. on Friday night. Already exhausted from the emotionally trying events of the day, coupled with the long drive, we found the energy to exercise the dogs and grab a quick dinner before we collapsed into bed after we groomed our Skyes.

The next morning, a nervous Dara awoke me at 7 A.M. I moaned, but arose to head to the show site early. The Skye terriers were not due in the ring until early afternoon. As Dara set up a table for grooming, we noticed a competitor from North Texas had brought her string of Skyes, three dogs and four bitches.

"Looks like she's trying to build points for her dogs. Dammit, I bet she planned to build this major for her puppies and points for her special," said Dara as she glared at our competitor.

"She does not look happy to see us here. She built three point majors for the Best of Winners with her dogs alone. I bet she's praying the judge hates drops. Hmm… I wonder if she's taking her string of Skyes to Pennsylvania?" I asked as I watched the young woman throw down an expensive brush and storm towards the ring. "She always has a frown on her face. That gal seems so angry."

Dara shrugged with another grimace. "Yes, especially if her dog loses. I figure she's headed to Philadelphia, too. I bet she hoped for majors along the way. She strikes me as one unhappy person based on her demeanor. Listen, can you focus when you are in the ring, or are you going to obsess about her being here?"

Dara almost looked worried. The key word was 'almost.' She definitely looked aggravated. She wanted the last point for Boze's championship before we got to Pennsylvania, and the North Texas girl better watch out if she tried to block Boze's win.

Trying to lighten Dara's mood, I grinned. "Not a problem. We will be fine. I'm a lawyer, I'm used to working under stress. We got a decent night's rest, even though someone made us arise with the hens. Her attendance at this show is nothing but a minor bump in the road. Listen, sis, you focus on getting the last point for Boze's championship. You focus on Boze, I will handle Hairy. Don't let her rattle you. Besides, you still have time to work with us if you are worried about Hairy and me. I can put Hairy up on the table for you to go over him, and I can take him down and back a couple of times for you to critique. Heck, Hairy is such a pro, I bet he could show himself. I'm just along for the ride. Jeez-Louise, you already approved of my attire. I'm wearing the Dara approved, sky blue Ferragamo flats with a sky blue Escada skirt and the matching pullover. I promise I will not fall down in the show ring, and even if I do, my pullover top will not pop open. That will never happen again. Besides, my outfit is Escada. It's first class all the way, and I look almost as fabulous as my dog looks."

Dara struggled to suppress her laugh. "You are so weird with your designer clothing. No one else wears clothing like you do to dog shows. Well, I still say that gaping blouse made the points for you the day you fell down in Waco, when your blouse came open—"

I smiled, pleased my distraction from our competitor worked. "Yeah, yeah, I know, but did the judge have to become infatuated with me?"

Dara snickered. "It was destiny. She swears you are her Earth Goddess. Does she still write you love letters?"

"Yes. Don't get me wrong. Edith is a lovely person, but I don't swing that way. Although given the choice between Jack and her? She would have been a better choice than Jackson."

When I fell in the ring in the Best of Breed competition in Victoria that cold winter day, Dara had the freaking audacity to tell the judge I preferred women and lusted after her body. Dara laughed for months afterwards about the judge's less-than-secret affections she directed towards me because of Dara's misinformation. Dara and I may co-own dogs, but I might have to raise her voice an octave or two if she ever pulls a stunt like that one again. So, help me, if she pulls anything like that again, she will sing soprano—or sing with the fishes.

Dara and I look alike, but the similarities end there. I am not an extrovert like Dara. I struggle to present the image of an extrovert at the courthouse, but in reality, my personality is as introverted as they come. That was one problem Jack and I had. He never expected me to react the way I did, and he never understood I do not crave to be the center of attention which he adored. Go figure.

Nigel, my hairdresser, owns two Morgan Point Skye terriers. The first time I met Nigel, I thought I had gone back in time to some old movie set and found a Cary Grant double. The man is drop dead gorgeous. Tall, slender, muscular, with a face composed of lean angles and clean perfection. He describes himself as having 'boyish good looks and a receding hairline', but he is so tall I can't tell where or if it is receding. Dara offered to get him implants, but the silly man laughed and said he thought his breasts were fine. He does the best hair color imaginable. I cannot imagine letting anyone else color my hair.

If he was straight, I would have run away with Nigel years ago.

We would have brought him to Montgomery if he could learn to dress and did not look like a Pee Wee Herman misfit. The last time I saw him in a show ring, he wore a God-awful madras sports jacket and these beyond-hideous, patent leather saddle oxfords he said he bought at the Salvation Army for a whopping $2.00. They looked like they originated in the '50s. Even that wouldn't have been a total disaster if he had left the tie with the hula dancer on it at home. His dog still took the points that day. Jeez-Louise, go figure. I wore an outstanding Chanel suit. It fits me perfectly, and let us not even talk about the price tag on that little beauty. Nigel's magic is with dogs and hair, even if his personal clothing style is appalling. That day, I was still a novice at showing. My inexperience showed even if I wore Chanel, and he was in Salvation Army rejects. He took the points, and I took best loser, or in correct dog show terminology, Reserve Winner's Bitch. It was one of the few times Bianca did not earn points.

At show time, I let my Hairy do his thing. His name is Hairy Potter, but Jack dubbed him Hairy J. Dog, with J. standing for Jackass. Leave it to my jackass husband to dub a dog he disliked 'jackass.' Hairy lolled his tongue at me, his dark eyes twinkling, and we went into the ring.

Dogs must win fifteen points, including two majors to complete an AKC championship. Boze received his fifteenth point that day with two to spare, since this was a major show. When a dog wins his class, he moves into Best of Breed competition. Dara bubbled over with excitement and enthusiasm as she brought Boze back into the ring for the Best of Breed competition.

Boze promises to be a fabulous special in another year or two. That day, Boze never had a chance to win Best of Breed against his sire. It is hard for a dog just a year old to compete against mature specials. Of course, in all fairness to Boze, some judges dislike drop ears. Go figure. It is the original ear set all Skyes used to have. Anyway, that Saturday in Lake Charles was Hairy's day.

Hairy has this incredible, coal black coat, with hair to spare, that long, crisp, luxuriant coat for which people know Skyes. Black is the rarest color in Skyes. As usual, Hairy trounced the other guys from beginning to end, once again taking no prisoners. He even trounced Boze, who took the best of winners to finish his championship. Dara appeared conflicted because Boze finished his championship, but he did not take the Best of Breed.

I admit that I especially loved it when my Hairy beat the other woman's special. You would think no one in the whole wide world could breed a Skye as good as hers, to hear her talk. Yeah, sure. She breeds beautiful Skyes, and her Duke is quite nice, but he is not 'the be all, end all' in the breed. I breed gorgeous examples of our breed, too. Hairy and Boze prove the merit of the Morgan Point Skyes.

Hairy Potter is the funniest dog I ever saw in the show ring. He looks asleep when it is not yet his time to perform. The dog has mastered the fine art of relaxation in stressful situations. He leans against my leg, slack-jawed, snoring, until I whisper, "Hairy Potter, it's Show Time." Then, my little man leaps into action. He gives a stretch and a smile before he flies around the ring with his ears up, neck arched, top line perfect, and his tail wagging with happy excitement. This Skye loves to show. He always puts on the Show to End All Shows for the judge, and believe me, judges eat that stuff up. I cannot make any other dog do it, but it is second nature for my Hairy Potter.

I wanted to leave after we showed in the class because I knew we could make it to New Orleans that afternoon if we boogied on down the road. We planned to enjoy a nice dinner at the Acme Oyster House and get some photos of the dogs in the French Quarter on Sunday before we drove on eastward. I rolled my eyes as Dara insisted we needed to wait for groups. She frowned when I took Hairy into the group ring, her lips pursed into a disapproving line and her foot tapping with nervous energy. After some discussion, she relented and 'let' me show my dog, but she appeared unhappy about it. She becomes quite proprietary about which of us takes our dogs in the terrier group competition ring.

When Hairy won the terrier group, I thought I would faint. To take my dog into the Best in Show competition, I had to negotiate with my bossy sister again. She acted like she might have a seizure when I insisted on taking Hairy into the BIS ring. By the time we were in the lineup for Best in Show, my hands trembled and my knees knocked ninety to nothing, but Hairy was too cool for school, as Mom says. When the Judge handed me the Best in Show rosette, Hairy leapt into the air, barking like a little maniac, while I tried my hardest to remain calm enough to stand on both feet. My God, I just won my first Best in Show! To be honest, Hairy won it while I held the lead. I stood there grinning like a total idiot while Hairy barked and danced around me on his hind legs, and the spectators clapped.

Hairy won Best in Show several times before, including once at the big Houston show in the summer, but I never handled him to those other BIS wins. Dara or my stepmom took him back in for the group and BIS. That Saturday, Dara stood ringside, mouth agape, in clear-cut shock. I held the BIS ribbon, grinning like an idiot. Boze stood wagging from nose to tail at her feet. As usual, Hairy ate it all up.

It surprised me to see the gal from North Texas clapping and cheering for us on the sidelines. I grinned and waved to her. She beamed as she waved back to me and then gave me a big 'thumbs up.'

"Interesting," I said to Dara when we left the ring.

"Very interesting. She seemed happy for you. I bet she asks to use him at stud when we get to Pennsylvania." Dara answered as she studied our adversary.

As we were finishing, a man spoke up. "Congratulations, Sara."

It surprised me to see a familiar courthouse face at a dog show when I glanced up. "Philip Martino, you gorgeous devil, what are you doing here? I didn't know you show dogs."

Tall, dark, and dashing shrugged and half-way grinned. His impeccable, jet-black hair fell over his brow in a charming, boyish manner. I somehow managed not to reach over and smooth that errant lock back into place. I always wondered if he trained his hair to do that so women will reach over to touch his hair. He tossed his head to flip the stray hair back from his brow. "I guess you didn't notice you whupped my ass in the Group ring earlier this afternoon."

I tilted my head and glanced down at the Airedale at his feet. "Oh, I remember your dog. Nice fellow, and he moves like a dream. It surprised and delighted me when the Judge placed Hairy Potter over him. But your Airedale took the group 2, so it wasn't a total wash for you."

When he laughed, I noticed the corners of his baby blue eyes crinkled with amusement. "Yeah, we won 'best loser.' I prefer a dog with a little more substance than your little ball of fluff."

Ball of fluff? And to imagine that I have flirted with this guy at the courthouse for years. I never dreamed those luscious sky-blue eyes hid the heart of a Skye hater. Of course, we never acted on our flirtation - although he let me know more than once that he wanted to take it to the next level. I made the mistake of going out to dinner with him after a trial once, and the man put some of the smoothest moves on me I ever saw. Thank God I did not have a couple of margaritas that night. Yes, he tempted me a time or two when Jack's most recent adultery ate at my soul, but I always somehow shrugged his suggestions off with a laugh and a wink. For me, our flirtation comprised nothing more than a mental exercise. At least, I always tried to think it meant nothing more than flirtatious mental exercise. I suspected Philip's flirtation meant more to him, but perhaps my suspicion was nothing more than feminine vanity.

My lips pursed as I frowned at Philip. "Have you ever gone over a Skye, or felt the bone on one of these guys? Have you ever looked at their jaws? They breed these 'little balls of fluff' to hunt badgers. Canadians call Skyes 'land sharks.'"

He laughed, making the laugh line creases at the corners of his eyes more noticeable. "Must be wusses. Look at that big, happy ball of hair. How could he catch a badger? Now, Graham is a real dog, all muscle and bone, aren't you, fellow?"

How could this man be so freaking adorable? I gave myself a mental shake to stop all thoughts of his adorableness. After all, this gal could not fall for another Skye hater.

Hairy growled as he stepped between the taunting man and me. I could see the ruff of hair around his neck rising. I flipped my hand at Philip. "Yeah, sure, whatever, Philip. Are you headed to Montgomery?"

He nodded. "Yes, he's the number one Airedale in the country. Are you guys headed north with the fluff balls, too?"

"Of course. Hairy is the number one Skye in breed points and group points. See you Thursday at Hatboro I."

Dara raised an eyebrow as she appraised Philip walking away from us. "Wow, look at his butt. He should advertise Levi's with glutes like those. Who was that hunk of masculine gorgeousness?"

Frowning, I shook my head. "Philip Martino is an attorney, but he works for the dark side. He is the Senior Assistant District Attorney in Galveston County. I did not know he even owned a dog, much less a terrier, or that he showed one. Now I guess I will have problems with him because Hairy beat his poor little Grahamsie-poo in the Group. Give me a break. Hairy won because he's 'the man.'"

Dara nodded. "You got that right, Sara. The dog won, not the handler."

"Damned straight," I answered, and we fell together as we laughed.

We had arranged for a late departure, so we did not have to pack the SUV early that morning before we headed to the show site. Dara left our bags with the concierge, who agreed to keep them for us until we returned. We hurried back to the hotel and loaded the rest of our stuff, and then we headed out for New Orleans. I could see it still miffed Dara that Hairy won BIS without her on his lead. She brooded in silence as she drove my SUV out of town.

We were about ten miles out of Lake Charles when she let out an ear-shattering scream. "Oh, sweet Jesus, no! I left Boze at the hotel!"

The next thing I knew, Dara wheeled around in the middle of the road to go back for her beloved boy. I screeched like a bat out of Hades as she wheeled my Lexus SUV around in the middle of the busy highway. The crates slipped and slid around. Hairy whined, and I cursed like a French sailor just denied entrance to a whorehouse. At least, my sister swore I cussed like a sailor locked out of the whorehouse, but do not ask me how she knew how sailors cuss when in that situation. A girl learns a lot of curse words when her dad is a cardiovascular surgeon, and your mother and your stepmother are both cardiovascular surgical nurses. You learn even more when your Irish stepdad, who used to be a sailor, now owns a bar.

Hmm, I would have to ask my step-dad if I curse like a sailor denied admission to a house of ill repute. She probably picked up the phrase from Kirk.

We raced back to the hotel for Dara's beloved dog. She rushed into the hotel, and found him waiting for her, curled up on the manager's desk watching television with him. I had not seen Dara cry since she was thirteen years old, when a softball smacked her in the face and broke her nose. The only reason she cried when the ball hit her was because her mom insisted she had to go to the ER, and Dara missed the final inning of the state finals. That day in Lake Charles, she cried big, wet, sloppy tears as she hugged her dog. When she threw her arms around his neck, Boze grinned and leaned close to her, his pink tongue hanging out of the side of his mouth. As she continued to cry, he licked the tears off her face.

I would bet it was the only time Boze ever saw her cry big, wet tears, too.

"Oh, shut up." She smashed the tears around on her face to wipe them off.

"I didn't say a word." There was no sense in arguing with her. I knew from long years of practice I could never win an argument with this woman. Once again, I thanked God she was not a trial lawyer.

"You were thinking them." She glared at me.

"Can't fault a girl for thinking. You do it all the time." I focused on looking out the window of the hotel as I struggled not to laugh.

"That's different. I think intelligent thoughts, but you get irrational. You heard me tell my dog I would leave him here if he didn't win breed today, and then I left him. Why did I even take him in the hotel? How can he ever forgive me?"

At that point, I could not help myself, and my laugh broke out. "You took him in for the same reason I took Hairy inside. It's too hot to leave the dogs in the car. And your precious little drop-eared Poopsikens adores you. Come on, sis, give me a break, let's go. I would like to reach New Orleans before midnight."

She sniffed. "His name is not Poopsikens. His name is Morgan Point Boze, as in Bozo the Clown. You ought to know, since you bred and named him. And now he is Champion Morgan Point Boze. Do not call him Poopsikens. You know I hate it when you call him that."

"Yeah, yeah, yeah, so please remind me why you call him Poopsikens whenever he makes you angry."

She glared at me again, because of the laugh or the truth in the statements I made before she snapped the lead onto Boze's collar. Then we headed out to the SUV again, this time with both dogs. After about ten minutes of silence, she spoke. "I don't always call him Poopsikens. I call him Bozo most of the time."

I chortled on that one. Her Boze is one of the sweetest Skye terriers I ever met, but he is a four-star clown.

Hairy told me again after we arrived in New Orleans that he intended to win Best of Breed at Montgomery and then to take Best in Show. I warned him it would not be easy with the many fabulous terriers in attendance and with most of them handled by top-notch professional handlers. Hairy reminded me had won four Bests in Show so far, including one at the big Houston show during the summer and the one in Lake Charles. He assured me via telepathy he could win Montgomery. I never saw my black dog so sure of anything as that prospective win.

The next morning, Dara and I took the Skyes through the French Quarter for some photos of our boys in one of our favorite cities. They looked adorable posed in front of the Cathedral, sniffing flowers in the park, and staring out over the Mississippi River. Dara and I both laughed and clapped when our boys sat up to beg for bites of the beignets. After we finished our beignets and café au lait, we headed out for the next leg of our journey.

As I drove out of New Orleans, I thought about the incredible journey which now led us to Montgomery with Hairy and Boze. Hairy was not breathing when born, and I resuscitated him. Fancy told me I was a fool to resuscitate him because she believed he was stillborn. I told her he was not dead; he was not breathing. Fancy laughed and told me 'not breathing' meant 'dead.' I asked her why they perform CPR on heart patients if 'not breathing' meant 'dead', and how she explained heart patients not breathing while on a heart-lung machine. I knew she saved many patients over the years with CPR or the heart defibrillator. She looked surprised by my question.

"Well, that's different," Fancy said, her eyes narrowed as she thought about my question.

"Why? Because your patients are humans and not dogs? Or because they pay Daddy big bucks to mend their hearts?"

Fancy laughed and shook her head, but she never answered my question.

Ignoring Fancy's claim about the puppy's viability, I performed CPR on the little fellow. To her surprise, the tiny puppy started breathing. I looked up at her with triumph and said, "That's why you perform CPR, Fancy. Cardiopulmonary resuscitation saves lives."

I tube fed the tiny puppy to supplement his nursing because he was the smallest in the litter. He would awaken me in the night, calling out to me. At first, I thought I imagined it, but when I would check on the puppies in the whelping box, he would be crying. I would pick him up and cuddle him while I warmed the formula to tube feed him. Our bond grew stronger as I became accustomed to the frequent telepathic calls of 'Mama, Mama, Mama.'

As the little black puppy grew and flourished, it became obvious my runt comprised the pick of the litter. I never saw a Skye with such beautiful, correct movement. He has the strongest front and rear of any Skye I have seen in fifteen years. He is as close to a perfect Skye as I ever saw.

We named him Morgan Point Hairy Potter because it must have been magic that let my runt survive to be the pick of the litter and able to communicate with me the way he does. Now, he had become the number one Skye terrier in the country, although Archer was only one point behind him, and Archer was drop dead gorgeous.

Jack hated Hairy. He called him Hairy J. Dog, and always stressed the J stood for Jackass. He was a good one to call anyone or anything else a jackass. My now-deceased husband resented my devotion to what he termed 'a mere dog.' I never knew a person jealous of a dog besides Jackson Talbott. I thought it was such unmanly behavior. Jack never comprehended Hairy and I had an unusual bond found rarely between a dog and the person he owned. Jack never understood Hairy owned me, body, mind, and soul. Then again, maybe the bond between Hairy and me was the reason Jack raged with jealousy over my beautiful black dog. My Skye became the baby Jack refused to give me. Hairy's registration papers might list me as the owner of Grand Champion Morgan Point Hairy Potter, but Hairy and I knew who owned who.

Hairy loved Show Time from the first time he entered the ring. I never saw a Skye love to show as much as my Hairy, and I can recall some fabulous Skyes who loved to show, like Buddy Goodman, Dexter, Desy, and Archer. Hairy would compete against Archer at the Pennsylvania shows, which made me more than a little nervous. Archer is a fabulous example of our breed, and he has a huge fan club. He is always owner handled, and Archer and Antoinette must have a bond like Hairy and I have because Archer shows with his heart and soul for the woman he loves. We would soon see if my Hairy was correct, and if he could beat gorgeous, cream-colored Archer.

It would disappoint me if Hairy Potter lost to Archer, but I had to admit he would lose to one hell of a fabulous Skye if that happened. My Hairy would still be the best dog there in my book. Like Fancy always says, you always take home the best dog no matter how he performs in competition or how the judge rules.

The long drive exhausted us, and we sighed with relief as we pulled into the hotel in Lansdale, Pennsylvania, on Tuesday evening. We liberated the dogs from their crates, exercised them, unloaded our bags and gear, fed the dogs, and then collapsed into bed. On Wednesday morning, we attended the seminars the STCA puts on every year to educate the membership. Antoinette and I put Hairy and Archer up on grooming tables and allowed members to go over our dogs. Later, Dara and I bathed and groomed our two dogs after the Skye terrier seminar. While Dara blow dried Boze, I ordered dinner from room service. We ate before we finished grooming our boys for the first shows at Hatboro I the following day.

I never understood why they held these four shows at four separate locations. It would be so much simpler to hold the four shows in one centralized location for the four days, like they do at most big shows I attend in the South. Houston holds six shows over five days in the same location. We rent grooming space for all the shows and set up once for all of them. It is easier than moving from show site to show site over the four days of shows. Of course, they held lots of those Southern shows in the summer in large, air-conditioned convention halls. Perhaps they did not have similar locales suitable for dog shows in Pennsylvania.

Oh well, we rented space to groom at these four shows. We had to set up our grooming stations every day and move on to the next site that evening, but we always had space reserved to groom each day.

The club always holds their meetings at the host hotel in Lansdale, so a bunch of us stay there every year. The host hotel is near the Montgomery County Junior College and the other show locations. I have attended these shows since I was fourteen. This would be the first year my stepmom did not go, too. My heavens, I realized with a start, that was half my lifetime ago.

Chapter 11
Sara

Thursday morning, we arrived at the show site with hours to spare before we showed the dogs. After we did our preliminary prep of the Skyes, we strolled among the two long rows of busy vendors since we already groomed our dogs except for a last-minute freshen up. Dara stopped to stare in amazement at a pet psychic with a lengthy line waiting to see her.

"Hey, Sara. Maybe you need to get your chakras checked." Dara flashed a sweet smile at me, but I could see the mischief behind her comment.

I shrugged. "Maybe. Who knows?"

Miss Santana, the pet psychic, smiled at me. "Do you need spiritual realignment, my dear?"

I nodded as I struggled to hold back my laughter. "I don't know. Last month, I had my tires aligned, but I never heard of spiritual realignment."

Miss Santana chortled while several of her admirers stopped dead in their tracks, stunned into silence by my irreverent words. It delighted me to see that the Head Mama Guru could enjoy my odd sense of humor, so I pressed on.

"Truth be told, I have even less idea what a reiki is. Could you explain how you treat a reiki? And what are those 'spiritual crews' the other lady was talking about, anyway?" I figured if I got dragged to her booth by Dara, I could at least find out what this stuff was all about.

As Miss Santana smiled at me, I realized she looked angelic when her face broke into a smile. I had some experience with an angel upon which to make such a bold statement.

"My dear young lady, that is without a doubt one of the most honest things anyone said to me in a long, long time. Come in and I will try to explain, although you must ask Gwendolyn what she means by 'spiritual crews.' I refer to 'the boys.'"

For the next hour, Miss Santana explained it all to me. Wow, did she ever! By the end of our talk, I realized a large group of people sat around us, listening to her talk. Other people wanted the straight poop on all this psychic stuff, too, not just me. I learned that 'reiki' is a Japanese word that meant 'universal life force energy.' 'Chakras' are spinning energy centers or nodes within the human body which are linked to sound and light. These are sometimes called the wheels of life. Balanced chakras can heal and bring us into alignment and balance. By being balanced, we can understand our place in nature, in creation, and our purpose in the universe. That sounded pretty darned fantabulous to me. She explained the Alchemy of Time sets it all in motion, whatever that meant. We have seven main chakras, many lesser chakras, and a life force, or what the Sanskrit calls a 'prana', and which the Chinese call a 'chi.' For our life force to be balanced, the seven main chakras or energy centers must be in balance as well. 'Aura' refers to the energy field emanating from the surface of a person or an object.

I cannot say I was an expert at the end of the hour, far from it. However, by the end of that time, she helped me understand who my personal 'boys' were, and I underwent a reiki session, which she said cleared my aura and re-aligned my chakras. When Miss Santana finished our reiki session, I felt balanced, because, girlfriend, I had not felt so good since the last time I had multiple orgasms, and believe me, that had been quite a while. Jack had not bothered to service my needs in our encounters of the sexual kind for more than a year. All he wanted was to satisfy his own animal urges. In fact, I felt so much better after Miss Santana adjusted me. I knew beyond a doubt this psychic stuff was not just so much hoo-ha. This was the real deal, in fact, it was realer than real. It was the Big Real, if that makes any sense at all. We talked about past life regression ("discover the errors you made in past lives and which you keep repeating"), soul reunification ("a way to heal the soul of past hurts"), and animal communication ("how to communicate with your pet more effectively using psychic powers"). It fascinated her to learn Hairy and I communicated psychically, and she suggested she would allow me to attend her elite group later that weekend called the Lotus Circle. She said the Lotus Circle was for people with special, innate abilities and skills which had not been developed, and she seemed sure I would fit in well.

I was not sure if this was going to be a new way of life for me, but I knew I felt better than I had felt in weeks. I did not want the emotional pain relief I found that day to disappear. I felt sure this stuff might help me find my own way through the Dark Night of Hell starring Jack and Robin, which I had been enduring. Without Jack Talbott, I was on my way to becoming whole with no one but myself except for my Hairy and my 'special guys.'

I looked over at Dara, expecting to see her listening to Miss Santana, too. I was mistaken.

"You are out of your gourd. Whatever dose you are on, cut it. Or double it, because this stuff just ain't right."

I bristled at her words. "You brought me here. You ain't right."

Dara shook her head, trying not to laugh at me. "To think I let you help deliver puppies."

I could feel my adjusted aura changing color at her words. I was not sure, but I thought a hole was forming out there in my poor aura from Dara's negativity. And to think my aura was swirling around me, all green and blue just a little while ago! "I did a damned outstanding job helping deliver those puppies. Admit it."

She laughed, her eyes sparkling with mischief. "According to who? Garp?"

"According to Fancy and you. And according to our girls, when they were in labor." Oh, yeah, sis, bring it on. Bring it on.

Dara shook her head as she laughed again. "Kara only thought about expelling the little wombats. It was her first litter. She rejected them, remember? She wanted nothing to do with those puppies. That's why she let you take them over."

It might be true, but saying so? Just plain rude. "Oh, shut up."

She grinned. "You shut up, you big dope. And go clear your stinky old chakras again. I intend to go eat chocolates. Godiva chocolates sound ever so much better than any sort of chakra balancing or cleansing act I have seen around here today. Jeez-Louise, Sara, you need to get a life. You ought to have enough sense to realize that 'your boys' are Hairy and Boze, and 'your girls' are Bianca and Kara. Not the Great Wombat or the Holy Archangel Smokey Eyeball or whatever. Give me a break, girl child, before I break something on you."

"You. Are. A. Heathen." I sniffed in total disgust at her limited mentality.

Dara did not even try to hold back her laughter at me. "No, but your new friends are, by definition. Chakras. Auras. And what was that other hoo-ha? Spiritual crews? Oh, yeah, sure. Give me a break. Sis, you cannot be serious." She began clutching her side as she laughed. "Oh, and I love this dog communication bull crap. I love it. You want to learn how to communicate with a dog? I'll teach you right now. Sit. Stay. Heel. Come here, and if you don't, I'll smack you upside the head with this fist."

Dara appalled me as she shook her fist in my face. This nonsense came from a woman who had never hit a dog in her life. I would never have expected her to make such outlandish allegations. I could imagine her hitting a person, but a dog? Never.

She glared at me for a minute before she continued. "That's how you communicate with a dog. For the love of dogs, I thought you knew better."

"I'll give you a break. Hairy and I communicate." I punched her in the arm.

She rubbed her arm where I had struck it. "Yeah, sure. Give me a break. We have all heard about Hairy's phenomenal ability to speak to your mind. Whatever, you whack job. Like I am going to believe your overgrown rodent could think his way out of a paper bag. Now, Boze? Maybe. But Hairy Potter? Nah. Oh, and stunts like slugging me ought to do wonders for the fine tuning of both your aura and your chakras. You are such a big dope. A certifiable big dope in need of serious long-term psychotherapy. You want to be a dog communicator? You need a mental health communicator. In fact, psychotherapy sounds like a good idea right now."

I struggled to hold back tears. Dara knew I attended therapy for years after our dad appeared in my life. "Don't do this to me, Dara Siobhan Winslow. I do not need to get upset right before show time."

She looked embarrassed for about a half a minute. Dara took a deep breath and put on what we all call her 'let's make a deal' face as she shifted gears while Philip Martino walked up, and she changed topics as she leered at Philip. "Well, hello, good looking. Have you shown your Airedale yet?"

"Yes, he took Best of Breed as expected. When do you guys show the fluff balls?"

I frowned and opened my mouth, intending to snap out a curt reply, but Sara laid a hand on my arm and kept talking. "We show in a half hour. Sara, tell Philip about that ridiculous circus in court last week."

I could not help it. The other circus over in family practice is my preferred arena. I laughed. While I do some criminal practice, I dislike it and do little. I dislike helping criminals. However, criminal practice makes up what I call 'bread and butter' work. It helps pay the bills and helps keep the puppies in kibble. "Are you serious?"

She nodded as her eyes twinkled with mischief. "Oh, yes, tell Philip the whole scenario, beginning with the fool with the crack-filled socks and ending with the other crazy case."

I struggled not to laugh. I grinned at Philip and winked. "The story about the hooker and the preacher man? Okay, here goes. My client got in trouble for public intoxication when the police officers got called out because he was arguing with his old lady in their apartment. They were too loud. When the officers arrived, he was balls to the walls wasted, and they dragged him down to the cop shop for public intoxication. They strip searched him while booking him, and the cops found crack cocaine in one of his socks. Not unusual, but my dumb ass client claimed, 'that's not my drugs.' Over the years, I have heard people claim they borrowed clothing, and the cops found dope in the pockets of the clothing they wore, but I never heard anyone claim the narcotics found inside a pair of socks a person wore was not their narcotics before this guy made the claim. I figured it would be hard not to know something is in your sock when it is in a plastic baggie inside said sock and next to your skin."

Dara laughed in near hysterics at this point. She knew from previous exposure to my criminal defense stories that my criminal clients are all nutzoid, and my criminal defense stories are off the wall. She loves my courthouse stories, the crazier the better.

Philip stood staring at me as he struggled not to crack a smile. He bit his lip and winked at me. "Proceed, counselor."

I paused a moment, grinned at him, and took a sip of water. "Well, with the drugs, my guy goes from being charged with public intoxication to possession of a controlled substance. The charge went from a misdemeanor to a felony. Not a good thing for my guy. So, he keeps telling me 'I don't use drugs, it wasn't my crack, I don't know how it got in my sock.'"

Philip frowned. "Oh, come on, Sara, quit stalling and tell what happened."

I smiled and batted my eyes at the handsome man standing before me. "Seems that my client had a 'lady friend' who dropped by for some late night 'company', and dropped him a little Rohypnol–"

"What's that?" Dara frowned as she interrupted again.

Sometimes, her interruptions can be quite annoying.

I rolled my eyes at her and sighed, impatient with my sister's incessant interruptions. "Rohypnol is called the 'date rape drug.' She dropped it into his Coca Cola, and the dumb ass man passed out. It turns out she's a hooker, and she intended to do whatever it took to raise her rent money. She strip searched the man for the money she needed to pay her rent. My client was her apartment manager, so the naughty little hooker intended to rob him to pay him. It infuriated her when she did not find any money on him, so she planted the crack in his sock in retaliation. He regained consciousness with his wife screaming at him, because she came in with this woman pawing over him. This big, noisy fight ensued. The cops got called, and like I said before, the officers arrested him for P.I., and dragged to jail, where they found the crack in his sock. Bizarre, hmm?"

Dara laughed, her amber eyes sparkling with mischief. "I just love it. Kirk should hire the thief. That girl has real potential in the corporate takeover world, let me tell you."

I rolled my eyes as I shook my head in disgust. "You think so, sis? Kirk owns bars. He's damned smart, but I would not call him the King of the Corporate Takeovers even though he owns a half dozen bars now. Oops, we no longer call them bars, we call them 'fine eateries' or 'dinner clubs.' Whatever. In my humble opinion, it would be a mistake to hire an unreformed hooker to run a bar. Anyway, the story gets better. My client's wife used to be a hooker. She changed her ways, but she knew this girl still worked the streets. The wife confronted the hooker with a street preacher. As the wife put it, the preacher man laid some conviction on the little hooker-thief girl, who broke down and confessed what she did to the preacher and to the wife. They all came to Court, gave statements, and voila! The district attorney dismissed the charges against my client. The word is a powerful tool. Wham, bam, thank you, ma'am. The preacher has a fine sermon on Hellfire and Redemption if you ever need to hear it. I understand the hooker is being charged with date rape for giving my client the Rohypnol and for the delivery of the crack onto his person while he was unconscious. The girl is looking at some serious time, and my client is going to be reduced back to the original P.I. charges if the district attorney refuses to dismiss the case against him, and I contend they should dismiss the charges. In his wife's words, 'Praise the Lord! It's a miracle!'"

Through it all, Philip remained quiet although his cheeks reddened with embarrassment. When I winked at him again, he shook his head as he struggled not to laugh.

"Sara, tell him about the other story, you know, the Rough Sex case." Dara grinned ear to ear.

Philip put his head in his hands. "For the love of all that is holy, Sara, are you going to tell that story, too?"

I grinned at him. "Sis, you just ain't right. Okay, here it is. Same day, same court, same Assistant D.A. They charged my client with domestic violence. In particular, they accused him of biting, hitting, and choking his wife. Pretty nasty, right? I read these charges, and I must admit, it grossed me out at first. It sounded god awful. Then I read it again, and my intuition or something kicked in. Oh, I know! It must have been my psychic awareness which kicked in."

It would not be possible to explain my friendly ghost planted the idea in my brain. I took another sip of water. "After all, Ms. Santana swears I am attuned to my spirit guides. "

Philip appeared confused. "I beg your pardon? What do you mean?"

As I laid a hand on his arm, I laughed. "It was like I heard this voice in my head say, 'rough sex, Sara.' I stopped and read the officer's report again. It read like erotica. It was not something I would enjoy, but to each her own, as I always say. I read it a third time, and then I pushed it over to one of the other attorneys and asked what he thought. He read it, grinned, and said it read like it might be a case of rough sex to him. Then damned if the idiot did not start talking about auto-erotica to me, and I just knew I would barf right there in the jury room where we all sit and talk about our cases as we wait to talk to the D.A."

"Ooh, gross! You did not tell me that scintillating detail the first time. Tell Philip what you did then." Dara looked both repelled and captivated by the story.

I glanced at Philip and cocked an eyebrow at him.

He rolled his luscious baby blues at me again. "Oh, by all means, tell us the rest of the story, Sara."

Biting back laughter, I proceeded. "I picked up the file, took it out to the wife, and handed it to her."

I took a deep breath and another sip of water.

"And then what?" Dara's eyes sparkled as she pressed for more of the dirty little details.

I grinned. "First, let me tell you, the wife is a beautiful, college educated woman. She works as a registered nurse in a major hospital in the med center. This lady is no moron. She should know better than to let any man hit her and choke her. When she read the officer's report, Miss Pretty, as I call her, turned scarlet. She could not look me in the eye, and she started stammering. After a couple of minutes, I asked her if it they were having rough sex. Miss Pretty looked me in the eye and admitted she likes it rough. She said she likes it the rougher, the better, and she loves it when her husband bites her, hits her, and even chokes her. He calls her 'his little freak.' I asked if she would tell the District Attorney about her sexual preferences. She blushed but nodded her head, and I saw she understood what I intended. She grinned as I went into the courtroom and handed the file to the Assistant D.A."

Dara's eyes grew wide with alarm. She looked from me to Philip and then back to me with amazing alacrity. "Oh my god, was it you, Philip?"

Philip blushed, shifted from foot to foot, and mumbled something I could not comprehend for the life of me.

I tilted my head to study him before I smiled. "Yes. Standing before you is the handsome and charming Senior Assistant District Attorney in the flesh."

Philip's blush deepened, but I could not tell if it was from the compliment or the story. "Thank you for the compliment, Sara. I admit I can be cocky. I imagine I looked damned smug when I made my outrageous offer to you. You know, five years on probation, 260 hours of community service, blah-blah-blah. Finally, Sara laid a hand on my arm. I stopped speaking when she touched me. With this sweet, innocent face, your sister said, 'Rough sex, Philip.' I must have looked at her like she had grown a third head or something. Unsure if she understood me, I repeated my offer. Sara then busted my balls when she announced, 'Philip, the wife loves rough sex.'"

I stood there giggling as Philip told that part of the story before I spoke again. "Poor Philip looked aghast. He recovered enough to ask if the wife was at the courthouse because he would like to interview her. I told him she was in the hall with their baby, and oh, did he know she expected another baby fathered by my client? The poor darling looked like he wanted to throw up his toenails."

"If only I were your darling, you naughty little vixen. Then, I could cope with this disgusting scenario. As it was, I thought I would vomit." He looked like he might puke standing there. "I still do. The entire case makes me want to hurl."

"Poor Philip then went out to talk to her. After about twenty minutes of talking to this lovely young woman, he looked like a deflated balloon—or a limp noodle. Take your pick."

Philip shook his head in disgust. "That's rough, girl. You should never compare a man to a limp noodle to his face."

Dara and I fell together as we laughed in hysterics. When I caught my breath, I continued the story. "He advised he would recommend the court dismiss the case. I could not resist asking if it was because his star witness told him she not only could not remember what happened that night because she got too drunk to remember, or because she enjoys rough sex, the rougher the better. Miss Pretty told Philip she loves to be bitten and choked. The cops pressured her into signing the affidavit, which she did not even remember signing. She pointed out to him the wording in the affidavit was not the language she used. It did not sound like her normal speech, and the statement did not read like a college educated woman phrased the words. The multiple spelling errors in the affidavit horrified her. Poor Philip had a Jack Shit case, and he knew it. He looked sick."

"Much like I do right now, I imagine," he muttered, shaking his head before he turned to walk away.

Dara and I struggled to hold back our laughter.

"You know, Sara, he is damned cute."

I made a gagging sound. "He is handsome, for an Assistant District Attorney, but for dog's sake, sis, the man works on the Dark Side."

Dara laughed again, but with speculation in her eyes. "Yes, I got that the first time, but he also has terriers, and like I said, he is not at all hard on the eyes. Is he married?"

Laughing again, I shook my head. "Look, Philip is a great guy, and I know he lusts after me, but—"

She smirked. "You're loyal to the memory of dearly departed Jack Ass Talbott? Yeah, sure, like I could believe that line of baloney."

I winced. She always cuts right to the chase. "No, bitch, but I am not ready for a new man. Although Philip Martino is something wonderful to look at, and we have flirted for ages."

Dara arched her eyebrow, like I have seen Fancy do many times. After a minute, We both broke into laughter again.

"And so? Nothing wrong with a fling with a good-looking guy while you are on the dog show circuit. You're single now, sis. And like they say, what happens on the circuit stays on the circuit," Dara said.

It was difficult, but somehow I managed to ignore the fact she wanted me to talk about men and resumed talking about my case. "Hmm, a fling? Whatever happens at the dog shows stays at the dog shows? Maybe for you, but it's not my style. And, so, to go back to my story, justice was served, and everyone enjoyed the day, except poor Philip Martino, Senior Assistant District Attorney. And the young couple rode off into the sunset to the strains of music from the Count Basie Orchestra, and the sound of a woman happy to be choked."

"Gag me with a spoon." Dara muttered as I made gagging noises.

An hour later, we showed, and Hairy took Best of Breed, and Boze went Select Dog at Hatboro I. Later, Hairy took a Group 1 to resounding applause. He then shocked the fire out of me for the second time in the week when he took Best in Show.

On Friday, at the Hatboro II show, Hairy took Select Dog, but he did not take Best of Breed. Dara kept telling me the judge cheated Hairy. I grinned and told her it did not matter. I could not get upset about losing to a dog as fine an example of our breed as beautiful Archer. It shocked me that my sister did not fuss since the judge did not name Boze Select Dog that day. Hairy was already a Grand Champion, and now his son, Boze, was a Champion. We were having a fabulous weekend, even with the losses of the day.

Early Saturday morning, we drove over to the Devon show site. As usual, they held the show in a driving rain and the hard, frigid winds of the first norther of the year. They hold the Devon show 'way out yonder in the pawpaw patch,' or, to be more precise, way out in the boondocks in a horse paddock. It floods like crazy when it rains hard, which occurs almost every year. I remember several years when they cancelled the show because of torrential rains. Fancy dragged us out there at the ass crack of dawn one year, and it was pitch-black outside when we reached the site. She set the alarm on her phone, and we hunkered down under blankets to fall sound asleep. When the alarm went off at 7:30, we realized the site had flooded. Fancy scrambled out of the car and learned they cancelled the show while we slept on the show site. God only knows why they would not move the show. It is the furthest from the host hotel and often proves to be the most inhospitable show site.

Boze does not like to show in the rain, but somehow he took Select Dog for more points towards his Grand Championship. Hairy loves the cold and rain, and once again took Best of Breed. He then took the Terrier group 1 again over a large, impressive terrier group. He did not take Best in Show, but it still thrilled me when he received reserve BIS to a gorgeous standard poodle. I tallied Hairy's points in my head and confirmed his ranking as the number one Skye terrier in the country. He ran nose to nose with Archer for months, vying for first place with the gorgeous, cream-colored Skye. Now, if Hairy could just pull off Best of Breed and a group placement at the all-terrier show the next day at the Montgomery County!

As we started back towards the hotel amidst bumper to bumper traffic, Dara and I talked with excitement about the preceding three days of shows, and our plans for Sunday.

"Sara! Hang on tight!"

It surprised me to hear Captain Johnny shout at me. As I tightened my grip on the steering wheel, I felt the first bump on the rear fender of my SUV. The dogs yelped, and I struggled to hold the vehicle on the rain-slicked, narrow road that dropped off to a river below on our side.

"Shit! What was that all about?" Dara yelped as she twisted around to see the car behind us.

I shook my head, let out a sigh of exasperation, and shrugged my shoulders. "That driver wasn't paying attention, and he bumped me. Don't worry, we're okay."

But about then, the blasted car hit me again, harder, knocking us hard enough that the impact sent my car skidding off the pavement. As I pulled the SUV to a stop on the edge of the shoulder where it overlooked the sharp drop-off to the raging waters below, I realized this was no accident. However, this was a problem. As Sonny Cangelosi would say, 'dis is a big problem, Mrs. T.'

As soon as there was a break in the traffic, I wheeled the SUV around and headed back towards the Devon show site. I knew another way back to the hotel. It would take longer, but I doubted our assailants would dream I would travel back roads and double my travel time. At least, I hoped that thought would not occur to them.

Almost two hours later, we arrived at the hotel, exhausted, cold, wet, and downright scared. As I picked up the room key from the desk clerk and glanced over a fax from Ashley, the young man asked, "Did your husband find you?"

My heart dropped to my feet as my head snapped up at his words. "What did you say?"

He smiled. "Your husband came in about an hour ago and said he wanted to surprise you. He said that you were not expecting him. I figured a lady who had been out in the rain and cold all day deserved a chance to fix up a little before her husband shows up, right? Anyway, I told him I couldn't give him the room key since you did not list him on the card. He said he would be back later. I wondered if you ran into him yet."

Dara and I stared at him, stunned by his words. I remembered Sonny's words again: He wasn't squeaky clean, Mrs. T. Your husband had enemies. You gotta watch your back.

"I assure you the man was not my husband, Carl. What did this man look like?"

The desk clerk looked surprised. "He swore he was your husband."

I shook my head. "No, I'm pretty sure that's not possible. He couldn't be my husband. Someone murdered Jack near Houston a couple of weeks ago, and we cremated him last week. Whoever showed up was not Jackson Talbott."

Carl blanched at my words. "Oh, my god, Mrs. Talbott, I did not know your husband passed away. The man seemed so nice."

Yeah, he seemed nice, I thought. Some wise guy tried to run us off the road, and then shows up at my hotel claiming to be my dead husband, and the desk clerk described him as nice. Fabulous.

Dara trembled, and my sister is unflappable. "Wh-wh-what do we do, Sara?"

Her response scared me as much as the fact that we had some *strozzo* hunting for us, who already tried to run us off the road earlier today. Tapping a nervous finger against my lips, I thought a second before answering. "Carl, darling, could you move us to another room? One where no one would know where we are?"

He hesitated a moment and then started looking through the reservations to see what he could do. After a lengthy search, the young desk clerk smiled. "Ah! Here is another room that no one has checked into yet. I don't have another suite, though."

Dara and I both sagged with relief. "That will be fine. Can I get a cart to move our things?"

He nodded. "Oh, yes, ma'am. Allow me to help you. It would be best if not too many people knew where you are."

Ten minutes later, we had moved to the new room, and we had the dogs inside. I started digging through my purse.

"What on earth are you doing? It is not the time to freshen up your lipstick, Sara." My sister shook her head as she stared at me, shocked disbelief all over her face.

"No, sis, you don't understand. I need to find the phone number Sonny Cangelosi gave me the other day."

Dara paled as her hands began trembling again. "You intend to call the Mob for help?"

Grim-faced, I nodded. "Damned straight. Now, where the hell is that damned piece of paper?"

Dara kept a watch out a crack in the curtain covering the window, as I searched for the number. In frustration, I picked up my phone and dialed Ashley. "Hey, girl, I need help asap."

"Sure, boss, what's the problem?" I heard her yawn over the phone.

"I need to talk to Sonny Cangelosi right away. It is an emergency."

"You what? Boss, you cannot call him. He's represented by counsel." The girl shouted the words at me. I heard genuine concern in Ashley's voice.

"Girlfriend, I do not give a flying rat's patoot right now. Besides, the Judge subbed Maggie as counsel last week. There should be no problem if I call Cangelosi. Give me the number, right now." I ended the demand by shouting way more than just a little.

Ashley sighed, but conceded, after contemplating the level of unexpected tension in my voice. "Okay, but I hope this is not a mistake."

"So do I."

I dialed Sonny's number next. On the third ring, he picked up. "What?"

"Sonny? This is Mrs. T. I have a problem here, and I can't find the phone number you gave me."

I could almost see him snap to attention. "What happened?"

"A car tried to run us off the road this afternoon. Twice. And then some guy came to the hotel and tried to get into our room. He claimed to be Jack."

"Shit, I was afraid somethin' like this would happen."

"Double shit. Anyway, when our car got hit, and we went off the road, my purse dumped over, and the contents became jumbled in my purse. I can't find that freaking slip of paper you gave me. Can you please give me your friend's number again? I remember his name, just not the number." I was careful not to say his name.

"Where are you?" Sonny asked, his voice tense and tight.

I hesitated before answering. He sounded concerned, but what if I should not trust him? Or if he is behind all this? I took a deep, centering breath. Oh, hell, I did not know why, but I believed Sonny Cangelosi. We were in danger, and he might help me. "We are at our hotel. They moved us to another room."

"I don't give a flying fuck where they moved you, you're still in danger. You gotta get out of there now, Mrs. T. Right now. Grab those prissy assed show dogs of yours and get the hell out of that hotel now!"

I winced as the man shouted at me. "Sonny, I ... I don't think—"

"Mrs. Talbott, Sara, I don't have time to explain this all to you. Let me be blunt. They threaten to pop a cap in that desk clerk's ass, and you don't think he's gonna turn on youse guys? Get out of there right now. I'll text you Ray's number. Head to Jersey, and call my friend when you get on the turnpike. But, please, for the love of God, lady, get the hell out of that room. Youse guys are sitting ducks right now. Grab the pooches and get out right now."

His words made me felt lightheaded. With a jolt, I realized someone tapped my shoulder. I smiled when I realized Captain Johnny was there. Johnny did not smile back. He looked worried. "He's telling you the truth, Sara. You girls need to get the doggies and leave right now. This hotel is unsafe for you. You girls need to leave, *prestissimo*."

I scratched down the phone number for Sonny's friend before Dara and I grabbed the dogs and their leashes to head out the door. The crates, table, and grooming gear were still in the SUV, as was a suitcase with a change of clothes for each of us. We sprinted to the SUV as if we were just taking the dogs out for a while. When we got into the SUV, I eased it out onto the highway towards New Jersey.

No one knew sure what kind of mess Jack had involved us in, and I did not know what would happen to me. But these assholes damned sure would not hurt our dogs. No way.

Chapter 12 – Sara

The night passed in a blur of fear and worry. I followed Sonny's instructions and called Mr. La Rosa once we were on the Penn Turnpike. He told us to where I should drive, and he put us up for the night. However, he was damned unhappy when we got up the next morning before five to head out to the Montgomery show grounds.

"Whaddaya crazy broads mean? You're going to a freaking dog show? Lady, there is a hit contract on your head. I can keep you safe if you let me keep you away from those wise guys. Otherwise..." He shrugged as he dragged a finger across his neck and made a noise supposed to sound like a knife slicing through a neck. Dara and I both cringed. His meaning was all too clear.

As I stared at my sister, I swallowed hard. "Dara Siobhan, I came to go to this National Specialty, to take home the title of BISS winner. I intend to do it. I owe it to Hairy."

She nodded. "Yeah, I know."

Mr. La Rosa snorted. "Oh, for da love of God. All you owe your fleabag is a dry bed at night and a bowl of kibble. You and I both know that mutt's gonna eat no matter what happens at that damned dog show today. Okay, listen, if I cannot talk you out of it, you at least gotta let me send a couple of my guys as bodyguards for youse guys. *Capisce?*"

I looked at Dara, who nodded, silent and white-faced as she had been most of the night. "Okay. We'll do that."

"And you're taking another car. No way you are driving one they know down there today. In fact, Lenny can drive youse guys. He's my number one driver. You gals sit back and try to relax." He turned to walk away. "Crazy broad says she gotta go to a freaking dog show, and she's got a Stelari contract on her head. Dames. Who understands them?"

"Wait, just a gosh darn a minute. Who is Stelari?" I demanded.

He turned and stared at me like I had grown yet another head. "Jesus, woman, you don't know?"

I shook my head. "Nope. I never heard the name before."

"Jeez, da woman don't got idea what the eff she done got her ass involved with. How do I keep a broad alive who doesn't even know what she's involved in?" He wheeled around and walked out of the room, still shaking his head in disgust.

I frowned and yelled my response. "Why don't you wise guys explain it to me?"

He stopped, turned around, and glared at me. He made the popular finger to the temple motion. "*Usa la testa, signora.*"

I glared at him. "You got *aqua in bocca? Nessuno nasci dutto tra stu nunno.* Nobody is born with learning in this world. *Che diavolo succede qui?* What the devil is going on here? Who the hell is Stelari?"

He stared at me as if dumbfounded. "You speak *l'Italiano.*"

"Duh. *Si, un po.*"

I speak pretty decent Italian, but my ability to speak colloquial Italian as used in Calabria and Sicily is limited.

He stared at me, trying to unravel the mystery. "Holy shit, you're her."

He wheeled around to leave the room. I rushed over and grabbed his arm. "What the hell do you mean?"

He slapped his forehead with the palm of his hand. "*Tu sei la principessa de la famiglia Franchetti. Tu capisce, si?*"

My mouth went dry. Before I could reply, he whirled around and began shouting orders at his men in Italian. He thought some wise guy named Stelari wanted me dead because I'm related to Roberto Franchetti? No, I must have misunderstood him. As *Zio* Roberto would say, *questo 'e pazzo.* That's crazy.

I shook my head, shrugged and resumed loading the dogs and equipment into the new car replete with two armed watchdogs Mr. La Rosa assigned to accompany us to keep us safe at the dog show.

Usually, I bitch and moan at early show times, but it delighted me to have to be ringside at the ass crack of dawn for this show. I hoped it meant the wise guys might not make it in time to 'ace their hit,' as Mr. La Rosa put it.

It was, as expected, cold and raining when we got to the show grounds at Montgomery Junior College. The morning light had not yet broken. I shivered as I pulled my mackintosh closer and buttoned it, pleased I remembered to pull on an extra pair of wool socks beneath my rubber Wellingtons that morning. My hands stiff with cold, I struggled to pull on my gloves, turned up the collar of the coat, and flipped the hood over my head. Perhaps the hit man would not recognize me in my rain gear, and would not spot Hairy or Boze. Fat chance, I thought. Boze was the most unusual Skye there, with his flashy platinum coat and beautiful, black fringed, drop ears.

It was the biggest entry of Skyes I could remember since the Diamond Jubilee. Forty-five Skye terriers and two hours later, the judge signed her judging book and pulled Hairy out for Best of Breed and Boze for Select. Dara and I danced what Fancy calls 'the happy dance' with uncontrolled excitement. We were both over the moon. Harry leapt into the air for a somersault when the Judge pointed to us.

"I had a hard time deciding between these two Skyes. You better watch out, young lady. This drop-eared boy will surpass your pretty black boy once he matures a little more. However, my task is to find the best Skye today, and that is your black."

"Thank you, Judge. Hairy is Boze's sire, and I know Boze will mature into one beautiful Skye."

The judge laughed. "Unbeatable, at that."

I thought Dara's eyes would bug out over the judge's compliment. "Thank you, judge."

Afterwards, Archer's owner came over to congratulate me. "Congratulations, Hairy showed like a dream today."

I pulled her close to hug her. "Thanks. That means a lot to me. Your boy is drop dead gorgeous. You know I love him to pieces. Truth be told, I'm shocked Hairy beat him. Delighted, but shocked."

She laughed and winked. "We still have the Eukanuba show."

I hugged her again as I laughed. "Indeed, we do. See you there."

Dara stood by, trying to smile, as friends from around the country congratulated us on the wins. Still, I could tell she was not pleased. "She robbed Boze," she muttered to me under her breath.

"Oh, deal with it." I snapped her favorite phrase at her with the speed of lightning. "His day will come. Right now, Hairy Potter is the number one in the country. We already decided Hairy retires after the Eukanuba Invitational. Let my boy enjoy his moment of glory. Besides, with these wins, Boze is the number five Skye in breed points, no small feat for a boy who started showing six months ago. Boze will win like mad with Hairy out of the running after the Eukanuba show in December."

Dara shook her head. "I don't know, Sara. The way Hairy's been winning, maybe we should not retire him yet. At least, not until after Westminster. Right now, both boys qualify to go. There is no telling what he could do there, if we can just get past all this crap."

I stared at her, stunned by her unexpected change of opinion on this much discussed subject. Westminster is an invitational show, and you can go to Westminster only if you are in the top five dogs in your breed. I nagged Dara about taking Hairy since he first made the top five in the country. It is an enormous honor to get invited, and I wanted to attend it with my gorgeous 'bred by exhibitor' dog. Some folks breed and show dogs for decades and never make it to Westminster with a dog they bred. A Skye won Best in Show there a mere one time in the show's history. Dara always insisted she wanted Boze to have his day, if he qualified. It can be harder for a drop-eared Skye to win than a prick-eared Skye, and Hairy proved to be a formidable foe in the show ring. Boze was an exceptional drop-eared Skye, every bit as nice as Desy or King Arthur, and perhaps as nice as Adalia had been, and believe me, that's saying a lot. Adalia was a fabulous drop-eared Skye from Finland we called 'Queen Adalia.' Yes, Boze deserved to be shown as a special. We call it a 'special' when we campaign for a dog who already won his championship. Now, Dara verbalized a change of opinion since both boys qualified to go to Westminster. It would be fabulous if either Hairy or his son could win anything at Westminster.

I opened my mouth to reply, but before I could utter a word, Hairy growled, his voice low, deep, and menacing. The hair on my nape stood up, as did Hairy's ruff. *Watch out, watch out, bad man, big stick, mama, bad man, big stick,* I heard my dog say to me.

"Look out, Sara!"

Nervous, I glanced around at the sound of Captain Johnny's voice, just in time to see a flash of light, like sunlight flashing off a gun, as Hairy barked with unusual ferociousness. Before I ever heard the report of the gun, I threw myself down over my dog. Indignant, his doggie pride wounded, Hairy continued barking.

"What the hell just happened?" Dara frowned sat up in the dirt from where I had shoved her down, and began wiping fist and debris from her face and hands.

Before I could reply, another voice chimed in. "Sara, are you okay?"

I looked up, more than a little stunned at the mellifluous tones of the voice I heard. "Philip? What are you doing here?"

He shook his head in disgust as he helped me to my feet. "It's Montgomery County, Sara. I came here for the same reason as you, to show my dog. I told you I'd be here. Graham is the number one Airedale in the country."

I glanced around and did not see the Airedale. "Where is he?"

"In his crate, thank heaven. Are you okay?" He pulled my hood back upright on my head and wiped a smudge of dirt off my nose.

I nodded as I brushed more dirt from my hands and arms. "I think so. What happened?"

Philip looked frustrated. He shook his head as his lips disappeared into a thin line. "Don't play coy, Sara Talbott. Someone shot at you. What did you think happened?"

Well, I knew it was gunfire, but I did not know if he realized it was a gunshot. Then again, he is the Senior Assistant to the D.A. I guess he ought to know the sound of gunfire. I bet they teach you to recognize things like gunfire when you work in the District Attorney's office.

"I-I wasn't sure. Hairy told me to watch out. We have a bodyguard today, and we wore disguises." It seemed best not to mention that Captain Johnny warned me. I did not feel up to trying to explain about my guardian-angel-in-training to Philip right then. I continued to run my hands up and down my arms, which were covered in dirt.

He snorted again. "Oh, yeah, like any moron would not recognize that dog standing beside you, not to mention that goofy-looking one your friend has." He paused a moment, and then continued. "Wait a minute. Did you say Hairy told you to watch out?"

I nodded as I inspected a scrape on my hand. "Yeah, why?"

He shook his head. "Women. They are all nuts."

Dara bristled. "I take offense at that statement."

Philip shrugged. "Which one? About nutty women, or about your silly looking dog?"

Dara's face flushed with anger. As she opened her mouth to say something rude to Philip, I held up my hand to stop her. "Cool it, sis. I thought we would be safe, or we would not have come today. I was wrong. Now what?"

Philip stepped aside and spoke with several off-duty police officers who were working the show for a few minutes. They appeared nervous, but nodded and then dispersed, milling through the crowd again. He walked back to me with a serious, all-business look on his face. "Are you determined to stay for group?"

I looked at him like he had grown a second head. "Hell, yes, I'm staying. Hairy is the number one Skye terrier in the country and he just took Best of Breed. I intend to win that group today, you idiot."

Dara nodded, somber and unusual quiet. "Yes, we intend for Sara and Hairy Potter to stay and win. It is the most important show of the year."

Philip sighed, rolled his eyes, and raked his hand through his beautiful hair. "Great, I figured as much. Remember, you still must deal with Marjorie's gorgeous Sealyham terrier and that big winning Dandie Dinmont terrier Gabriel handles to take the group, not to mention my Graham. Hairy and you will face tough competition in the group ring."

I raised my eyebrows. "And your point is? We beat them all yesterday, as well as on Thursday."

He let out a sigh of exasperation and raked his hand back through his now tousled hair again. "I was afraid you would say that. That means we need to step up security and hide you out until then."

I blinked. "Wait just a gosh darn minute, Philip Martino. What do you mean, 'we'? You got a mouse in your pocket? And what do you mean, 'step up security'? What in the blue blazes is going on here, Mister?"

His face reddened, and he tried to avoid looking me in the eye. "Well, uh, Sara, you see—"

"Have you guys been watching me?" I felt my cheeks redden with embarrassment, frustration, and a dose of good old anger. Dammit, he must know the Jersey mobster rescued us yesterday.

For that matter, why didn't he rescue us then?

He nodded, which chagrin written across his face. "There was initial concern you hired the hit on Jack. Since then, we have pretty well determined—"

"Pretty well determined?" I yelped. "You still don't know beyond a shadow of a doubt that I was not involved in Jack's death?"

Philip stared at me a moment before answering. "Sara, you had a damned good motive."

My throat constricted as the tears burned at my eyes. "Hell, I might have wished Jack would just drop his ass dead, but I hoped you, of all people, did not think I could have killed Jack no matter what shenanigans he pulled. It is just not in me. Besides, if you want to put it that way, Sonny Cangelosi had a pretty good motive to kill Jack, too."

"I know, but Cangelosi is the number one reason we don't think you did it."

Stunned by his words, I blinked. "You don't mean you think—"

He shook his head, impatient with the entire conversation. "No, no, no, I never said that. However, he came into the office, and he told us he was worried about you. Based on what he said, we believe Jack was the victim of a hit contract, and that you could be in danger, too." His chuckle sounded wry. "Looks like Sonny hit that one on the head."

"Jeez Louise, I feel nauseous." As the bile rose in my throat, all I could do was manage a bare nod. I pressed a hand against my mouth, afraid I might puke right there. I figured they made me attend Jack's autopsy to see how I reacted. Sonny and La Rosa both told me the same thing, and Johnny warned me again of impending danger. Sonny must have somehow convinced the DA's office of our innocence.

In my wildest imagination, I never thought I would appreciate Sonny Cangelosi for anything. I realized I would have to remember him in my prayers from now on.

Someone killed Jack, and it appeared the person who killed Jack wanted to kill me. I sat down, hard, on the folding chair I take with me for shows. "Wow."

"Come on, let me get you out of this tent. Listen, why don't you let your sister show Hairy in the group?"

Dara perked up at that, and as she opened her mouth to speak, I began shaking my head. "No, Hairy performs better for me. Besides, Hairy's my dog. We're bonded."

Dara rolled her eyes. "Sara claims Hairy can read her mind. They communicate with one another." She made air quotes when she said 'communicate.' Dara tapped a finger against the side of her head and rolled her eyes. "Mentally."

Lips pursed, I cut her a sharp look before replying. Dara knew I did not discuss my special relationship with people outside our family. They laughed at me about it enough. I let out a sigh of exasperation. "Well, we have been winning like mad, too, little missy, and don't you forget it."

Her lips narrowed, but she bit her tongue. Well, at least until she stuck it out at me.

Philip choked back laughter as he shook his head. "You two are nuts."

Philip rounded together a half-dozen men I learned were Fibbie agents interspersed around the show rings to help protect us. The Fibbies walked us out to an RV that they used as their 'headquarters away from home.' I sighed as I sank into a plush upholstered seat, where Hairy laid his head on my lap.

"Thompson, let us know when they call the terrier group for judging." The FBI agent frowned but nodded before he turned to go to watch for the group to be called. I tried to ignore the tense note in Philip's voice, and I worried even more. I ran my fingers through Hairy's long coat. As always, the feel of his luxurious hair almost hypnotized me to a calmer emotional place. As my breath and my pulse became steadier, I could feel the tension eking out of my neck and shoulders.

Hairy licked my fingers and gave me a quizzical look. *Bad man gone, Mama?*

I nodded, not even aware that the dog had communicated with me. I patted his head as I answered. "Yes, sweetie, the bad man left. Mama promises everything will be okay."

Philip's eyes narrowed as Hairy whined and thumped his tail against the chair leg. "What did you just perceive that dog to tell you?"

I laughed, embarrassed, because Philip caught me talking to my dog. "He asked if the bad man left. He has always communicated with me since he was a tiny puppy."

Dara chortled. "Oh, you just gotta tell him the story, Sara. It's priceless. Plus, I am sure hearing how you communicate with Hairy will enhance your trustworthiness to the DA and the FBI."

She made the air quotes again. I bristled at her sarcasm, since she knows the special bond I share with Hairy. I took a calm, steadying breath and began my story. "Four years ago, one of our champion bitches gave birth to six in her first litter. Hairy was the last one born after she had been in labor for almost 10 hours. Hairy was not breathing when he was born. Since it was my first litter, like a fool, I did not know better than to resuscitate him."

Philip's eyebrows raised. "So, Hairy was stillborn?"

I sniffed in disdain as I shrugged. "I prefer to say he was not breathing until I resuscitated him. Stillborn sounds so harsh."

Philip struggled not to burst into laughter. "You're dead if you can't breathe, Sara."

I flipped my hand up and shrugged again. I did not intend to have this conversation I had with Fancy again with Philip, at least not right then. "Whatever, Philip. Anyway, Hairy was the runt of the litter, half the size of the other puppies when he was born. Dara thought his dam conceived him in a later breeding than the bigger pups. On day two, I realized he was not nursing well, and I put him on supplemental feedings. On day three, Fancy and I decided bottle feedings were not cutting it, so I started tube feeding him. He had a poor swallow reflex then."

He let out a low whistle. "That's a lot of work. How long did you feed him by tube?"

"Three weeks of tube feeding the little bugger every two to three hours, around the clock. Jack often complained I wasted my time caring for a sickly puppy when I could have been out sailing with him. Hairy went to the office with me, to court with me. You name it, he accompanied me. I didn't know enough then to know what an impossible task I had taken on. I just kept saying, but he might be my best in show winner. Well, it looks like I was right."

He nodded and smiled at the memory. "I remember you carried around a basket with a puppy in it now that you mention it. In fact, I remember you heated a rice bag in the little microwave in my office once to keep your puppy warm. It looks like everything worked out great. Would you ever do it again?"

I smiled down at my dog as I stroked his hair. Hairy smiled back at me as his tongue lolled out of one side of his mouth. "Everything worked out great. I would think long and hard before I did it again, but my Hairy proved to be worth the effort. Look at him, Philip. He's the number one Skye terrier in the country and my absolute best friend ever. Anyway, by the end of the first day I tube fed him, I would go to him before he woke up and cried for food. I would have his tube of formula ready by the time he fussed. It seemed like I could hear him calling to me, telling me, 'hungry'."

Philip arched his brows at me again, but he said nothing.

"A few times, as he got a little bigger and started eating more, I realized he 'told' me he ate too much, and his tummy hurt. He would cry and let me know he wanted me to hold him close to my heart. I would hold him on top of the warm rice bag I used to help regulate his temperature when he was small. The sound of my heart comforted him. He still likes to go to sleep laying across my chest."

Hairy sighed and snuggled closer to me as he laid there with his head in my lap. He turned his face up to mine, smiled his silly little dog grin, and then closed his eyes. In seconds, he fell asleep again, snoring.

"Fascinating. And then what?" Philip asked.

"At about two and a half weeks, his eyes opened. As tiny as he was, half the size of the other pups, his eyes opened first of them all. As he looked at me with those little blurry baby eyes, I realized he communicated with me again."

Philip smiled. "What did you perceive him to be saying to you?"

"Mama. He has called me 'Mama' ever since then."

Philip pondered my words in silence. I figured he was not sure if I was a total nutcase or just especially bonded with the dog I love so much. Man, if this rattles you, I hate to think about what you would say regarding my ghost. Or my guardian angel.

After a few minutes, Dara spoke up. "Craziest thing you ever heard, hmm? A dog that talks to her in her head. I told her she just wants a baby so bad that she dreamed this whole crazy thing up."

Philip shook his head. "Not really. Craziest thing I ever heard was the proposal that Sara Winslow Talbott killed Jack Talbott because he cheated on her."

Dara nibbled on her lip as she cut her eyes at me. "Sara did not kill Jack. She's afraid of guns."

My mouth went dry all over again at his words. "Philip, I did not kill Jackson."

I bit back the next sentence. He might have deserved for me to kill him, but I did not kill the Jack Ass. Those were words best left unsaid.

He reached over to pat my back. "I know, I know. I never doubted you. The DA is still considering everything."

It felt like something punched me in my gut. I looked at Philip for a long minute before answering. "So, just why are you here, then? If the DA does not believe in my innocence?"

He grinned. "I already told you. I had a vacation letter to bring Graham to the dog shows. When this mess blew up, I phoned a friend at the Fibbies and called in a favor. To tell the truth, I was worried about you. Damned worried. Looks like my concern was damn well justified."

Anyone could see Philip was interested in me for several years. Like I said, we flirted, like lots of attorneys do with one another. He asked me out for dinner and drinks a time or two. I rebuffed his attentions with laughter and told him that, as attractive as he was, I would not cheat. I suspected he knew Jack cheated. Hell, I suspected everyone at the courthouses in Galveston, Harris, and maybe Brazoria Counties knew Jack cheated. Philip never said a word to verify my suspicion before today. Believe me, Philip Martino presented sore temptation for me to give in to my lust and have some rousing, fabulous 'pay back' sex. I cleared my throat. "Listen, Philip, I did not kill my husband, and I damned sure did not pull the trigger. Like Dara said, I'm afraid of guns. Understand?"

He nodded. "Yes, I understand."

"But Cory thinks I am involved?" Cory De Leon was the District Attorney.

Philip shrugged. "Corey remains suspicious. He suspects everyone. That's his job. The facts are stacked against you. Except, now someone is trying to kill you, too."

"So, I will prove my innocence if I get killed? Not an acceptable resolution in my book." I took another deep breath as I struggled for words before continuing. "Will you tell me where I stand?"

He grinned and stood up. "I hope alive. Come on, gorgeous, it's time for the group. Let's go."

Graham took Best of Breed that morning, so Philip would show Graham in the group. The Fibbies and my sister tinkered with my hair and makeup while we waited, and I had to admit I did not look like myself. Maybe like some tart all dolled up in a pound and a half of makeup and my designer clothes, but the reflection in the mirror looked nothing like me.

But it was not so much a matter of the hit man not recognizing me. The problem was Hairy. The dog's name is Hairy Potter. Anyone who knew Hairy would recognize he was my beautiful black dog. He is one of a kind. The Skye Terrier Club of America could have written the standard based on Hairy's exquisite conformation. He is an exceptional Skye. Add that striking true black coloring, and you cannot miss my boy. I damned sure hoped the shooters missed today if they stayed around the show so they could shoot again. I paused for just a moment before I entered the ring and took a deep breath.

"You sure about this?" asked Philip.

I nodded. "Yeah. Come on, Hairy, it's Show Time."

In most dog shows, you have breed judging, then group, and then Best in Show. Montgomery County is an all-terrier specialty show. Terriers comprise one of the seven groups at most shows. Since all the dogs at Montgomery are terriers, the judging just goes straight from the breeds to the group for the highly coveted Best in Specialty Show win. The dog who takes a group 1 (best terrier) at Montgomery County wins Best in Specialty Show, or BISS. It is an enormous show, and thousands of terriers attended this show. I damned sure wanted to win it. Hairy swore we would win it that day. I hoped he was right. We were about to find out if my dog was blowing smoke or if he was correct.

Philip shook his head. "I just do not get it. How can a judge pass over a proper terrier for that little dust mop?"

Hairy barked and tossed his hair back over his eyes. I laughed. "None of that negative talk, buster. The judges know quality when they see it. They bred these dogs to go into holes and kill badgers in Scotland. Badgers, foxes, otters, and rats. They are tough, gamey little bastards. What can an Airedale hunt? Oh, they are not very effective when hunting to ground. They are too big, right? Yeah, I would love to see an Airedale do earth dog work. What a laugh. How could they go in a hole after their prey? But I guess one could kill a rat if push came to shove… above ground."

Airedales can hunt and could do an outstanding job on lots of prey, but I embarrassed Philip because he blushed. Adorable, I thought. He was even cuter with flushed cheeks. It made the blue in his eyes appear more vibrant, more… alluring.

Ooh, Mama likes the man.

I looked down at my dog and grinned again. "Caught me, hmm?"

Hairy barked again. *Nice man, Mama. Hairy likes him, too.*

I laughed. "Even when he calls you a dust mop?"

Hairy looked nonplussed. *Well, maybe not then, but he's a great guy most of the time.*

We headed into the ring for the final judging of the day. The Judge was an old hand at this, who knew her dogs and the standards for terriers to a 'T.' My heart pounded as the judge pulled out us for the short list. "Okay, Hairy, this is it. Strut your stuff, man. Show her what you are made of. This is the big time. Show Time, baby."

And, true to form, the dog who acts like he is comatose at home on my sofa understood what it meant when I told him Show Time. My Hairy loves to show, and always gets the Judge's attention early on. After we made the last lap around the ring, Hairy barked, and then sat up, doing what we Skye folk call 'sitting pretty.' The Judge spotted him and smiled, just as Hairy leapt into the air, circling in a backward flip, as he barked again with excitement. The Judge laughed and then broke her routine to walk over to him and ran her hands over Hairy again. "He's a beautiful Skye. He has the correct coat, a great top line, the best front I ever saw, and fabulous bone. Take him down and back again, please."

"Thank you, judge." I burbled and nodded, my heart in my throat, unable to respond with anything else that was even semi-intelligent, as I struggled to hold my emotions and not to cry. OMG, she likes my boy.

Dara would never let me live it down if I cried.

And then, as we came back to our position in the lineup, the judge walked to her book and made her entry.

"Okay, boy, here it is." I whispered to my dog, who self-stacked himself in a perfect pose at my feet, ears pricked, his elegant neck arched, long tail wagging, eyes sparkling, the absolute epitome of a perfect Skye terrier.

The judge picked up the ribbon and the trophy and turned towards us. The air was ripe with anticipation as we waited for her to speak.

"The Skye terrier."

I swear I thought I would faint. I did not think a Skye had ever won at Montgomery County for Best in Specialty Show before. As I released the breath I had been holding for God only knows how long, Harry barked and then did another backwards flip, catapulting himself through the air, and then danced merrily on his hind legs as the crowd went wild. The Judge laughed again as she handed me the ribbon and trophy, and the cameras began snapping all around us. "This dog is all attitude. I never saw a Skye love to show this much. He stole my attention from the moment he surged into the ring."

"Oh, Hairy, I can't believe it! We just won the National Specialty and BISS! We won the whole kit and caboodle!"

He tossed his facial hair, what we call 'the fall,' out of his eyes. *Of course, Mama. You wanted to win, didn't you?*

I bent down and patted his head, and then I pulled him close to kiss his face. "You know I did, my darling boy. Your Mama is so proud of you, too."

Then, what's wrong?

"Nothing. Nothing is wrong. Why?"

I sighed and answered him through our mind link. *Now if I just knew who killed Jack, and if I could prove I had nothing to do with it.*

Hairy barked and slurped a big kiss across my cheek. *That's easy, Mama. Bad man, big stick.*

I looked down at the dog dancing at my feet, stunned by the communication he had just shared with me. "What?"

Bad man, big stick hurt Jack, Mama. Came to the house and argued with Jack there. Didn't you know?

"But how do you know it, Hairy?"

Hairy can smell it in the house. Bad man smelled funny. Jack smelled scared. And then, I think the bad man with the big stick made Jack go with him.

"Sara! Look out!"

My heart clamored inside my chest. Just then, another shot rang out across the ring, and once again, I threw myself down across my dog for the second time that day. Captain Johnny saved us again.

Chapter 13
Sara

Well, as we say around the courthouse, that was when the fertilizer hit the ventilator.

When I dared to raise my head a fraction of an inch and peep around, I saw Fibbies everywhere, along with a host of near-hysterical people who showed their beloved dogs. I figured the attendees would hate me for the rest of their lives and the Skye Terrier Club of America would ban me from ever attending the National Specialty again. Dogs looked rattled, but not as upset as their owners and handlers.

I raised myself a little and looked down at the dog beneath me. "You okay?"

Hairy slurped his tongue across my face. *Bad man, big stick, Mama. Don't let him hurt you.*

I stifled back a sob and hugged Hairy close as I showered his hairy little face with kisses. "You silly dog, I'll be okay. You are who matters. Are you okay?"

He barked and slurped another kiss across my cheek. *I fine, Mama.*

"You can get up, Mrs. Talbott." A Fibbie agent reached down to help me up as Philip stood hovering nearby. I noticed his face was pale as a sheet.

I could not believe it. The mob marked us to be killed.

Correction. They marked me. And with me, everyone else was in danger. Mortal danger.

We piled back into the Fibbie RV. I rode in silence as Philip and the Federal agents got us away from the show site. I held my dog close to my heart while my sister sobbed as she clung to Boze.

"Ms. Winslow, get a grip on yourself. Your relentless crying just makes this worse on everyone." Philip's voice sounded quiet but stern.

She sniffled. "I'm only doing what everyone wants to do, Philip." She shuddered. "I can't do this anymore. I... I... I didn't sign up for this crap."

Philip frowned. "For the love of God, woman, shut up!"

I cringed as tears streamed down my stalwart sister's cheeks again. "Leave her alone, Philip. She never cries."

I pulled my sister close to my shoulder, shut my eyes, and swallowed. I wanted to give way to tears, too, but I needed to remain calm. Maybe my calmness could help Dara. Damn, this was so hard. How could this be happening? Why were these people trying to kill me? "Hmm. All this crap makes me wonder: why was Jack killed? I swear, if Jack still lived and I could get my hands on Jack Talbott right now, I would kill him. I bet I could tell God he died, and God would believe me."

Dara nodded. "God would believe you, sis. I swear, Jackson Talbott was the freaking gift that keeps on giving. Hell, I don't know what the Jack Ass did, but he deserved everything he got and then some."

I must have dozed off, because when I awoke, it was dark, and the big Sprinter van was still moving. It embarrassed me as I realized I snuggled up against Philip in my sleep, but he did not seem to mind. As I raised up, I rubbed my eyes and looked around. "Where are we?"

Philip kissed my forehead. "Hello, gorgeous. We are on the New Jersey Turnpike. Why?"

I frowned as I sat upright, pulling away from Philip as I moved. "New Jersey Turnpike? Where are we going?"

Philip's lip raised a fraction of an inch in what could be a smile. Not much of a smile, but a teeny, itsy-bitsy smile all the same. "If I tell you, I might have to kill you."

I shrugged. "Yeah, and so what's new? People already tried to do that four times. Where are we going?"

He laughed, the corners of his eyes crinkling as his blue eyes twinkled with amusement. "We head to Boston. We ought to be there in a couple of hours."

Dara stretched and yawned. "Boston? What did we lose there?"

"Nothing, if I know you two. My dad lives in Boston. He already expects us. I called and explained we ran into a minor problem, and Dad said to come on to the house with the entire gang. Why?"

I peered back over my shoulder behind us. "A minor problem, hmm? I'd hate to see a big problem if this is little. What if the hit men follow us?"

His lips narrowed into a tight, thin line. "They won't."

I frowned. "But Philip-"

"Believe me, babe, they won't follow us. We changed vehicles, and they would have no reason to suspect we would go to Boston. Some officers will see that your SUV gets back to your home in Texas. Everything will be fine."

I could not help it. We had a rather unusual day, and I felt damned nervous about the entire situation. Every few minutes, I kept looking back, peering out into the darkness. I guess I hoped I would see something, while I was terrified what to do if I saw anything out of the ordinary. You know, like hit men aiming their guns at us. Stuff like that. "What about all of our gear?"

"All taken care of. Don't worry. Everything will be fine."

I fell asleep after we drove across New York and entered Connecticut. I awoke to find I clung to both Hairy and the sleeve to Philip's expensive, custom-made sports jacket. I had been rubbing the wool back and forth between my fingers, the way I sometimes see Fancy do when stressed. I think our therapist in Georgia said it was a method of disassociation. Therapists might not recommend it (ours said dissociation comprised a waste of time when he tried to help Fancy stop doing it), but it sure seemed to sooth my nerves. If rubbing fabric makes Fancy feel this calm, I understood why she does it.

I knew Hairy should ride in his crate, which had appeared as if through some sort of Fibbie magic, but I needed to touch my dog. I needed the reassurance that the touch supplied to confirm my boy was safe. He could make this trip laying across my lap. Anyway, it seemed like only a minute or two later, and Philip shook my shoulder.

"Wake up, babe. We're here."

I shook my head as I heard Dara snicker. "Don't call me that."

He tilted his head as he looked down at me. "Why not?"

"She hates to be called 'babe,' Philip, although it's okay for the parental authority figures to call her 'baby girl,'" said Dara.

I hate it because Jack called me babe. And he betrayed me.

Oh, yeah. Like I was going to tell any man that. I shrugged my shoulders. "Philip, I just don't like the nickname. I prefer people call me Sara." I rubbed my aching back. Throwing myself on the ground twice that day had been two too many times, and my back was telling me about it from my neck to my tailbone. "I need to have my chakras balanced again. My chi must be out of whack, and God only knows what color my aura must be after all this crap."

Dara chortled. "Crazy nutball."

Philip looked perplexed. "What are you talking about? Do you own a chihuahua?"

Dara smirked as she rolled her eyes. "Oh, God, no. The Skyes would eat a Chi. Psychic mumbo-jumbo is what she is prattling about. Sara is all into this New Age stuff. My best guess? She needs her back adjusted, not her chakras. Her back already bothered her before today."

I bristled at her words. "Oh, shut up. You are such a heathen."

Dara laughed for the first time in hours. "No, you are the heathen. As I told you before, you are a heathen by definition."

As I opened my mouth to make a snappy comeback, the car door jerked open. "Need any help in here?"

I blinked as an older, tall, handsome, silver-haired man smiled down inside the humongous van at us. Philip smiled back. Jeez Louise, he looked just like that actor who played Tony DeNozzo's dad on NCIS. "Hi, Dad. I would like to introduce you to Sara Talbott and Dara Winslow. Ladies, I'd like to introduce you to my dad, Jim Martino."

Dara blinked as her eyes widened in surprise. She flipped her luscious hair back, pasted on her best sultry sex goddess smile, and held her hand out to the handsome man at the door. "Senator Martino, what an unexpected delight. Thank you for your hospitality, sir."

I cut my eyes at Philip, who avoided my look. As Dara stepped near me, I whispered. "What was that all about?"

She smiled like a cat who had gulped down the Ultimate Canary. "You idiot, James Martino is the retired U.S. Senator from Massachusetts."

I frowned. "I'd have sworn that was Ted Kennedy. For about a kajillion years."

Dara tossed her long hair back over her shoulder. "Don't show your ignorance, Sara. Ted Kennedy is dead. James Martino was the other senator from Mass. Don't you remember?"

"Uh, not really." About that time, we had progressed into the foyer, where I peeked into the exquisite formal living room. I saw a stunning family portrait hanging over the fireplace of Mr. Martino and Philip, with a beautiful woman sitting between them. She had an engaging smile, bright blue eyes, and dark hair. A golden retriever sat by her side, with his head on her knee.

And then I remembered. I could almost see the news write-up and photos in my mind's eye. 'The wife of newly elected Massachusetts Senator James Martino was murdered today. Senator Martino ran for office on a strong anti-crime platform. Infamous Mafioso Carlo Stelari made threats last month against Senator Martino's family, if elected. This morning, hours after the news reporters announced the election results last night, Alessa Martino died in a car bombing, believed to be a Stelari gangland hit.'

"Oh, my God. His mother died in an explosion the morning after they elected his dad." I whispered the words to my sister.

She nodded, her face grave with worry. "Murdered in a gangland hit."

Alessa Martino's death comprised more than murder. The mob assassinated her in retaliation for Mr. Martino's election to the senate.

"Oh, my God, a Stelari mob hit." I cringed.

It was like I told Hairy. We were smack dab in the middle of this shit storm. The man brought me home to 'protect me' when the mob murdered his mother in this city years before. The same mob which hunted for me now.

Could it get any worse?

Never ask a question if you do not want to hear the answer.

The next day, Philip and his dad took us to the Fibbie offices in downtown Boston. After way too many hours of interrogation, we were leaving when it happened.

Dara had crossed the street and waited to get into Senator Martino's ultra plush limo. I will never know why she decided to enter the limo on the street side, but as I stepped into the street, I heard Johnny loud and clear. "Sara! That car! Watch out!"

In retrospect, I don't know if Captain Johnny shouted at Dara or my name, but I realized a black Cadillac was bearing down on my sister. Her head snapped up at the sound of my voice shouting at her. As she paled, immobilized like a deer in the headlights, I raced the last steps, and then threw myself at her. I knocked her back out of harm's way.

Unfortunately, the son of a bitch hit me.

I felt myself being tossed through the air as the fender clipped my hip. Ow, ow, ow, ow, big, big, big owie. Oh, fuck, oh fuck, oh, fuckety fuckety fuck. The last thing I remembered was stars fading into darkness as my head hit concrete, with Dara and Philip both screaming my name.

***

I awoke later on the gigantic French Provençal bed in the beautiful, feminine room in the Senator's gorgeous home where I had stayed since we arrived. I moaned as I tried to raise up and fell back on the bed. If there was a place to hurt, I hurt there, but I have to admit, my hip and my head seemed to hurt a zillion times worse than all the other spots together.

"Are you okay?" Philip sounded more than a little worried.

Hell, no, a car hit me and I hurt like crap, I wanted to say, but somehow I withheld the snotty retort. I tried to nod, and then winced as pain shot through my temple. "Yeah, I guess I'm okay. God knows I hurt everywhere, but I am alive. And every day you wake up and don't have dirt on your face is a good day, right?"

He kind of laughed, his voice taut with worry. "Yeah, I guess so, babe. No broken bones. Waking up alive sure seems to beat the alternative."

I grimaced. "Don't call me babe."

Philip snickered and leaned over to kiss my forehead. I felt my lips disappear as I frowned. "I mean it, Philip."

It pleased me to hear I sustained no broken bones in my flight by car. "Did you guys catch the driver?"

He shook his head with a wry frown. "No, the son of a bitch got away, but we will find the sorry rat bastard, I swear."

I raised up and looked around. When I saw Hairy laid right at my feet on the bed, I relaxed a little. I patted the coverlet beside me, and he wriggled his way up to me like a Skye terrier inchworm, to cover my face with doggy kisses before he sighed and laid his head across my chest. "Everything will be okay. Won't it, Philip?"

He nodded again, but I noticed a tightness around his eyes. "It has to be."

"So, what the hell do these idiots want, and why involve me this way? Why don't they just ask me for it?"

Philip hesitated a moment as a flash of uncertainty crossed his handsome face.

"Oh, come on, now, mister. These bozos tried to kill me five times now. Twice on the road after the Devon show. Twice when they shot at me at Montgomery. Today, this yahoo tried to run me down, coming out of the freaking FBI offices. Oh, I forgot: they tried to get to me at the hotel, too. I lucked out when the desk clerk refused to give 'my husband' the room key."

I made air quotes when I spat out 'my husband.' "The poor desk clerk looked sick when I told him someone murdered Jackson last month. Philip, if I'm not safe there, where will I find safety? I deserve a little honesty from the government. Why can't I be told in what unholy fucking criminality my dead husband involved his stupid ass? I deserve to know why the freaking mob wants me dead."

Silent, Philip stood chewing his lip. I felt a sense of genuine panic gripping my chest. "Philip? Don't I deserve that much?"

It must have been the break in my voice that got to him. His eyes clouded over, and he wet his lips before he began. "Jack worked with the Stelari family, smuggling art treasures into the U.S."

My brow wrinkled as I frowned. "Just who are the Stelaris?"

He frowned, and a look of surprise at my response crossed his face. "You don't know?"

I shook my head. "I don't have the foggiest idea who they are, other than they want to kill me."

He paused again, and I could see he felt conflicted. This must be good, I thought.

Philip let out an inaudible sigh. "The Stelari family is the premiere mob family in the States."

"Shut the door!" I exclaimed as my jaw hit the floor. "Aw, come on now, get real. Jackson Talbott worked with the mob? That man would chase anything with a vagina, but he was so squeaky clean in his business dealings that it is not even funny. Hell, he was an expert witness appointed frequently by the courts to evaluate the net worth of businesses. He had to be squeaky clean. Are you sure we are talking about the same man?"

Philip nodded, and I noticed his face appeared grim. "I'm sure as death, Sara. Old Squeaky Clean branched out from his court appointments and worked a deal to act as an intermediary for the Stelari family. They sent him stolen artifacts from Europe, and he acted as go-between with antiquities dealers. His stellar reputation kept our eyes from him for years. The fool started a little free enterprise from his original deal with the Stelari family. He pilfered off certain pieces for his own resale purposes. Unfortunately, he kept the wrong item, and he pissed them off, big time. And as we both know, they are not a family to enrage."

I thought for a moment. "Fine, so Jack was an idiot and got involved with the Mafia, and then he became an even bigger idiot because he stole from them. Why am I involved? Just because I married him?"

Philip shook his head. "No, not only that."

I frowned. "I don't get it. Then why?"

Philip sighed and raked his hand through his hair. He got up, and walked over to the window, and stared outside a long moment before answering. "Do you know a man named Roberto Franchetti?"

So help me, I felt like my heart dropped right down to my toes. I feared this would be bad news about my kinfolk. I tried to clear my parched throat. "My Uncle Roberto? Uh... How is he involved?"

"He's the head of La Cosa Nostra in Calabria."

"Get out of here. Not my sweet Uncle Roberto." As I laughed, I realized he was serious. I rubbed my forehead and frowned. "But I thought their name was Stelari?"

Philip shook his head. "Stefano Stelari is the head of *la famiglia* in the United States. Your uncle is the head of the mob in Calabria."

"Well, shit." I sat down hard on the edge of the bed, stunned by the unexpected news. As I thought back over my trips to Italy, I remembered the unusual respect the townspeople lavished on my uncle when we visited, both when I was a kid, and four years ago when Jack and I visited him in Calabria. People came to ask him for favors, and he loaned them money, lots of money. Uncle Roberto kissing babies in the streets. People kissing his hands, in apparent gratitude.

Hmm. It all made sense. My Uncle, the Godfather.

After a long, awkward pause, I asked the question bothering me. "Okay, so let's assume *per arguendo*, for argument's sake, that Uncle Roberto is the head of the Mafia there, and this Stelari guy is head here. How is Uncle Roberto tied in with the Stelari family?"

Philip tried to smile. "His mother was Stelari's father's sister. They are cousins. One heads *la famiglia* in Calabria, and the other one heads it in the United States. They called his mother 'La Reina.' Rumors named her as the head of *la famiglia* in Calabria before her death."

As I remembered Nonna took me to Italy when I was twelve to meet her family, I felt nauseated and dizzy. It was the only trip I made to Italy with Nonna, and she wanted me to meet *la famiglia*, as she called it. I remember Uncle Roberto told his workers, "This is my niece, Sara Catereina. She's named after my mother." Only my family ever called me Catereina, a variant of the Italian version of Katherine, which is my middle name. The man's eyes got big, and he said, "*La Reina?*" Uncle Roberto smiled. "*Si, la regazza e' la proxima regina.* Treat her with utmost respect, Carlo. This young lady shall be our next Reina." I remember I laughed, because 'Reina' means Queen in Spanish, and it was so incongruous that anyone would liken me to a Queen. I remember thinking, there is no Queen of Calabria. Now, years later, I realized what he had been saying, and why the Fibbies were so interested in me.

Hell, maybe this was why I intrigued Jack years ago. It was not my great beauty, intriguing eyes, sparkling wit, or charming personality. Jack wanted my contacts with *'Ndrangheta.*

Jeez Louise, I am a freaking Mafia Princess. Now if I only looked like Susan Lucci. Maybe I would have to go dark with my hair color instead of light.

I took a deep breath. "But members of the *'Ndrangheta* are men, and they recruit based on blood relationships. They expect sons to follow in their fathers' footsteps. They go through a grooming process in their youth to become, oh, what did my professor called them? Oh, yeah, they call them *giovani d'honore*, or boys of honor. They enter the ranks as *uomini d'honore*, or men of honor."

Philip's mouth fell open in shocked surprise. "How on earth do you know that?"

Embarrassed, I chuckled. "I took a class on international crime syndicates in my law school classes. *'Ndrangheta* became a worldwide crime syndicate in the 1950s, when a series of earthquakes caused many Calabrians to move elsewhere. The *'Ndrangheta* fascinated me because of their recruitment techniques. Very few Calabrian members of *'Ndrangheta* ever turn on *la famiglia* as *pentitos*, or repentants. *'Ndrangheta* avoid confrontations with the Italian government, and have a powerful grip on the economy and governance of Calabria."

"I take it you never suspected you might be part of their family?" he asked.

I shook my head. "Never. I understood my Italian family raised olives and grapes. I did not know they also raised criminals. Okay, so if I am related to the Bad Guys, why do they want to kill me?"

Philip shrugged his shoulders. "Good question, but I don't know. The Stelari family may think you know where Jack stashed the goods he stole from them. They would consider that to be a betrayal to the family."

"Well, bull hockey! I don't know where the stuff is. What do I do? How do I convince them I do not know what they are looking for, or where the hell it is? What in the great blue blazes of hell did my Jack Ass husband steal from them?"

Philip extended my cell phone towards me. "Listen, I suggest you call your uncle. I hope he can tell you what is going on. Better yet, perhaps he can stop all this before it is too late with a phone call to the Stelaris."

Philip sat there, silent, holding the phone out to me, waiting for my next move.

I gulped as I stared at the iPhone in his hands, hating the idea my beloved Uncle Roberto could have had anything to do with murdering anyone, much less issuing an order for me to be killed. I loved this man for years. He was my Nonna's brother. I refused to believe Uncle Roberto wanted to have me killed. I prayed he realized I did not know doodle squat about all this. But, then again, maybe not. There was no telling what Jack ever told anyone about my involvement in this fiasco. I took a deep breath, took my phone from Philip's hands, and scrolled down my directory for Roberto's number. After only the slightest hesitation, I punched in Uncle Roberto's telephone number. On the third ring, someone answered.

"*Pronto?*"

"This is Sara, Signore Franchetti's niece in America. I need to speak to my uncle, *per favore.*"

The harsh voice laughed. "Why you think he wants to talk to you?"

Anger welled up in me. "Because I am *La Reina Nuova. Io sono parte de la famiglia. Nostra famiglia* depends on each other, and I am calling *mi zio* for help, *per aiuto. Capisce?*"

It shocked me to realize I shouted at the end of my diatribe. The man hesitated a moment, and then I could almost see him nod. "*Si, bene.* I will tell him you are on the phone. You wait."

It seemed forever before Uncle Roberto came to the phone. "Sara? How are you, *cara?* I have not heard from you in a long time."

Oh, yes, like for two freaking weeks. Sara, hold your temper. You must handle this with care, I thought. Be careful not to alienate the man. After all, *Zio Roberto* is the Calabrian Godfather.

I choked back a little sob. "Not so good, *mi zio. Non cosi buono.* Things have been rough here this past month. *Molto brutto.*"

"Tsk, tsk, tsk. Tell me about it, *carissima.* What can your old *zio* do to help?"

I took another deep, ragged breath and struggled to control my crying. "Last month, someone murdered my husband—"

"Yes, we talked about that before." His voice sounded flat, emotionless, cold.

It surprised me when he admitted to it. He sounded so cool. Perspiration poured off me, and it could not have been over 40-degrees that day in Boston. I licked my lips, and cut my eyes at Philip, who nodded at me, as he mouthed, "Go on."

I nodded back and took another deep breath. "*Zio* Roberto, this is hard for me. It embarrasses me."

"To ask for help from *sua famiglia,* Sara? No, *mi Reina,* you must not feel shame."

"No, no, *mi zio,* not to ask for help. Family is to help in times of trouble. Thank God above I have *mi famiglia* to call, to depend on." I could almost see the old man nodding with pleasure at my words. "*Zio,* I feel shame my husband stole from his, uh, business associates."

I could hear the sharp intake of breath on the other end of the line. "What do you mean, Sara?"

I stammered as I struggled to reply with some modicum of sense. "Well, *Zio* Roberto, you see... okay, it's like this. Nonna used to say, '*qui cum canibus concumbant cum publicibus surgen*t.'"

He chuckled. "Do you know what the phrase means?"

I nodded. "Si. Remember, I am an attorney. *Io sono un avocatto.* The Latin phrase means 'when you lie down with dogs, you get up with fleas.'"

Uncle Roberto began laughing. "Yes, you understand the Latin phrase. Are you saying ...?"

"I'm saying my husband associated with people he should not have cheated. Jack laid down with dogs and got up with fleas. He did a terrible thing. He thought he could mess people over, and he got caught. But, *Zio* Roberto, now they are after me...”

“What?” he growled. “What you mean, *mi Reina*, they are after you?”

I cried. I had not meant to cry, but the tears would not hold back any longer. “*Zio* Roberto, there have been at least five attempts to kill me in the past week alone. Jackson took something from these people, and they think I know where it is. But, *Zio* Roberto, I don’t have any idea where it is. I swear I know nothing about it. Heck, I don’t even know what he stole from them.”

“*Merda.*” The vulgar curse was soft, but I heard it. “This was not supposed to happen.”

For the first time in days, I relaxed the tiniest bit. At least Uncle Roberto did not order the hit on me. “*Zio*, if I knew what he took, and if I could find it, I would return it. I swear I would.”

“What you say, Sara? Do you have it?”

The quiet hunger, the raw greed in his voice stunned me. Oh, my Jack Ass husband must have stolen something unbelievably valuable. Obscenely valuable. If he wasn’t dead, I would kill Jackson Talbott with my own hands.

“That is not what I said, *mi zio*. What I said was I do not even know what he took. If I knew, maybe I could find it. It might be right under my nose, and I would not even know it.”

He thought about that a moment before answering me. “The word on the street is that this thing he took, it is *molto, molto pregiato*, you know, how you say? Very high of value. There should be no question to anyone that you were involved. You are *mi famiglia*, my sister’s grandchild, you are like *mi figlia*. But, since the fools think you are involved, then yes, I think if you could return *La Sforza*, it would help very much, as a show, of how you say? *sua intentos bona fede*, your good intentions.”

La Sforza. I thought I had heard the name somewhere before, but where? I was not even sure what it meant. “What is *La Sforza, mi zio*? How will I recognize it if I see it? For all I know, it could sit right in my living room, and I would never even know it.”

"You remember *La Sforza, mi cara.* You saw it when Jack and you visited here."

My heart dropped. I should recognize this thing, but what the hell is it? "Where, *mi zio? Dove?* Where was it? Where did I see it?"

"In *El Museo de Calabria,* in Reggio. We went to see it. You must remember, *carissima.*"

Chapter 14
Sara

It hit me like a sack of shit. Oh, fuck. Oh, double, triple fuckety fuck. Jeez-Louise, he could not have done this. The damned man could have done nothing this insane. I swallowed, and then swallowed again. My throat felt as dry as the mountains of southern Italy, infamous for the Mafia that roam through them, regulating their odd sort of justice there. "The exhibit of Greco-Italian treasures."

"*Si, si, essatamente.*" Uncle Roberto sounded excited when I remembered it.

My heart sank down to my toes, if not lower. "*Zio* Roberto, please tell me he did not steal that gorgeous urn discovered the year before we came."

"I am sorry, *cara*. That is what he stole from the Stelari family. They sent it to him to resell for them. He never sold it. He kept it."

"Oh, my dear God in heaven above." I closed my eyes and leaned my head against my hand.

La Sforza was an eighth century Greco-Roman treasure. The Calabrian archeological team unearthed it in a pristine condition the year before we visited Uncle Roberto. We stood in line for over an hour to get to see it - astonishing when you consider my uncle was the head of *'Ndrangheta*. You would have thought we could have waltzed right in any time we damned well pleased since we were in the company of the Calabrian Godfather. I figured the museum knew not to leave the chickens with the foxes. Leave it to my husband to help steal one of the greatest Greco-Roman art treasures ever unearthed in Italy from underneath the nose of *'Ndrangheta*. If I remembered correctly, the damned thing was worth the insane amount of fifteen million euro. Jack sure as hell did not list 'art treasure worth millions' on his inventory. To add insult to injury, I might get my ass killed over the blasted stolen urn. No wonder Jack became so excited when I said I would not go after him for undisclosed items on his inventory. I struggled not to hurl. "*Zio*, I did not know my idiot husband involved himself in the theft of this precious art treasure. I have not seen it since that day we visited the museum. Is that why they keep trying to kill me?"

"They were not supposed to harm you, *cara*. You are part of *la famiglia*. But, yes, I am sure that is why they have been after you. Jack's business associates are terribly upset about this. It is a very substantial monetary loss, you understand, not to mention, a blot to our name, this theft of *un tesoro nazionale*. We have a close relationship with the Calabrian government, and I refuse to allow this theft to damage our close ties. I know everyone would very much appreciate the safe return of the urn. It would be, uh, how you say? I would consider it to be a personal favor if you could return it."

Enough to call off the hit on me? And what if I cannot find the damned thing? My mind reeled and my chest ached with the pain of my husband's latest betrayal. I took a deep breath. "It is only right. I should return it to them. Jack had no business taking it. But, *Zio* Roberto, I am not sure I can find it."

"Try, Sara, try hard. It may mean the difference in life ... and ... death."

Yeah, and I knew whose life he meant. I felt faint. My stepmother would say I 'swooned'. Whatever it was, I did it, as everything around me darkened and my field of vision narrowed. I bent over and took several deep breaths.

My uncle heard me. "*Reina, va bene?* Are you all right?"

I nodded. "I will be fine, *Zio*. Can you fax or email me a photo of *La Sforza*? It would help me search for it."

After only the briefest hesitation, he assented. "*Si, como no*. I will send it today. I will try to talk some sense into some people, let them know they make an enormous mistake when they mess with *mi famiglia*. But you be careful, *cara*, and stay safe. We will get through this tough stretch, hmm? Then you will come to see me again, like old times."

I sat numb after the call ended, not knowing what to say or where to start. Philip cleared his throat, and then spoke. "So, what did he keep?"

Idid not answer right away as I struggled to figure it all out. Finally, I replied. "Art treasure."

He laughed, an odd, tight little laugh. "Yeah, I thought so, but what did he call it, *La Sforza?*"

I nodded again. "Yeah. I remember Uncle Roberto took Jack and me to see an art exhibit at the Museum while we were there, to see this famous urn worth a veritable butt load of money. Jack stared at it for ages. Leave it to my Jack Ass husband to steal it from the freaking mob. I never would have thought Jackson Talbott had it in him."

Philip let out a low whistle. "Shit, I knew the urn went missing, but I didn't know Jack was involved. I'm sorry, Sara."

I snapped my head around at him, my eyes narrowing, as I realized what Philip had told me only moments before. "Now, wait just a minute, mister. What do you know? Why couldn't you have told me this was about a missing art treasure? Did it occur to you that maybe I knew where it was?"

He stared at me a moment before answering. "I had orders not to tell you anything early on. So, uh, do you know where it is?"

I shook my head. "No, damn it, not a clue. Believe me, I damned sure wish I knew where it is. Maybe I would not be as likely to wake up dead tomorrow."

When he remained silent, I turned to face him. "Orders, hmm? Shit, now I'm beyond scared. What if we can't find this damned thing?"

He pulled me to him. "We will, babe. We will find it."

He felt so good and smelled even better. I hated to spoil the moment, but I had to say it. I pushed back a little as I looked up at him. "Please, Philip, don't call me babe."

He tensed at my words. He tousled my hair with one hand as he grinned down at me. "Why not? It's just a term of affection."

"Come on, Philip, just humor me. The mob wants to kill me, and I only need to find a multi-million-dollar artifact to get them off my ass. This is a little thing. Don't call me babe. Please."

I could almost see it go through his brain as I frowned and ran my hand across my hair to straighten it. All the shit on the table for me right now, and for what godforsaken reason was this so freaking important to me? I could not bear to tell him Jack used to call me babe. Jack's betrayal of me was still too raw. I could not handle a man using the damned pet name.

And I had to admit, it was not just about Jack. My Nonna always called me that and she died. People who called me 'babe' never stayed around long. They died or left me.

Oh, hell, it was more than even that. I could not handle it from this man. It mattered to me what Philip thought, what he said. Philip mattered to me. Damn it, I did not want him or any man to matter to me. It hurt too much to care. I did not want to risk anyone—especially him—hurting me again, like Jack hurt me. So, maybe, just maybe, if I did not let him get too close, maybe if I did not let him call me babe, then maybe he could not hurt me. Maybe it would not hurt so bad if—when—he disappointed me, too.

I did not think I could stand it if Philip hurt me the way Jackson did. The mob would not have to kill me. His betrayal would kill me. I could not risk getting any closer to this gorgeous hunk of man than I already was. And that meant he could not call me 'babe.'

And then when I had determined not to let myself get involved with him, the damned man just had to do it. He pulled me close to him and tilted my face to his. Oh, no, Philip, I thought, no, oh, no.

I tried to turn my face away from him, but he turned me back towards him and did it, anyway. He lowered his face to mine and kissed me and with a tenderness I had only dreamed about, only read about in romance novels, only seen in the most tender, enchanting movies. Now, I understood why Dad's mom wrote that the moment of a first kiss was when you might lose your heart forever. I tried to turn my face away from him, but he would not let me. And, once his lips claimed mine, I melted into what was without a doubt the sweetest, dearest kiss I ever received from a male in my entire life, not counting Hairy's big wet slurpy kisses, of course.

Yes, I figured that was the last moment I could call my heart my own.

His kiss even made my knees go limp. Could my knees go limp? Mine felt limp. I felt limp all over. Limp as a wet noodle.

"Did you know who I was all along?" I asked as our kiss ended.

He frowned. "What do you mean?"

I shook my head, impatient with the whole mess. "One of Uncle Roberto's sisters was my Nonna. And, as you pointed out to me, their mother was Catareina Stelari before she became Catareina Franchetti."

He nodded. "*La Reina*, yes, I know. She came from the Spanish branch of the family."

My eyes narrowed as I studied him. "How do you know *La Reina* came from Spain?"

"*Reina* is Spanish for Queen. I figure they would have called her *La Regina* if she had been Italian. They used to call her the Queen of Calabria."

I did not explain it was her mother, my great-great-grandmother, who immigrated from Spain to Italy to marry Matteo Stelari, or that all the first-born girls had Catareina as their middle name. I also failed to mention that my uncle called me *La Reina Nuova*. Some things you do not share, even if you are swapping spit.

And just then, Dara stormed into the room. "Sara, what the hell is going on here?"

I jerked away from Philip faster than a proverbial speeding bullet and looked from him to my sister, with my face burning bright scarlet. "Uh, what do you mean, sis?"

"I have been in a car that was almost run off the road into a raging river. Someone shot at me..."

"Actually, they shot at me," I replied, my voice rather droll if I say so. "Twice, if I remember correctly. But don't let a little thing like the truth slow you down."

She stopped long enough to give me The Stare. She won when I had to look away.

"We had to change our hotel room because the Mob was after us. And now, I damned near got run over."

"Oh, excuse me, but I was the one who got run over. Enough is enough for the love of dogs. What is the problem? Spit it out."

She stared at me a moment before she replied. "Well, that's just it. I want to know what is going on. Why are people trying to kill us?"

I looked at Philip, and he nodded, almost imperceptibly. Almost. Dara caught it and exploded.

"Oh, great. So, you must ask him if you can tell me, and I'm your own flesh and blood? I have been your sister for how long, oh, yeah, something like all your freaking life, and you have been lip locking this guy for what? A day? A minute? Give me a damned break, Sara. What the fuck is going on?"

"Jack was a bigger jackass than anyone suspected. He stole from the Mob."

She stared at me for a long time. I guess three, maybe five minutes. After an uncomfortable silence, she spoke. "Well, shit."

As she wheeled for the door, I grabbed her arm. "Dara, talk to me. What are you thinking?"

It stunned me to see tears in her eyes, and to feel her shaking when I grabbed her. I tried to pull her close, to comfort her, to tell her it would all be okay, but she pulled back as a tear slid down her cheek.

"Sara, baby, I can't do this anymore."

See, there is that 'baby' business again. Why do the ones who use a variant of this freaking 'term of endearment' with me always wind up breaking my heart? I keep on telling people not to use it, but they do. This happens every stinking time. Damn it.

I felt a surge of panic, the likes of which I only felt a few times before in my life. The night my Nonna died, the first time I learned Jack cheated, the day I learned I would never have a baby. The day I learned about Jack and Robin and their Little Bundle of Joy, who is on the way. I grabbed Dara's arm, struggling not to let her go. "You don't mean this, Dara Siobhan Winslow. You cannot mean this. Please, please, don't go, Dara, please..."

She pulled back and stared at me again. My mouth went dry as I waited for her next words.

Please, Dara, please, don't go. Do not go. Please don't leave me. Please don't abandon me. Not like this.

"I'll take the dogs with me. There's a storm in the Caribbean. It is already a class 4 hurricane. I'll ship the dogs to Mother. I need to go home for the other dogs in case the hurricane hits our region. Once I get the rest of the dogs, I will go to my mom in San Antonio. Hell, maybe I'll get lucky and keep them all alive through this shit."

I pulled my dog close to me in a protective stance. "Not Hairy. You're not taking my Hairy."

She glared at me. "Fine, I won't take your precious Hairy. God forbid anyone tries to separate you from your fur ball. I just hope you do not live to regret keeping Hairy with you, Sara. I won't take Hairy from you, even if I do co-own him with you and have every right to do so. After all, he's your baby. I hope the freaking Mafia does not decide to hurt you through an innocent dog. Hairy deserves better than that."

I winced as the sarcasm dripped from her words like acid. Dara shook off my hand and slammed out the door. I collapsed after she left the room. As I started sinking towards the floor, Philip grabbed me and held me close in his arms, crooning to me. I cried for what felt like an eternity, mourning the loss of my dearest human friend. What would I do without her? Dara had been in my life since I was twelve years old. She was my only friend who knew me before my mom married Kirk and before Nonna died. Dara was with me through all of my life-changing events. And now she was gone. I cried myself into a restless sleep.

Chapter 15
Johnny and Tamsin

"I'm worried about her, Johnny. This last betrayal could break her." Tamsin's brow wrinkled with worry as she chewed on her angelic lip.

Captain Johnny nodded, but he never took his eyes off the sleeping woman. "I agree. These problems keep mounting. Sara never expected Dara would abandon her in her time of need. I fear the lass cannot bear much more."

Tamsin took a deep breath. "The Lord does not allow Satan to send humans more than they can bear. He says what doesn't break you -"

"Strengthens you. Yes, my love, I have heard Him say that. Tammy, we need to double our watch over her."

She frowned. "But Johnny -"

He shook his head. "No, my love. We must succeed with this assignment so I can remain with you for eternity."

Tamsin nibbled on her lip. "I pray it is not too late to save the girl."

He sighed and nodded. "I know. If only it's not too late."

He worried in silence whether the circumstances had already progressed too far for them to save Sara Winslow Talbott. He uttered a silent prayer that he was wrong.

Chapter 16
Sara

It would be a gross understatement to claim I moped around Senator Martino's gorgeous old house for the next couple of days. I lacked enough energy to crawl out of bed, much less to think about finding the godforsaken urn, or to do anything else. With all I had been through of late, including Jack's murder and the repeated attempts on my life which culminated with the hit and run, my sister's abandonment about pushed me over my limit. I did not have the energy to put one foot in front of the other, much less make a viable plan for my future. Three days later, I caught the news on the television, and realized I had to get up. A hurricane barreling down on the Texas Gulf Coast got my attention, and I somehow dragged my ass out of the big, comfy bed. I took the bath, which I needed, and dressed. Clad in clean clothes, with fresh hair and makeup, I almost felt human again. Almost.

Philip jumped up from his chair as a smile spread across his face. He looked surprised I came downstairs. "Well, I have to admit, I was getting pretty damned worried about you. I am glad to see you up again. You look great. Do you feel better?"

I nodded. "Yeah, sure, whatever. How do we find this freaking artifact?"

He looked uncomfortable with my words. "We have been talking about that."

"Yeah, I'm sure you have. I've thought about not much of anything else for the past three days except how my dead husband fucked me over, even in death, with this damned stolen urn. I could still wind up dead over it all. I swear if Jack wasn't dead I would kill him for the hell he has put me through, the sorry son of a bitch. Now, I must find and return it to those people, as the Italians say, *prestissimo*. I just want my freaking life back."

Senator Martino walked into the breakfast room to listen to my tirade, his intelligent blue eyes taking in everything I was saying. When I finished my impromptu rant and rave session, he replied. "It's not that simple."

I shut my eyes as I shook my head. Please do not tell me I can't have my life back. "Why not?"

"You cannot go home because the hit contract is still in effect. The Stelari family wants you dead. They think you betrayed their family. Your uncle is working on it, but the bottom line is you cannot go back until you return the urn. It would be suicide." Philip's dad sounded sincere in his concern for my safety.

I stared at him a moment before replying. "Well, that is just peachy. Don't you guys understand they know I'm staying here with you? Hell, they tried to kill me as we left the FBI building. I don't know where the blasted thing is. Believe me, if I knew where it was, it would thrill me to tell you. Jack and I owned a good bit of real estate. Have your guys searched all of our properties? He had to have the damned thing hidden in plain view somewhere. The bottom line is, I must go home. I have a law practice to manage, and it looks like the hurricane will hit the Galveston area."

I turned to walk out of the room when his dad spoke. "We know Jack and you owned properties. The FBI dug through them for any sign of the missing art treasures for weeks now, with no luck. They have gone through his office records, his storage facilities, everything. No sign of it."

Well, shit, I had not expected that. "Did you check Robin's house?"

Of course, but it is not there." Mr. Martino looked frustrated as he tried to convince me not to return home.

I frowned as I stood, trying to make some sense out of this crazy mess. "Did you check on his sailboat?"

Philip and his father both nodded.

"We checked the sailboat the first thing. Of course, if it had been on the boat, it's gone now. Remember, he sailed over to Red Fish Island the night they killed him," Philip said.

As my heart sank, I nodded. Only I knew anyone was on the boat with him that night. "You checked his office? His rental houses? His condo in Austin? How about the hotel room where Robin hid from Sonny?"

"Yes, we checked and rechecked all those places. We found nothing, zip, nada. It is not in any of those places. God knows I wish we had found the damned thing in one of those places." Philip interjected into the conversation his dad had commandeered.

I frowned. "Hmm, he loved Red Fish Island and went over there often. Why did he go there that night? Robin's son was sick and she couldn't go with him. Could he have gone over there to retrieve the urn?"

Philip shrugged. "If he did, the urn wasn't on the boat when they found it moored at the Hilton."

And who accompanied him on the boat? I had an idea or two. Perhaps I should have verbalized them, but I pushed those ideas out of my mind. It made little sense, especially considering Hairy claimed a man forced Jackson to leave the house. I struggled to make sense from chaos, not to delve into deeper chaotic messes. I needed to focus on something concrete that I could deal with, here and now. Getting home and practicing law, taking care of my dog, getting ready for this storm. I longed for and needed to do those tasks right now.

I stared at Philip and his dad for another long minute before replying. "What part does a United States senator play in all of this?"

His dad smiled. I guess it comprised a smile, since he looked sad. Bittersweet. What you could almost call a smile. "Carlo Stelari killed my wife."

I shut my eyes tight. Ouch. Well, dumb ass, ask and ye shall receive. Yeah, I knew a mob contract killed his wife, but I avoided making the link about who would have ordered it. Now it was official: Uncle Carlo kills women. "I thought Stefano headed the Stelari mob syndicate."

Mr. Martino nodded. "Stefano headed the Mob earlier. After he suffered a massive stroke, Carlo took over. Carlo is his son."

"Great. That makes them a politically correct mob. They are gender neutral and do not discriminate about whom they will kill based on the gender of the potential hit. Hmm. I wonder if they killed my Nonna, too."

Senator Martino's eyes narrowed. "Why do you think they might have killed your grandmother?"

Mom swore a hit-and-run driver killed Nonna. I asked Mom if it was possible her death was intentional, but Mom refused to accept that her mother's death was anything other than a horrible accident. Now, all my questions at the time of her death came rushing back to assail my poor, overtaxed brain. "The timing. It seems strange a hit-and-run driver killed the sister of the head of the *'Ndrangheta* within twenty-four hours of when they murdered your beautiful wife."

Senator Martino paled at my words. "Oh, my god. And my wife would have been your grandmother's second cousin."

I reached out to steady myself as vertigo swept over me. "Wh-what?"

"My mother-in-law was a Stelari before she married. My wife was ashamed of her family's criminal links, so I swore to take them down if elected. They swore there would be hell to pay if the citizens of this fine state elected me. The morning after the election, Alessa's car exploded on her way to church to offer prayers of thanks for my election."

I grew lightheaded as I contemplated his words and felt the blood drain from my face. Nonna died the same day as Alessa Martino, and both women were related to the Stelari family.

In a flash, Philip was at my side, pulling me to him as I swooned. Oh, how I wanted to depend on those beautiful, broad shoulders, to lay my problems there and to know he could take care of my worries and concerns for me, but that would not be fair or right.

Plus, I was not sure I could trust him. I was unsure I could trust any man, no matter how much I wanted to trust this gorgeous hunk of man, no matter how badly I longed for his touch. Did he want me, or just want to the damned *Sforza*? Or did he just want to catch his mother's killers?

After I reveled in his musky, masculine scent, the feel of him, the very closeness of him, I took a deep breath and pulled away. "So, what are you guys suggesting? I have a home and a law practice. In case you do not remember, that means I have legal and ethical responsibilities to my clients. I am due back in court next week. Plus, the hurricane made its way into the Gulf, and it's a class 4 hurricane with winds 150 freaking miles per hour. The projected landfall is Galveston."

"Well, Sara, I wanted to talk to you about that. The Agency thinks you shouldn't go home yet. We think—"

"You don't think I should go home?!" I yelped. "Who the hell do you think is going to pay my bills? Or make sure my cases are safe? Who will tie up Jack's damned ritzy ditzy sailboat? I don't give a crap about the boat, but it is worth $40,000. If that damned boat gets loose during this storm and damages someone else's property, I would be liable for the damages. And who is securing my house against this storm? You need to remember I live on Morgan Point, right smack dab on the freaking bay. Philip, I have no choice. I must go home. I need to shutter windows and put away lawn stuff. My god, I need to protect my case files. You should understand I must do those things since you're an attorney, Philip."

He waited until my rant ended before he tried to reply. "Are you done?"

I nodded as I pressed my hand to my breastbone, while I struggled to catch my breath.

"If it hits the Galveston area, the courts will close for days, if not weeks. Remember when Ike hit Galveston?"

I shook my head. "I have heard about it, but I didn't live in the area then, thank heaven."

That slowed him down, but not by much. He took a big breath and resumed his speech. "The Galveston courthouse flooded, and the courts closed for weeks. Heck, the roof of the First National Bank in Alvin collapsed. The lawyers there could not get to their files for a month by order of the Alvin Fire Marshall, although some lawyers sneaked in at night to retrieve their files. Similar things occurred throughout our region. I told Ashley to send letters to all the Courts and tell them someone injured you in a hit-and-run accident, that you are under a doctor's care, and we expect you to be out of pocket for a couple of weeks. We bought you some time. All the Judges in Galveston County know about this situation and back you 110%. Ditto for Brazoria County."

"You did what? Oh, Philip, who do you think you are telling my legal assistant to do anything? She works for me, not you. Those are my cases. The clients hired me to handle them, not someone else. I must return home, Philip. If not this week or next, I have to go home soon. I have no choice. It is imperative."

He stared at me a minute before answering. "My priority is to keep you alive."

I shut my eyes and rubbed my forehead. It was just my luck that I get migraines like Dad. I took a deep breath and tried to force myself to relax so the headache would lessen. "Oh, bull crap. My priority is to find this stupid *Sforza*, so maybe I can keep myself alive. If I cannot hunt for the damned urn, I am good as dead right now. If this hurricane blows that damned urn away, I might as well chuck it in right now."

Philip reached out and took my wrist in his hands. "I cannot let you go home, babe."

"Don't. Call. Me. Babe." And then his words hit me. "Why can't you let me go home, Philip? Why do you think you can stop me from going home?"

Philip looked at his dad, who cleared his throat. "Phil is a senior investigator for the Federal Bureau of Investigation. He's tracked this group for three years."

It took about thirty seconds for that to sink in. "Three years? You've been trying to catch my husband for three freaking years?"

Philip shook his head. "I've hunted for the smugglers for three years. I knew they were Stelari-related, and I want to bring down their organization for killing Mother. About eight months ago, I learned about Jack's involvement."

I sat down hard. Jeez Louise! Eight months ago was when my relationship with Jack changed from bad to untenable, and he became even more secretive and guarded with me.

And that was when Philip began wooing me with more than casual interest. I felt my cheeks flush as I remembered the evening he took me out for dinner and drinks. Holy crap, I almost gave into temptation that night. Was I never more to Philip than a way to catch his mother's killers?

As I struggled not to cry, I remembered the words he uttered to me that night in the lovely, candlelit restaurant overlooking Galveston Bay. Sara, I love you. I think I fell in love with you the first time I met you. Thank God I did not give in to his persuasive words and charming ways and…

And then, of course, I learned about Robin a month ago. God only knew how long Jack's sordid affair with her went on.

At that point, the argument went to hell in a hand basket. Three hours later, Philip and his dad still insisted they could not—or they would not—allow me to leave. I still insisted I had to go home.

I knew something had to give. It was not just about preparing the house for the storm or work. I had to go home and find *La Sforza*. If I did not, I was dead in the water. If the storm hit and destroyed the damned thing before I found it, I was dead meat. I was not ready for death. At least, not yet.

Every day without dirt on your face is a good day. I did not want to wake up with dirt on my face.

I gave up arguing. Nonna always said, 'you cannot win an argument with a rock.' I had already made my plane reservations, and I was packing when Philip discovered what I was doing.

"What the hell are you doing?"

I shrugged and kept on folding my clothing. "Packing. I thought that was obvious."

Philip hurried across the room and took the t-shirt from my hands. "Sara, it's not safe in Houston right now. You don't understand."

I pulled the shirt back from him and laid it in my suitcase. "No, Philip, I understand. I have responsibilities and I need to go home. We cannot find the evidence needed to save my life sitting here. I don't have a choice: I must go back. Oh, yeah, believe me, Philip, I understand."

He shook his head. "Not a possibility. We expect a class 4 hurricane to hit Galveston within the next 48 hours. They began evacuating Galveston County and the low-lying areas of Harris County yesterday. And you want to go home? That is insane. I doubt you can get to the house if you try to go home. You could waste the trip and risk your life. The hitmen must watch for you. It makes little sense for you to go home now."

Before I uttered a word of protest, Philip grabbed my shoulders and pulled me up close to him. As my eyes widened in surprise and my heart raced, he laid a lip lock on me like I had not experienced in years. Hell, maybe forever. It was better than the first kiss, and I had not thought I would ever receive a kiss better than that one. I will give him this: Philip Martino is one world class, fantabulous kisser.

I always knew I would be in Big Trouble with a Capital T if he ever kissed me.

Remember movies where the couple look at each other, the sparks flew, and they jumped each other's bones? That describes what happened next.

My shock gave way to this incredible, unexpected burst of fiery lust that flared up, as they say, from 'deep within my loins.' I realized I kissed him back with unexpected eagerness, like a woman who had just completed the forty days of Lent without chocolate and broke her fast. I did that. Jack and I had not been intimate in months. We had intercourse the last night we were together, but it involved no real intimacy. It comprised pure angry sex and nothing more. It had been a proverbial raccoon's age since Jackson Talbott and I even kissed, much less done anything that I consider shared sexual intimacy. And, believe me, Jackson Talbott never, but never, made me feel like Philip Martino made me feel that night in Boston. I sizzled with passion, from my little pink toenails that curled up in ecstasy to the top of my head, where my hair stood on end. I was sizzling with a Great Big Capital S.

The next thing I knew, I was climbing ol' Phil like a starving monkey climbs a tree for a banana. Again, after a proverbial forty-day fast from bananas. We both shucked clothing while clinging to each other. We hung on to one another as if our next breaths depended upon continued physical contact.

I had forgotten that French kissing felt so wonderful. Hell, maybe I never knew it could feel so wonderful. Jack, the quintessential man whore, hated tongue kissing and always said the whole concept of someone's tongue being in his mouth seemed nasty. Jack obsessed about germs. Go figure. He would do the horizontal mambo with any willing female, but feared germs.

Now, in the thralls of passion, I obsessed on the sensations in my mouth. My tongue danced with Philip's, and I reveled in the now sexy taste of peppermint and feel of the man as he teased me without mercy, *a' la francaise.*

While I clung to him, Philip tried to balance me, kiss me, fondle me, and unzip his pants all at once. Being more single-minded, I tried to suck his tongue out of his head. It surprised neither of us when we tumbled over and fell. Fortunately, the heap of pillows lying on the floor cushioned our fall. Seconds after landing, I ripped my shirt and panties off, and I flung myself back down on the man beneath me.

"Slow down. We can enjoy this." Philip smoothed my hair back from my face and studied me for a long moment as my breath came hard and ragged.

I shook my head. "No, I don't want to slow down. I ...I..."

I felt like a woman crazed, my thirst for him almost desperate in longing.

He smiled at me as he smoothed his hand down my cheek again. "Slow down. For a long time, I wanted you in my arms like this. Since the first time I saw you, I wanted you. I knew from that first smile and the coy little wink you gave me we should be together. I intend to enjoy this."

My eyes widened in stunned surprise as he lifted me up from the pillowed floor as I remembered his past attempts to engage me in an affair. I clung to his neck and snuggled right up, burying my face in his shoulder as he carried me to the bed.

"Take a deep breath, Sara. We have all night."

We did not have all night. He did not realize I still intended to catch the Red Eye back to Houston. However, there are times when silence is golden, and I kept my mouth shut about my plans.

I sighed with pleasure as he laid me down on the plush down comforter and fondled one of my breasts. My hand raised up to cup his own. I wanted to keep it right there, doing just what he was doing. "Don't stop. That feels fantastic."

He chuckled. "Sometimes you forget you're exceptional. This is your reminder. I love your breasts. You don't know how long I wanted to pleasure you like this."

My eyes flew open, and I tried to focus as Philip lowered his mouth to my nipple. I grabbed his hair and pulled him back. "What do you mean? My little bitty titties could never move a man to passion."

Philip's eyes smoldered with anger. "I don't know who told you that, but your breasts are perfect. Just big enough, not too big. Don't you know more than a mouthful is a waste?"

I laughed. I heard that line before, but I did not believe it. "Jack said a girl couldn't have too much. He tried to get me to have implants, but I couldn't do it."

Philip snorted. "Jackson Talbott was not just a four-star idiot; he was an asshole."

I giggled. "That is why I called him my Jack Ass."

Philip stared for a second before he began laughing as well. "Your Jack Ass, huh? Well, Jack Ass Talbott didn't deserve a treasure like you. Haven't you heard good things come in little packages? You are one hot little package, babe. I wouldn't change a thing about you."

As I wrapped my arms around him again, I ached and rejoiced at his cathartic words. As an adult, I yearned for a man to tell me that. For once, I did not even fuss when Philip called me babe.

I agreed with Philip's assessment of Jack. Just as I opened my mouth to tell him so, he sucked my nipple into his hot, wet mouth and flicked it back and forth with his tongue. I moaned, as I forgot all about Jack. Hell, I forgot Jack ever existed. If Philip asked me about Jack right then, I would have replied, 'Jack, who?' I gyrated beneath Philip as I clutched his beautiful, dark hair like a lifeline to a boat.

After a while, Philip stopped sucking on my breast. I moaned again, in disappointment, but my disappointment lasted only a moment, for he trailed that magical, hot, wet mouth of his lower and lower down my belly. By the time he reached Down There, I became a squirming, hysterical mass of quivering flesh. I would have done anything for the man who relit my little personal pilot light.

Then Philip slid a finger inside me. And then another one. I would have sworn I died and went to heaven as I trembled at his touch. I lay gasping, unable to catch my breath by the time he thrust himself deep inside me.

Dara had been after me to get a battery-operated buddy, a 'Bob' she called it. I kept telling her I didn't need one. She thought I resisted. She did not realize I already had one. Philip Martino was better than my friend, 'Bob.' Oh, yeah, he was better than any battery-operated friend I ever owned.

Hours later, Philip lay sound asleep when I slipped out of the bed. I knew he hoped I would fall asleep, too, and I would miss my plane. But a gimongous storm headed to the Galveston–Houston area, and I had to go home. Crazy, huh? The first major hurricane slated to hit the Galveston area since Hurricane Ike, a hit man after my ass, a total hunk lusting after me, me lusting after him, and like a moron, I go home. Go figure.

Don't ask me why, but I knew I could not live with myself if I did not search for that damned *Sforza* urn, and if I did not protect my home. Plus, I needed to see Nonna's house again, if only one last time.

I prayed it would not be the last time I saw Philip Martino.

I thought about leaving Hairy, but my selfishness won out. When Hairy looked at me with those big, soulful eyes of his and whined, I caved. "Fine, come on."

I looked back at Philip with more than a little regret. I would miss that man. When he realized I had left, I wasn't sure if he would want to see me again. I swallowed hard and sat the note down beside him on the bed.

I must go. Please don't be mad, Philip.

Your Babe.

I hoped he would know by my signature what I meant, but I did not know if he would. I blinked fast, determined not to cry. I closed the door without a sound as Hairy and I slipped outside to the waiting taxi. We entered the cab as I wiped the tear from my cheek. "Logan International, please."

Please don't be too mad, Philip. Please don't hate me.

Chapter 17
Sara

The plane landed in Houston before dawn. I rented a car for Hairy and me, thinking I could drive to the house before the traffic got heavy. However, no traffic was going out of town towards Morgan Point. All lanes headed north and westward, away from the storm.

Like a fool, I headed towards Morgan Point.

I remembered reports of bizarre traffic a few years ago, in '05, when everyone thought Hurricane Rita would hit Galveston the month after Katrina devastated New Orleans. Rita did not hit Galveston, but it took three days to drive from Houston to Dallas. Traffic was like this again when Ike hit Galveston in '08. I did not live in the area when either storm hit, but I remembered the newscasts. Plus, friends told me about living with no electricity for weeks after Ike. That was why we purchased the whole house generator while remodeling my old house.

I admit I felt scared. 'Scared' does not describe the level of terror I felt as I drove to the house by myself. This would be my first hurricane, and I would be alone with my dog in a 130-year-old house overlooking Galveston Bay.

My house sits right on Morgan Point, but it survived countless storms, even the big hurricane in 1900. I had no intention of fleeing this one. It took Hairy and me three hours to creep the twenty miles home, what with traffic stops and generalized traffic insanity.

I knew we would have problems with food at home, so I brought canned fruit and meat, bottled water, and kibble with me from Boston. We had enough food and water for a week. I paid for overweight luggage, but I knew it was the one bit of foresight that might save us.

By the time I reached my elegant old house, the incoming hurricane was all over the news. They projected the hurricane would make landfall in Galveston during the night. Jim Acosta on CNN news told how high the waves were already. He must be nuts to stand on the seawall as towering waves crashed over it to lap at his feet. I feared the waves would wash him over the seawall. I wondered if he would stay in a local hotel to record the sounds of the hurricane as it blew into Galveston.

I told Hairy for months we were in the heart of the storm, although I knew most people called the middle of the hurricane 'the storm's eye.' The eye, or the heart of the storm, is quiet as it passes overhead before the fury of the hurricane renews. I couldn't believe things could get worse than they had been for the past few weeks, but we were on the edge of a powerful hurricane. We would be in the storm's heart. I cringed again at the thought about going weeks with no electricity, like after Hurricane Ike. With my whole house generator, loss of power would not be a problem for me. I could call Ashley after the storm to see if she wanted to come to Morgan Point, but I might prefer to go to her home in Alvin, depending on how my house fared through the storm.

When I remodeled the house the year Nonna died, I realized the shutters on all the windows were functional. The contractor ensured they all worked and could shut each from inside each window. I would have no problem in case of a storm to shut them. It took little time to close the shutters.

I rushed on, moving valuable artwork into the safe room. I hoped the art would not get wet and be ruined. I wished again I could find *La Sforza*. Little brown jug, where are you? I saw nothing that looked like an eighth-century Greco-Roman art treasure in the safe room or anywhere else in my house.

Like I said before, when we remodeled, we built a 'safe room' that was supposed to withstand hurricane-force winds. I made sure all the foodstuffs, water, and Hairy's kibble were in there. I intended to hole up in the safe room when the storm made landfall.

The double set of French windows in my bedroom opened out onto an enormous deck overlooking the Bay. When we built the deck, I had an electronic shutter installed in case of storms. It has a manual override in case I waited too late to put it down and the storm knocked out the electricity like my friends told me it did during Ike. Later, we added the whole house generator so I should never have to worry about or deal with an electricity failure. I could keep the shutter open until the last minute and be able to see what happened on the bay. In case of an emergency, if I waited too late, I could crank it down by hand. We also had installed internal shutters, so I could shutter the French doors inside and out when the storm made landfall.

Just in case.

My phone started ringing about 5 A.M., the time the plane landed. Each time it rang, I hit the 'ignore' button on the cell phone. The caller identification showed it was Philip, and I knew there was nothing I could say that would make him accept my decision to come home. When I realized Mom and Dad were both calling, too, I silenced my phone. When I did not answer, they started bombarding me with text messages. I ignored those as well. The phone calls stopped around five p.m. in the afternoon as they gave up on getting me to answer them. I sighed with relief. I had too much to do to dilly daddle around chatting on the phone.

Frantic to get everything finished before the storm hit, I worked to move everything I deemed essential to the safe room in case disaster struck at Morgan Point, although I hoped 'the just in case' never occurred. Before the storm made landfall, I carried forty gallons of water upstairs to the safe room, along with bread, canned meat, protein bars, a case of sodas, and kibble for Hairy. He wanted to help, and was right beside me as I shoved the toolbox, a crate for Hairy, a mattress on which we could sleep from the guest bedroom, and plenty of clean bedding for us into the safe room. I charged the house phone and my cell phone, and I placed an extra charger in the safe room. We moved all the art plus several valuable antiques I did not want to lose, my laptop and printer. I hauled designer suits and shoes into the safe room as well. Yes, I realize I am vain, but those clothing items comprised a sizeable investment, and I would need clothes for court in the weeks to come. I threw in a couple dozen boxes of treasured books and my jewelry box. Last, I stashed the box filled with Hairy's most recently won ribbons and awards, including the ones he won in Pennsylvania, in the now empty gun safe.

Hairy stayed right there with me. Hairy and I were a team. He would go nowhere without me, knowledge that terrified me and gave me hope. I could survive the storm as long as Hairy was by my side.

Next, I tried to call Robin, but she did not answer. More sensible than me, she left while she could. Oh, well, if I survive this, we can talk.

I looked down at the dog waiting by my feet, and I felt a tug of guilt, and not for the first time that day. As Hairy smiled up at me, I gulped and I reached down to pat my faithful friend's head.

We would survive. I did not intend to die in a hurricane.

Around 10 p.m., I locked the house and set the burglar alarm. Hairy and I trudged to my bedroom, where I locked the door to it. We collapsed across my bed to listen to the latest news about the hurricane. It felt sure I forgot something, but I was too exhausted to figure out what else needed to be done. The hurricane was only about a hundred miles offshore by then and we were already getting hit with bands of intense winds of over 100 mph.

I fell asleep with the TV blaring while I listened to the weather reports. The meteorologist said the hurricane would move on shore by morning. He projected the storm would land in the next few hours with winds of at least 150 mph., and the eye would pass over Galveston Bay soon after.

"Boy, do I know how to pick 'em, Hairy?"

He barked and wagged his tail.

I thought the eye of the storm sounded more like a wonderful place with each passing hour as I watched towering palm trees shudder as they bent over from the powerful winds.

I fell asleep and slept hard. In my dream, I heard barking and sirens. There was a problem, but I could not awaken. I kept trying, but I could not open my leaden eyes. As I struggled to awaken from the dream, the air felt so hot, so thick, I could barely breathe. Funny, I wanted to sleep forever.

And then I dreamed Captain Johnny shouted to wake me. Something grabbed my arm to shake it as Hairy whimpered. *Wake up, Mama, wake up.*

At last, I awoke from the dream with a start, my heart pounding, drenched in sweat. Hairy barked, as he scratched at me and licked my face while he danced from nervous energy on the bed. As I opened my eyes, he cut his eyes over to the door of my bedroom. The air felt hot and heavy, just like in my dream.

Wake up, Mama, wake up, wake up. Hairy slurped another big, wet one across my face. *Come, Mama, come. Now.*

I took a couple of deep breaths and nodded as I struggled to raise up. "I'm awake, baby, I'm awake. Let's get a drink. Maybe that will help."

Hairy growled and grabbed my wrist in his mouth. Surprised, I looked down. "What's wrong, Hairy?"

Bad man, Mama, bad man. I smell him. He made it hot in the house. We gotta go, Mama. Go, now. Mama, come, heel. Mama, come, heel, right now.

I laughed as my dog gave me obedience commands and then realized what he said. "How did he make it hot, Hairy?"

I don't know. I was sleeping, too, but now the house is hot, Mama. Hairy smells the bad man. He was here. Hot, hot, burn Mama. Burn Hairy. We gotta go now. Mama, come, heel. Now. Johnny says we gotta go now.

That got my attention. "Johnny told you that?"

Hairy growled again and took my hand in his mouth. *Come, Mama. Come now.*

With a start, I realized my dog was right. I smelled smoke. I jumped up and grabbed for my clothes.

Hairy again grabbed my hand with his mouth. *No time, Mama. We gotta go now. Heel, come. Now. We gotta go. Danger, danger, Will Ranger.*

Any other time, I would have chuckled. My dog loves the old Lost in Space television show, and always called the boy 'Will Ranger.' That night, my eyes snapped open when he uttered those words.

As I sat up, I heard a crash from somewhere down the hall. My heart sank as I realized my Nonna's beautiful old house was on fire. It survived the 1900 storm. My house survived Hurricane Audrey, Hurricane Debra, Hurricane Alicia, Tropical Storm Claudette, Tropical Storm Allison, and Hurricane Ike, but this old house was not likely to survive this. The sorry rat bastards set my house on fire. If I had not awakened, the world would have thought it burned up in the storm.

I knew the history of the area. We know the area from Galveston and up Galveston Bay as Hurricane Alley. Memories of the historical record of Hurricane Alley bombarded me.

The 1900 storm killed 8000 people in Galveston alone. They estimate the 1900 storm was a Category 4 storm. They built the seawall afterwards and raised the level of Galveston.

Hurricanes hit our area again in 1909, when forty-one died, and in 1915, when 275 died from the storm. Storms hit again in 1932, 1934, and 1942. No people died in those storms. A hurricane hit in 1943, and killed nineteen. Hurricanes hit in 1945, 1947, and 1949, with no fatalities.

Hurricane Audrey, the first named hurricane, had winds of 110 mph. Two years later, in 1959, Hurricane Debra hit. Those storms claimed no fatalities as well.

In 1979, Tropical Storm Claudette dumped 45 inches of rain on the area. It hit Alvin, Texas, so hard that boats only could access Alvin for a week. Claudette caused four hundred million dollars of damage.

In 1983, Hurricane Alicia struck the area, and it caused three billion dollars of damage and killed twenty-one people. It destroyed ninety per cent of the dwellings on Jamaica Beach when the houses blew off the piers. Many glass buildings sustained heavy damage.

Hurricane Jerry killed three and did over seventy million dollars of damage in 1989.

Tropical Storm Allison dumped 36.9 inches of rain, which resulted in fifty-five deaths and nine billion dollars of damage in 2001 as people drowned in the fast rising waters in underpasses while they struggled to get home.

Hurricane Ike hit Galveston with winds up to 145 m.p.h. It resulted in 214 deaths. It did 38 billion in damages. Attorneys told me they closed the Galveston Courthouse for weeks due to storm damage. Boats washed up from the harbor to the mainland to be dumped on Highway 45, where the elevation increased onshore. Friends told me they cut holes in their roofs to escape the fast rising flood waters. The roof of the First National Bank in Alvin collapsed. The fire marshal locked the attorneys who officed there out of their offices for three weeks.

In 2017, Tropical Storm Harvey hit, dumping up to sixty inches of rain in some locations. Many attorneys had told me about the extensive damage their homes sustained because of the huge rainfall. It caused one hundred twenty-five billion dollars of damage, with more than one hundred deaths. It tied Katrina as the costliest tropical cyclone on record, and was the wettest on record with peak accumulations of 60.58 inches. The resulting floods displaced 30,000 people and prompted more than 17,000 rescues. We came through it fine, but lots of my friends were displaced from their homes. We all suffered financial losses at the very least.

Good grief, I thought, seventeen storms in a little over a hundred years. No wonder my sister, Bella, was terrified of hurricanes while Miguel and she lived on the Island. I used to laugh at her about her 'silly fears.' Bella's fears seemed anything but silly as I struggled to figure out what to do. What on earth was I thinking to come home for this storm? My family didn't know I came home. Now, my home burned, and I prayed my beloved Hairy and I could survive somehow.

With a sinking heart, I realized the 'bad man with the big stick' gained entry to my home because I forgot to set the pins in the security hinges of the exterior doors when I came home. God only knew how I set the pins in the security hinge to my bedroom door I had installed after my last sexual encounter with Jackson.

I grabbed my cell phone and tucked it inside my bra. As I clutched my dearest companion close to my heart, I reached to open the door to the hall.

Hairy fidgeted and nipped at my hand as I reached for the doorknob. *No, no, no. Stay, Mama, stay. Hot, hot, hot. Burn Mama, burn Hairy.*

With a deep breath, I laid the back of my hand on the doorknob, only to jerk it off. I realized my dog was smarter than me. "Jeez-Louise, the handle is red hot. You're right, Hairy, we can't go that way."

It's a hell of a comeuppance to realize your dog is smarter than you are.

I looked around the room as panic welled in my heart. Philip told me not to come back, and Dara told me to send Hairy with her, but I refused to listen to them. I had to do this my way. Now I would burn to death in my beautiful old house, and my beloved Hairy would burn to death with me. Shit. Double shit. Hell, double, triple fuckety fuckety shit. And all because I was a stubborn bitch who just had to do this my way.

Trembling, I swallowed hard and looked at the expansive French windows. I forgot to shut the interior shutters or the exterior metal shutters, so I knew we could still get onto my deck. No stairs led down from the deck, which extended out over the water. I did not know just how long it would be safe on it, both from the incoming storm and the raging fire within my house. I didn't know if we could get down from the deck without killing the two of us. I could not shimmy down, much less jump, holding Hairy. The safe room was out of the question now. We would never make it through the inferno burning the other side of my door. I looked around the bedroom, desperate for something I could use to get us out of this awful mess.

We were on the second floor, but the deck extended from my bedroom out over the bay. I built it that way on a whim, so I could sit out on the deck and watch Jack when he went sailing. You could not access the deck any other way than through my bedroom. My heart leapt as my eyes landed on the rope ladder, lying across a corner of my bed. I forgot to put it in the safe room, too. I shivered. It would be a terrible risk, but it was our only way out. Even if I climbed as far down it as possible, we would still have to free fall to the water below in the dark. I would have to hope and pray we hit water, and not the cliffs below the deck.

I looked around, heart pounding in fear, and sighed with relief when I spotted Hairy's little red life jacket hanging on the peg on the wall in my bathroom. Skyes do not swim well. They have too much coat, and my dog was in full show coat. His beautiful hair hung to the floor. Thank heaven I always insisted Hairy wear a life jacket if he went out on the water. His doggie life jacket hung there since the last time Hairy and I went sailing with Jack many months before. Hairy didn't like to wear it, but he would not fuss. I put on my life vest and got Hairy into his. I clipped the two vests together with a cord like the ones surfers attach from one leg to their surfboard. I picked Hairy up again, kissed his face, and gulped. It swear I had a lump the size of a cantaloupe stuck in my throat.

Maybe I should call Philip, I thought, with a little sob. But why? To tell him he was right? To tell him goodbye? I could not even try to utter the words burning in my heart.

To tell him I think I love him?

No time for regrets right now, I thought. I forced myself to push those thoughts out of my mind. I needed to focus on our survival.

I shoved Hairy's long facial hair out of his eyes so I could peer right into them when I spoke to him next. Hairy needed to see me as I told him what I had to say, and I damned sure needed to see my dog's eyes.

"I love you, Hairy Potter. Mama's here, and I won't leave you, but we gotta go swimming. I know you don't like the water, but we gotta go in it, baby. We have no choice, but everything will be okay. I'll climb down the rope ladder and drop to the water when we reach the end of the rope ladder. Remember to take a big breath before you hit the water, and hold your breath until we come up again. Don't breathe under the water, baby. Swim for the shore if you come loose from me when we hit the water. Mama will be right behind you, I promise."

It okay, Mama. I'm your heart dog. Everything will be okay. He slurped a kiss across my cheek.

I choked up, hoping and praying my dog understood me. It was a lot of words to bombard him with at one time. I kissed him once again. "Yes, my love, you bring calm to my heart in the midst of this hideous storm. You will always be my heart dog. Remember to take a big breath before you hit the water. Mama loves you, Hairy. Let's go."

I hugged him tight and kissed my dog again. I took a big breath and before Hairy could reply, before I could think, before the damned cell phone could ring again, I slung my dog over my shoulder, threw the rope ladder over the edge of the deck, and I climbed down. That is not a simple task while you struggle to balance a thirty-five-pound dog on your shoulder, let me tell you. When I reached the end of the rope, I turned my head and kissed my dog one more time.

It's okay, Mama. Hairy will take care of you.

That's my dog. He always wants to take care of me. I nodded. "I know, baby. Let's do this."

I let go of the rope ladder, and we fell into the darkness below as I clutched Hairy to my chest.

Chapter 18
Johnny and Tamsin

"Hurry, Johnny! We have to help her get to shore or they will drown! Poor little Hairy Potter can't swim much longer." Tamsin rushed to the unconscious woman and the little dog who struggled to pull his beloved mistress to the shore.

Captain Johnny swept down from above to help push Hairy and Sara to shore. "We mustn't let that happen, my love. Not on our watch."

Once to shore, the angel and the ghostly pirate helped the exhausted dog pull Sara out of the water onto the driest bit of land they could find.

Tamsin sank down with a gasp of exhaustion. "There. We are about twenty feet above sea level now. It's damp, but not underwater. I swear, Johnny, that was the most physical activity I have had in years."

Johnny laughed. "I imagine it was the most rigorous activity either of us has experienced in over two centuries, my love."

They sat watching over Sara and the tired little dog until human help came to Sara's aid late that night.

Chapter 19
Sara

I awakened to the disturbing sound of me crying.

I became more aware of the surrounding sounds, as well as the level of pain I was enduring. Raw, blazing red pain raged through every cell of my body. It was all I could do to keep from screaming. Or barfing. Or both.

As I pried open one eye, I saw Philip sat beside me, holding my hand, as he whispered to me. Strange, I thought, Philip never talks like this to me. He says, 'do this,' 'do that,' or he is sarcastic. He never utters soft words and caresses.

Except that one time.

I struggled to form words. What happened? Where was I? Would I be okay? And the important one. Where is my dog? Is Hairy okay? With what felt like extreme effort, I gasped out, "Hairy..."

Philip's face broke into a smile. "He's okay. Your dog saved you, you know."

I arched an eyebrow at Philip. "H-How?"

He smiled again, the dimples in his cheeks flashing, and bent to kiss my hand. Of course, I melted. "When you jumped, you hit the piling. Hairy swam for shore and dragged you with him. He pulled you out of the water. Otherwise, you would have drowned."

I tried to say something, but my heart was up somewhere between my tonsils. I was pretty damned sure I was about to cry. I nodded. "Good... boy. Wh-Where is... he?"

"In the other room. I'll go get him for you."

I arched my eyebrows at him again. "W-Why did you come?"

"Oh, yeah, like I wouldn't come after you? You left in the middle of the freaking night, a hurricane about to hit shore, and the Mob after you. Did you think I wouldn't come after your sweet, adorable little ass? Get a grip, woman. Of course, I came. Your parents are frantic. You wouldn't respond to any of us. When I got to Morgan Point and saw your house on fire, I thought I would die. Thank God, I heard Hairy barking. I hunted until I found you two."

I frowned. "How's my house?"

"I won't even lie. It's a hot mess. The house looks damned bad, but we can deal with the damage later. First, you get better. Then we have to identify the idiots trying to kill you."

I nodded. "Where are we?"

He laughed, as if embarrassed. "When I found you, I wanted to get you to the hospital. We never made it that far. The storm raged then, with winds of 160 mph, and flooded streets. I turned in here to La Isla to get rooms. They boarded the doors up—"

"So where are we?"

He grinned again. "I told you. We are at La Isla. I drove my Jeep through the door. There was a skeleton crew inside. Let me tell you, they were pretty freaked out when I stormed in with you and the dog. They said we could not come in, but I asked, 'You and what army plan to stop us?' I looked serious, and they let us in. I threw them my credit card, demanded a suite, and voila! Here we are. Like the old saying goes: money talks, bullshit walks. I talked their language with the American ExpressCard."

The La Isla Resort is this tres posh, tres pricey hotel and condo on Clear Lake. Everyone who is anyone wants to stay at La Isla, at least once. The suites are to die for. I admit these were not the circumstances I had dreamt about for my fantasy La Isla holiday. I frowned and struggled to raise myself in the bed. "Jeez-Louise, I hurt all over, even worse than after the car hit me in Boston. How did you find us?"

He shrugged and flashed me his adorable, boyish grin again. "Like I said, I followed you here. I was not about to leave you alone at that damned house like a proverbial sitting duck, during a storm and with the Mob after you. It's good I came, too. Otherwise, you would be dead this time, Sara."

I was missing something. Hmm… "But how did you find us?"

"I heard Hairy howling, and I followed his voice. You two were in the little cove south of your place. I don't know how he hauled you there, but now I appreciate the dust mop. He's tougher than I suspected. Anyway, we had the dickens of a time getting you up from the cove, but Hairy and I managed."

I nodded and tried to absorb it all. Philip opened the door to let Hairy in the room. My dog let out a yelp of joy and leaped on the bed. I laughed as he licked my face. "Take it easy, boy. I'm okay now."

Hairy snuggled up to me as he continued to lick my arm. *We saved you, Mama.*

I chuckled. *Yes, Philip and you saved me, Hairy. Well done.*

Hairy stopped licking me. *No, Mama, not Philip. He came later and we brought you here. The pirate and the pretty lady helped me. They made sure they got us out of the water.*

My eyes narrowed as I gave him a sharp look. *Captain Johnny and the Tamsin lady? The pretty angel?*

He nodded and barked. *Yes, them!*

My eyes narrowed. I knew the cove Philip mentioned was below the water level during storms. *Did they help you get me to the cove?*

Hairy shook his head. *No. They helped me get you all the way to the street. It was wet, but it wasn't too bad. The cove was full of water.*

I frowned. Why would Philip lie about where he found me? Something did not fit right. Now, if I could just figure out what it was.

"It's a damn shame the house burned. I guess we will never know if *La Sforza* was in it or not."

I turned my head to face him before I answered. "Maybe. It just depends."

He frowned. "It depends? That makes little sense, Sara. How?"

I wet my lips as I thought about both the question and the answer. Do I trust you? Shall I tell you? After a long pause, I sighed. I had to trust him. Who else could I trust? No one besides my dog, Daddy or Kirk. Neither of my dads weren't here. I trusted no other person in town. "We should check the safe room."

He frowned. "A what? I don't understand. What's a safe room?"

I tried to smile. "When I inherited the house, it needed to be remodeled. During the renovations, we added a 10 x 10 room right in the middle of the house, built behind the stairwell. It encompasses two stories, with a circular staircase connecting the two floors. It's supposed to be hurricane and fireproof. We made it through Tropical Storm Harvey fine in there, and I always kept valuables in the safe room. I intended for Hairy and me to hole up in there during the storm when the fire started."

His mouth fell open. "Well, I'll be damned."

I had not searched the safe room for *La Sforza* before the storm. If there was one place the Fibbies and the Mob overlooked, it was the safe room. "You miss the button to open it unless you know it's there. You enter through the alcove beneath the stairs on the first floor. The door is behind a Murphy bookcase. You swing the bookcase open, punch in the lock combination for the inner door, and are in the safe room. Another bookcase hides the entrance on the second floor. It is possible Jack hid *La Sforza* in the safe room. Of course, it might not be there. When I moved stuff in there before the storm, I didn't see an eighth-century Grecian urn lying around. I had other things on my mind. I figured I would have time when the storm made landfall to hunt for the damned urn. It all depends on whether it was there in the first place, and if it survived the fire. I hope the room protected the contents like it was supposed to do. We didn't have a fire during Harvey."

"But the urn might be in there, right? We need to go back and check this out, Sara."

"Tonight? Jeez Louise, Philip, I feel like warmed over crap."

He nodded, his eyes sparkling with excitement. "Tonight, babe."

My eyes narrowed as I stared at Philip. The raw hunger in his voice disconcerted me. "I take it the prospect of finding this urn excites you, huh?"

He stopped in the middle of my words and stared at me like I had sprouted horns. "Well, of course, babe. If we find it, we may save your life. Think about it."

Believe me, I was thinking about it, but I did not say another word, not even to complain about him calling me babe. I bit my tongue and nodded.

Later, we drove over to the house after I called my parents and assured them I was okay. Hurting and limping, I would have appreciated a couple of days to recuperate from my stunt before I ventured back to the burnt shell of what used to be my house. Philip insisted we should get over there before anyone else found the safe room and *La Sforza*. Of course, the Bad Guys and the Fibbies had been through my house repeatedly and missed the safe room. I don't know why he thought someone might find it now.

I could grow to hate that blasted urn.

As we approached the house, my heart sank. The fire destroyed my beautiful home, I thought, my heart heavy with dismay. Nonna's exquisite Victorian mansion looked like a post-apocalyptical crispy critter.

"Hairy, stay in the car. You could get hurt in this mess. There is burned wood, glass, and nails everywhere."

Hairy emitted an unhappy groan. He looked none too pleased, but he obeyed.

I struggled to hold back tears as we walked past the incinerated yard, now stomped into a blackened, muddy quagmire, post-fire, and post-hurricane. The bare skeletal remains of my house remained upright, the bricks and wood charred beyond recognition of its former beauty. As we crept inside, I did not know whether to laugh or cry when I saw the safe room remained intact. "Let's see if the contents remained safe through the fire and storm."

Philip looked stunned as I pulled him into the niche beneath the stairs. I pushed aside the burned remnant of the bookcase and I punched the code into the steel door lock.

"My god, we went through this house with a fine-toothed comb, and no one spotted this."

We did, huh? I wondered if he realized he incriminated himself among those who had searched my house for the blasted urn. Of course, I didn't tell him Nonna taught us to always have a safe room, and how to hide it from the view of intruders. Instead, I forced a smile. "You weren't supposed to spot it. Come on."

We grinned at each other as we heard the lock shift. The battery backup to the electrical system still worked despite the damage from the fire. It took a couple of tries, but Philip shoved open the heavy door with a hard push.

They designed the safe room steel vault door to sustain fires of up to 1700 degrees Fahrenheit and to keep the safe room below 350 degrees. Philip and I both began coughing as the door swung open. A thin film of grey dust covered the surface of everything inside the room. Hairy and I could not have survived if we were there when the fire broke out. The temperature would have soared too high to sustain our lives. It would have baked us alive.

"What caused the layer of dust?" Philip sneezed, and then another bout of coughing seized him.

"It looks like there was some minor burn in here. The fire must have been hotter than 1700 degrees in the house."

Philip raised an eyebrow and let out a low whistle. "Damn, that was one hell of a scorcher of a fire. More proof the fire resulted from arson. Babe, there's a lot of stuff in here. I didn't realize it extended to the second floor. Where should we look first?"

"I imagine it was pretty damned hot. After all, it was arson." I grabbed a couple of lanterns from the wall just inside the safe room door and handed one to Philip. I stashed them there because I figured I might lose electricity during the storm. It's blacker than a starless night in that windowless room once the door swings shut. I turned on my lantern and made my way through the items stacked inside the room. "Let's look through the boxes. Let's drag Hairy's crate and kibble out. We might want the bottled water, too. It could come in handy. Jack and I labeled most of the boxes. I hope we labeled them correctly. I guess we could start with the unlabeled boxes first."

He nodded as he knelt and opened his first box.

Two hours later, Philip sighed in frustration. He wiped his hands across his chinos and then arose. "It's damned hard to see in here, even with the lanterns. Did you find anything?"

I nodded. "I found some stuff I want to keep, but no art treasure, except for the art I placed in here before the storm hit."

He pulled a handkerchief out of his pocket, blew his nose, and wiped off his sooty face. "Look, I need a break from all this residue. My nose is running like crazy because I am so blasted allergic to dust. I'll get some allergy medication from the car. Plus, I need to make a couple of phone calls. Be back in a few minutes, babe. Okay?"

I nodded. "Yeah, I will call you if I find anything special."

I decided I'd been through enough for the day a few boxes later. As I turned, I heard a ghostly voice.

"Sara, look over here."

I turned towards Captain Johnny's voice and spotted a box marked 'dog ribbons and trophies.' I grinned and bent over to pick it up. As I carried it to my 'keep' stack, I realized there was already a box there with my dog things I packed the day the hurricane hit. In contrast, Jack wrote the label for this box in his neat, military-precise handwriting. It was not my illegible chicken scratches.

Jack had beautiful handwriting. Maybe it was typical of people pursuing his career. I never met an accountant who did not have nice, crisp, clean printing, and Jack was no exception. Even I cannot read my handwriting half the time. While my handwriting looks like an aberrant form of Swahili written by an extra-terrestrial, Jack's handwriting looked like teachers wanted me to write as a kid. I never came close to perfect handwriting like Jack's. Everything he wrote was picture perfect. My pulse quickened. In all the years we were married, Jack never once helped me pack a box with dog stuff in it. Not my duck, he would say as he waltzed out the door to his sailboat.

I eased the box down, and using my box cutter, sliced inside the tape that sealed it shut. Disappointment washed over me as I realized there were dog show ribbons in the box. I guess Jack helped me pack these things, I mused. As I reached for the packing tape to secure the box again, the contents shifted inside. My heart clamored in my chest when the ribbons moved, revealing an odd-shaped object wrapped up in a velvet bag. The bag looked like the dust bags in which I store fine handbags. I swallowed hard and pulled the velvet bag out of the box. With bated breath, I opened the drawstring to the bag and peered inside in the now dim light of late afternoon in the darkened room.

La Sforza.

After a minute or two, I remembered to breathe. I tugged the velvet bag shut around the priceless treasure and slid it back into the box which cradled it in a nest of dog show ribbons. I felt so excited, so nervous, that it terrified me to think about lifting the box to carry it outside. The beautiful ancient relic awed me so much I could not call out for Philip. *La Sforza* deserved reverence.

My hands trembled as I lifted the box. I started toward Philip, who had wandered outside. He stood talking on his cell phone with his back towards the house. I did not want to interrupt his call. I would wait until he completed his call to share my exciting news. I stood in the shadows on the remnants of my porch in the fading twilight.

At first, I reveled in my discovery, formulating what I would tell Philip and Uncle Roberto. *Mi zio*, I found it! Philip would be so proud and happy I located the priceless treasure. Now, we could get the hit contract called off. Maybe we could get on with our lives. I smiled as I realized I thought of a future with Philip.

I frowned when I realized Philip argued with someone on the phone. He kept his voice low and controlled, but I could tell something upset him. I was nosy enough to perk up in attention to listen to Philip's end of the conversation.

"No, Dad, enough is enough. Don't ask me to do it. I can't do it. You don't understand. I care about her. I can't do this anymore."

I blinked, surprised by his words. Without thinking, I turned on the record feature on my phone as I stepped back into the darkness. I got into the habit of recording Jack when he skulked around chasing tail. As Philip spoke with his dad, I turned the volume button up as loud as it would go and strained to hear what Philip said next.

"I found her in the cul-de-sac in front of her house. The water got that high, or the dog pulled her there somehow."

With a sinking heart, I realized my dog was right. Philip lied to me. He did not find me in the cove.

As he started talking again, I shrank into the shadows seconds before he turned towards the house.

"Well, gee, Dad, I'm sorry she didn't have the common decency to die in the fire. Yes, dammit, I know that was your plan. I know what you intended. Her death was always your plan. Don't you think I realize who was behind those attempts on her life? Yes, I heard you, dammit. I need to find the urn and dispose of the problem. But, Dad, we can't find the blasted thing ..."

Tears sprung to my eyes, and I struggled to breathe as I covered my mouth with my free hand. I shook my head, unable to believe what I heard. No, this could not be happening. Could Philip have been involved with the attempts to kill me? As a horrifying awareness swept over me, I realized I had been sleeping with the enemy. I wanted to beg Philip to deny what I overheard, but I knew I could not if I valued my life. I just heard him say his dad wanted me dead. Philip was supposed to 'dispose of the problem.' My stomach lurched in spasm as I comprehended Senator Martino demanded Philip get rid of the problem named Sara Talbott. Hands shaking, I slipped further back into the darkness, terrified Philip would turn again and somehow see me standing there.

A lone tear slid down my cheek. I knew I should never have let him call me babe.

Just then, I saw his shoulders sag. "Yeah, I understand. Her family killed Mother, and you want retribution. You think this is perfect payback. But Dad..."

Now, it made sense why Philip was always there when the attempts on my life occurred. He was supposed to ensure they killed me. Who said there is no such thing as coincidence? Philip was always Johnny On The Spot because he was the brains behind the schemes.

As I returned to the safe room, a few tears escaped from my eyes, and I pulled my shirt up to wipe them away. I did not intend to have to explain tears to him. I grabbed some loose papers and threw them in the box with the ribbons on top of the priceless velvet bag. With a furtive look towards the vault door, I threw in two of my expensive designer suits to help pad the urn. I grabbed my duct tape and sealed the box shut. I set it with the other boxes to go in the car when Philip returned, thin-lipped and nervous.

"Find anything else?"

I shook my head. "Another box of dog stuff, that's all. I want to keep those things. I'll put the box in the car. Gosh, my nose is running, too. Must be all the dust."

"That would be my guess. Here, I'll take the box, babe."

My heart lurched in alarm as Philip lifted the box from my arms. "Philip, you don't have to carry it."

He bent over and kissed my cheek. "Not a problem, sweetheart. So, what all is in it?"

I shrugged as I feigned indifference. I could not let him know the value of this box. My life depended on it. "Okay, thanks. It's just a bunch of Hairy's things. Ribbons, catalogs, and the prizes he won at various dog shows. I guess it's silly, but I want to keep them. I don't imagine he will ever show again, and it was pretty special to win those Best in Show prizes besides the BISS at Montgomery."

He rubbed my back with one hand while he balanced the box against his chest with the other. "It's not silly, it's sweet. And yes, it's pretty damned special to win BISS at Montgomery. Come on, let's load this stuff up and blow this joint. It's creepy out here in the dark."

Without a word, I nodded, numb with grief and fear.

Philip slipped the box into the trunk of his SUV and turned toward me. "Dad thinks it is not safe for you to be here. He suggested we return to Boston while the Fibbies sort this all out."

Startled, I looked up at him. If I had not heard him talking with his dad, I wondered where they would have killed me in Boston. Did I imagine the whole thing? There was not a freaking fat rat's patootie of a chance in Hell I would go near Senator Martino or Boston, and I intended to get away from Philip as soon as possible. I took a deep breath and nodded. "Okay. Let's go. This place spooks me tonight, too."

He turned and cast a wistful look back towards the safe room. "I wish we could have found it."

Yeah, I bet you do, you murderous son of a bitch. I smiled at him again. "We can come back tomorrow and try to find it, darling."

He looked uncertain. "Well, maybe. We need to leave pretty soon. I'm not sure it's safe for us to be here. I'm concerned the rest of the structure might collapse at any minute. We should get out of here as soon as possible."

I chewed my lip for a moment as I thought about how to best answer him. "Okay, but I need a new health certificate for Hairy to travel on a plane again. I'll run to the vet in the morning and get a new one."

You need a health certificate from a vet that verifies a dog can fly. The certificate lasts for ten days, so the one I had when we came home was still valid for four more days. I pretended I needed a new one to get on another plane. What he did not know would not hurt me.

I saw Philip sag with relief. "Yeah, that would be good. You take care of the health certificate in the morning. I'll make the plane reservations, run into the office and wind a few things up before we leave. We'll fly back to Boston tomorrow night."

I stared at him a moment, desperate to beg him. Please don't betray me, Philip. Not like this. But I knew he already had. "Sounds like a plan."

I would have a couple of hours the next day to myself. I could leave before he realized I slipped from his grasp.

Of course, Lover Boy wanted sex that night. I grit my teeth and obliged. I could not risk alerting him I was on to his nefarious scheme. Oh, well, I learned how to fake sexual pleasure with Jack.

The next morning came all too soon. Philip's alarm clock went off at 6 A.M. I moaned and pulled the pillow over my head. He laughed and bent over to kiss my cheek. *You sorry excuse for a man. You'll kiss me, fuck me, and then wham bam, thank you ma'am, you intend to kill me if you get the chance.*

"Go back to sleep, babe. The vet won't open for a couple of hours. Get some rest while you can."

I moaned and nodded, as I pretended to snuggle back into the down comforter to sink back into my slumbers.

As soon as I knew he had left, I climbed out of bed. "Come on, Hairy. We have things to do."

He tilted his head at me and yawned. *Like what, Mama?*

"We are going to blow this joint. We have people to see and places to go." *Why?*

I whispered the words to my dog, in fear that anyone else might hear me.

"The bad man works for Philip, baby. We have to go, or the bad man will find us. If Philip knows where we are, we're in danger."

Hairy's ears pricked up in surprise. *Are you sure, Mama? Hairy likes Philip. He's nice.*

I nodded. "Yes, I'm sure. Believe me, I wish I was wrong. Now, come on. We have lots to do today."

I pulled on jeans and a t-shirt and called Uber to carry us to my house. I could fetch a couple of suitcases and more clothing from the safe room. My rental car came through the storm fine. Don't ask me how it eluded flood waters and a raging fire. I fished the keys out of the safe room, and changed into the chestnut brown Ungaro pant suit, cream-colored silk blouse, and brown suede Ferragamo boots which I stored in the gun safe before the fire and which I spotted the night before. I knew I would look sharp in that stylish Euro chic way, not too dressy, but still within the range of my normal style. I must blend in with the locals, both in the States and abroad, in short order. I did not need to look like an ugly American. I packed my jeans and t-shirt along with some other favorite outfits and shoes into my suitcases and then loaded the bags into the car. I packed it full with Hairy's crate, the box holding *La Sforza*, the boxes of dog show goodies, an extra bag of kibble, Hairy and me.

Next, I drove to my office where I locked the door after I pulled it shut. The electricity was still off, and the interior was dark and silent. Ashley sat at her desk, trying to salvage bits of cases that had been water damaged in the storm.

I strode to the inner office and to my desk, where I slid down to the floor behind it. I rolled the expensive Bakhtiari rug back from underneath the desk, and I lifted the panel of flooring the rug covered that laid underneath the desk to reveal the safe built into the floor of the office.

Only Jack and I knew the safe existed, and now Jack was dead. I guess you could say I am OCD about security. Nonna raised me that way. Now I knew why. My Nonna, the Mafia Princess, taught me well.

I had a good feeling that the Fibbies or the Mob bugged the phones and my office to locate the damned *Sforza*. I needed to make phone calls, but I did not intend to make them from the office or my cell phone. The camera or bug wouldn't see the backside of my desk. If I remained quiet, they would not know what I did. Besides, the bugs should not work without electricity. I opened the safe and removed my jewels, passport, and the cash inside. Fancy and Dad gave me some beautiful antique jewels over the years, and I figured they were valuable. Jack surprised me with nice jewelry when he felt guilty over his latest affair. I grabbed Hairy's passport and the blank international health certificate forms I kept at the office. I learned veterinarians do not always have international health certificate forms when I took Hairy to the World Show. Now, I keep copies of the forms in case I go to Europe again. I also grabbed his registration papers and shot records.

Since I owned the building where my law practice was located, I saved every penny of cash my clients paid me. I dipped into the cash when a client's check bounced, but the cash deposits grew over time. Every few months, I bought prepaid AmEx cards. I had 100 in the safe, each worth $500, or $50,000 in total in prepaid AmEx cards, plus some additional U.S. currency, euros, and gold coins. I pinned the folding money inside my bra. The money would get us far away from the duplicitous, evil, wicked, mean, bad and nasty Philip Martino and his murderous, bloodthirsty father. I tucked the AmEx cards into my handbag along with the passports, blank international health forms, Hairy's shot records, and his registration papers. I tucked the gold into my jewelry case. It would go into the hidden compartment in my carryon luggage. I grabbed a large, locking wheeled trunk from the store room. I figured I could put the box containing *La Sforza* in the trunk. I was able to put Hairy's prizes from Montgomery in it, too. The trunk was too big to carry onboard. I padded it well with bubble wrap and some more of my designer clothes to keep the valuable urn and Hairy's prizes as safe as possible during my travels.

I replaced the flooring, smoothed the rug back into place, and eased the desk and chair back into the spots where they rested on the rug. No one could tell I moved the desk, chair, or the rug. Next, I wrote out a check for Ashley, with a hefty bonus, and checks to pay the bills for the next three months. I stuck my debit card and some extra checks in my bag to transfer funds later. I left Ashley a note with the checks that told her I was going into witness protection and Aunt Maggie would love to rehire her. She should tell no one where I went. I handed her the envelope holding her paycheck, the note I had just written to her, and the other checks I had filled out to pay bills. I started back out the door. Halfway out, I turned back to hug her.

She looked both stunned, startled, and concerned by the hug. "Hey, boss, what gives? Are you okay?"

I nodded, although I knew I would never see the girl again. "It's nothing, kiddo, I'm fine. The storm and near drowning shook me up. You never know what might happen. Watch your back, kiddo. See you later, alligator, and remember, I love you."

Based on prior experiences, I knew she would not open her paycheck until Friday. By then, she would know I was long gone. I would email Aunt Maggie, tell her I was going into witness protection, and urge her to hire Ashley. I knew she would love to have Ashley back. She already told me she needed to fire her receptionist. Now she could. Plus, Ashley and Linda always got along great.

I drove to one of the local phone companies and picked up a new iPhone equipped with international dialing capability. It was not my regular provider. I wanted there to be as little chance as possible that Philip could trace me through GPS on the new phone. I would hang onto the old phone a little longer, before I would ditch it later on my trip. I planned to do anything possible to make the situation more confusing for the son of a bitch and hard for him to find me.

When I returned to the car, I called my uncle from my new phone. "*Zio* Roberto? I found the urn, but I have a problem. I need advice on how to handle it."

"Of course, *mi Reina*. What can this old man do for a beautiful young woman?"

I told him what was going on. "So, what do I do now? I have money and my passport, but I don't want anyone to find me before I get someplace safe. I'm afraid to call Mother or Daddy. I don't want to put my family in any danger."

"Of course, my darling girl. Do not call your mother or father right now. You call them in a few days once we get you to safety. Here is what you do..."

Chapter 20
Sara

I drove us to Hobby Airport to return my rental car. Hairy's fancy schmancy crate has built-in locking wheels. It will not roll unless you want to move it. I pushed the crate holding my dog with my luggage stacked on top outside and called for Uber to drive us to Intercontinental Airport. Once there, I took Hairy to air freight and checked him in for the flight to New York City. My uncle secured the boarding pass for me while I was in transit. After I scanned the blank international health form, I sent it to my uncle via the new phone. I could print the forms out, fill them in with the dog's name and destination, and who was supposed to pick him up at the next airport. I worried the entire flight to New York that Philip would figure out what I was doing and catch me before I left the country.

I talked to Philip twice by phone when he 'checked in just because he loved me.' The first time, I explained I had to drive across town to get a new health form. The vet could not see us until 3 that afternoon. I 'forgot' to tell him the name of the Houston vet. He sounded irritated, but he accepted my explanation. I turned off my old phone when I boarded the plane a little before noon.

Gag me with a burnt chicken wing. I knew he wanted to keep track of me. He would die if he realized I flew the coop from beneath his nose while he did paperwork at the DA's office. I kept my old phone with me to cover those calls. I already knew how I would ditch it later.

Once the plane landed at JFK, Hairy and I traveled by cab to Times Square and exited our cab. We waited by the side of the busy street until the cabbie drove away. Five minutes later, I hailed another cab, which took us the short distance to the Waldorf Astoria. Hairy and I strolled in and proceeded as directed to the concierge, where I picked up a package my uncle had waiting for me. I smiled as I gave the young man a huge tip. I slid a fingernail into the seal of the package, opened it, peeked inside and grinned. Uncle Roberto sent me everything I needed and then some, with three passports, several credit cards, and multiple driver's licenses in the same names as the passports. He even sent three dog passports and international health certificates for our various legs of our journey. Not bad, in less than a day. These must have cost my uncle a proverbial arm and a leg. I pulled out the first passport and proceeded to the front desk.

"*Bon jour*, I am Lilliana Montrachet. I reserved a room for this evening." I batted my eyelashes and smiled as I handed the desk clerk my passport while I spoke with my best Parisian accent.

The clerk checked his list and then smiled at me. "Welcome to the Waldorf Astoria, Mademoiselle Montrachet. May we help you to your suite?"

I flashed him my sexiest smile. "*Oui*, that would be lovely."

Hairy tilted his head at me. *Why are you talking funny, Mama?*

It's a game, Hairy. I'm pretending to be someone else. And you pretend your name is… Hmm… How about Georges?

One of the international health certificates listed his name as Georges.

His tongue lolled out of the side of his mouth. *Okay, Mama. I know a poodle named Georges, and his mama talks funny like that, too.*

Smiling, I nodded. *Perfect, baby. You pretend to be Georges, just like your friend the poodle. Now, act prissy like Georges, and we will be ready to play this game all the way to Gay Paree.*

Once in our rooms, I poured over the instructions and the packet of documents. While I did, my phone rang again.

"Where are you, babe? It's getting late." Philip sounded nervous.

I smiled, thrilled my ruse was working, and he was worried. I bet sweat poured off him by now. "On the Beltway. I had a flat tire, but it's okay, I changed it. My dad taught me how to do lots of things. I'll be back in a little while now, not more than an hour."

We chatted a few more minutes before I hung up. Realizing he could trace my location with the old phone, I knew I needed to hang up as soon as possible. I could picture the sorry bastard fantasizing about how he would try to kill me the next time. I calculated I still had a couple of hours before he realized I flew the proverbial coop, during which I could answer calls, before he would try to trace me with the GPS. Gosh, I wished I could have a picture of his face when he realized I slipped through his fingers. I had been so excited to have GPS on my phone when I first purchased the phone that could track my location. I had to be careful now or my much treasured GPS would bite me on my tiny little hiney. As a shiver of apprehension trickled down my spine, I turned the phone off again and slipped it into my handbag. With a bittersweet smile, I took a deep breath and then exhaled slowly. I felt tension slip out of my body as I did the breathing exercise two more times. I could check in with Philip later. If he asked, I would tell him the cell phone battery died. Better safe than sorry.

A beautician arrived thirty minutes later to color and style my hair. While the colorist did her magic, a manicurist worked on my nails, applying gel overlays and gave me lovely new fingernails. I wrecked mine in the past stress-filled weeks. A personal shopper showed up to let me select new clothing. Choose things which are very Euro, Uncle Roberto stressed. You do not want to look like an American tourist when you are in a disguise.

That evening, Hairy and I would catch the flight to Paris. From there, we would fly south to Naples. From there, I would rent a car, using another passport and driver's license, and drive to Calabria. Each leg of the trip, I would use a different passport, a different name, and a new identity, until I reached safety with *mi famiglia* in Calabria.

While the hairdresser restored the natural titian red color of my hair, the manicurist tinted my nails a deep, sexy fuchsia. I grinned when the manicurist painted Hairy's nails to match mine. She giggled like a schoolgirl as he slurped a kiss across her cheek.

I selected two gorgeous suits, one Ungaro, one Escada, a couple of coordinating tops, and a hot little Roberto Cavalli red knit dress. Believe me, the Cavalli number could light a dead man's fire. It was *molto* sexy. I figured it might just come in handy when I crossed the state line into Calabria. Being me with a shoe obsession, I also chose several sassy new pairs of Prada pumps, and a gorgeous pair of Louboutin boots I could not resist.

After everyone left, I pulled out my laptop and drafted my email to the DA. I sent blind copies to Maggie, Ashley, and my parents.

When I noticed an hour had passed, I turned the phone back on. The phone rang almost immediately, and I picked it up on the third ring. "I know, I'm late. The damned traffic is bumper to bumper."

He said nothing at first, and I figured he struggled to control his temper. It takes a lot to make his temper to flash, but I saw him go off on an attorney or two at the courthouse. The fury was not pretty. "Okay, sweetheart, just be careful. There are nuts out there, you know."

"I understand. See you soon." I smiled. Yeah, baby, I know more about those murderous nuts than you suspect I know.

When I completed the email, I hit the send key before I dressed for my flight. I figured Cory would not open the email until the next morning at the office. The DA's office was working with a skeleton crew since the hurricane, so it was possible it would be several days longer before Cory De Leon saw it. I was not sure they were working at the courthouse yet since it took on water from the hurricane. It flooded during Ike, and they closed it for weeks. I realized I needed to be as far away as possible when Cory called Philip in to discuss my allegations. In contrast, my family and friends would have the email tonight.

Oh, well. You snooze, you lose, Lover Boy. I no longer snoozed, and it was time to rock and roll. This Mafia Princess gig might be fun.

I texted my parents to tell them I slipped from the clutches of the evil man. Melodramatic? Perhaps, but true. No one should tell Philip a word about me, but act like they knew nothing. I would contact them later with all the details. They should delete all text messages and emails to and from me upon receipt of that one, although they should print out the long email I blind copied to them and put it in their safes. With a lighter heart and a sigh of relief, I turned the laptop off and packed it into my carry-on luggage.

When Hairy and I left the hotel thirty minutes later, I did not think my mother could have recognized Hairy or me. Hell, I did not recognize us.

For starters, the outfit I wore into the posh hotel earlier was now packed away in my new designer carry-on luggage, along with the rest of my new clothing. The change was more than a change of clothing.

The modest, conservative lawyer who checked in that afternoon looked nothing like the bombshell who slipped out of the hotel in a form-fitting, fuchsia Escada suit, with just enough plunge to the neckline to distract any flirtatious ticketing agent. Who would dream an under-wire bra could give me the curves I always wanted? I looked even sexier wearing the four-inch, black patent leather Prada slingbacks. They made my legs look like they were a decent length for a change. As Jack would have said, my legs looked like they went all the way from my ass to the ground. I never quite understood the phrase, but men seemed to understand he meant 'long legged gal.' The hairdresser put extensions into my freshly reddened hair and coaxed it into a high fashion style I never imagined possible for my bone-straight hair. My new, Irish-red hair brought out greens in my amber eyes I had forgotten existed. After the hairdresser fixed my makeup, I realized I had cheekbones and full lips, not to mention those brilliant eyes flecked with green. The look was further enhanced with two carat, princess-cut, cubic zirconias in my ears, a four-carat honker on my ring finger, and another humongous one dangling in my cleavage. I looked like one hot heifer on the prowl. The black faux fox stole draped around my shoulders added to the picture of a rich French bitch. I looked like a smoking hot Parisian model, clad in haute couture designer apparel.

Even the black dog beside me looked straight off the runway, with coordinating nail color matching mine, and a blinged out collar and leash the same color as my outfit. His change was complete with a sassy little fuchsia velvet coat and a matching tam-o'-shanter perched on his head. We looked foo-foo, or as Dara would say, we were the shits. Baby, we were hot! Hairy Potter and I were ready to hide in plain sight.

Upon arriving at JFK, I checked Hairy (now called Georges) in at air cargo to be shipped to Paris. I provided the airlines with one of the new international health certificates my uncle provided, which verified my little Georges was a Scottie mix, in excellent health, with no known health problems. I tried not to chuckle as everyone oohed and aahed over the beautiful Scottie. Mademoiselle Liliana Montrachet then checked in with the airline and settled back to enjoy a cocktail while she waited for her flight.

As I picked up my martini (extra dry, with an onion instead of an olive, *s'il vous plaît*), my eyes widened in surprise as I saw two familiar faces from home rushing up to me. I prayed I had not allowed recognition to cross my face at the sight of the Foxworths.

"Sara Talbott! Isn't that you, Sara? Whatever are you doing in New York?" Sadie Foxworth gushed on and on, excited to see me.

Heart in my throat, I tilted my head at her, as if I did not understand what she was saying. "I apologize, madam, but my English, um, it is not so good. How you say, um, my name, it is Liliana Montrachet. I, um, I do not know this person of whom you speak."

With that, I allowed the fox to slip into my cleavage. As Sadie's jaw hit the ground, I knew the contents of my stomach were about to hit the floor. After a pause, her husband took her by the elbow and began pulling her away, but not before I noticed the randy old goat salivating at the sight of my precocious, perky little boobs.

"I'm sorry, ma'am. I told my wife you were not that little gal from Morgan Point. In fact, you don't look a dad-gummed thang like her. Sadie, darlin, Miss Sara is nice enough to look at, but she's a lawyer. She looks like a lawyer. Very prim, proper, professional, if you know what I mean. I reckon you must be one of them there French high fashion gals, cause you're about the purtiest little thang I ever laid my eyes on. Now, come on, Sadie, let's leave this purty little gal alone. My gawd, woman, you ought to realize this woman is not Sara Talbott. This woman is drop dead gorgeous. I never saw a redhead so purty in all my life, and you know I love redheads, my little rosebud. Heck fire, Sara could only wish to look this fabulous."

It thrilled and annoyed me to hear Buster Foxworth go on and on about Sara's plainness and lack of attraction, and Liliana's incredible beauty. My ruse worked, and it thrilled me. It annoyed me because I am Sara, damn it, and I am beautiful, too, so there, you horny old goat. Anyway, even though I felt torn and confused by the entire conversation, angry and delighted to hear how successful my deception was, I stayed in character. I made my best imitation of that Gallic shrug we all expect from The French, with my fox wrap slinking deeper and deeper into my cleavage. I batted my false eyelashes and flashed him what I hoped was a seductive smile. "It is not a problem, *monsieur*."

My heart beat so hard I thought it would explode in my chest. Thank God I already checked Hairy onto the plane, because Sadie would have recognized him even with his ridiculous little shi-shi outfit. I took another sip of my martini--not something I drink. After all, I am a margarita girl. Believe me, I wanted a margarita right about then. I said something clever to the bartender *en francaise*. Thank God I studied French for four years in high school and in college in addition to a year in Paris as a foreign exchange student. We both laughed at the mere idea that *les Americains* thought I was one of them. From where? Some place called Morgan Point in Texas, of all places!

I cruised through the duty-free shops on my way to the plane, buying enough to slow me down and keep me out of the path of the Foxworth's. A girl never knew when she might need a new Fendi bag or a bottle of Chanel's latest scent.

I had already put my old cell phone into a FedEx envelope addressed to a distant cousin in Toronto. She would turn it off and mail it on to Mom. As I walked through the duty-free shops, I slipped the little package in the FedEx drop box right there at the airport. I was sure Philip would call soon, wondering where I was. If he couldn't reach me, he would check on the GPS, unless I was mistaken. I had better lose the trail in New York, or else I would have big trouble when I landed in France. I figured by the time he tracked my phone down, via New York to Toronto, and then on to Blue Ridge, Georgia, I would be long gone to Southern Italy and the protection my family could provide. *La famiglia* in Calabria would protect *La Reina Nuova* from danger.

I wasn't sure what I would do if I wound up next to the Foxworths on the plane. They must not have been on my flight to Paris. If they were, they damned sure were not in first class, because they were not sitting next to me when the plane took off.

Chapter 21
Philip

"Damn it, Sara, answer the phone." Philip worried when Sara was not back at the hotel at 8:30. She had been gone for twelve hours now. This was ridiculous. Philip slammed down the phone after the voice mail picked up again. He raked his hands through his hair as he stared out into the Texas night. "Something is wrong. Something is most definitely wrong."

Was it possible she figured it all out? How could she have realized what was going on? He worked too damned hard to perfect his pitch. Philip raked his hands through his hair again and glanced at his Rolex for the umpteenth time. She had to show up. She must come back.

He stopped in his tracks and rubbed his aching forehead. The dratted woman gave him a headache. He sighed as he rubbed his temples while he pondered the situation. Hell, maybe she found the damned urn, took it, and ran. Dad would shit little green apples if she pulled that off.

His shoulder slumped as he sighed. He did not know whether he should yell or weep. Or maybe cheer her on.

Philip resumed pacing.

Chapter 22
Sara

The flight from New York to Paris took about five hours, in real time. Air France proved to be a delightful trip, with gourmet food and wine in first class. After dinner, I slipped off my heels, snuggled under my plush velvet blankie, stretched out on my ultra-comfy reclining seat, and fell into what was the best sleep I experienced in weeks if not months. As the plane flew over Ireland the next morning, I awoke just in time to see the sun rising over the lush green countryside below. After my typically French *petite dejeuner* of hard rolls, cheese, a boiled egg, and French roast coffee brewed to perfection, the plane landed at Charles de Gaulle Airport, where I retrieved Hairy. We hailed a cab, which drove us to the posh Hotel du Crillon.

I wanted to stay at the Crillon for years, reputed to be the finest hotel in Paris, if not all of Europe. Jack refused to spend the money for a room there. It delighted me when my uncle booked me a room there—until I realized I was supposed to check in, change my disguise, and then slip out the back. Once outside, my instructions said I should hail another cab and go to the Ritz, where I would spend the night using a different passport.

Once I arrived at my dream hotel, I picked up a packet from the concierge and then got to spend about half an hour in my beautiful, luxurious room. The contents of the packet horrified me, but it would make one hell of a disguise. Hairy and I rolled all over the bed and took a nap before I took a bubble bath before I assumed my new identity. I peeled off the false eyelashes and scrubbed off all my makeup. Cringing, I covered my beautiful Irish red tresses with a wig cap and pulled on an unattractive mouse brown wig. The hideous wig looked like it had been used to scrub floors. As if that wasn't bad enough, I next pulled on a cheap polyester blouse. The frumpy smock-type blouse looked like something Nonna wore working in her garden twenty years ago. I changed into my brown Escada pantsuit and pulled on my boots before I trundled everything downstairs through the freight elevator. Once outside, I called for a cab to meet me across the street from the side entrance.

Thirty minutes later, a cab picked up a frumpy, middle-aged woman with a short, mousey-brown hairdo, the ugliest blouse in Paris, gimongous, horn-rimmed glasses and her funny looking dog to take them to the Ritz. No one who saw me check in as Liliana Montrachet would suspect the unattractive little mouse who left by the side door was the same woman, just like the Foxworths could not believe Liliana and I were the same woman.

Damn it, I hated to give up that Liliana persona. That gal was hot!

Chapter 23
The District Attorney

Cory De Leon sat at his expensive mahogany desk, pensive as he reviewed the email. Perhaps a ploy, but Cory realized it could be true. There had been several attempts on the woman's life since her husband's death. Cory sighed as he pushed back from his desk and loosened his expensive silk tie. The overworked District Attorney shook his head. He had to investigate her allegations. "Margie, get Sim Lake in my office right away. I need the skills of the best investigator we have. Tell Philip Martino I need to see him in my offices, asap, and he needs to bring Mrs. Talbott with him."

"Phil's not here, boss. He is still on vacation."

Cory's frown deepened. "I don't care if he is on his honeymoon. Hell, I would swear he was here yesterday morning. Get him in my office pronto. This is important."

She frowned. "But boss ..."

"No buts, Margie. This is important. Tell Mr. 'I'm Too Sexy to Come to Work' to get his butt in here now, and to bring that blasted Talbott woman. It is high time I had a talk with little Sara Talbott about her husband's untimely death. Understand?"

The legal secretary nodded as she bit back a grin at her boss's words. "Yes sir, Mr. De Leon. Anything else?"

Cory thought a moment before answering. "Yeah, get me the ballistics reports on the bullet that killed Jack Talbott, and on the bullets recovered from the attempted shootings at Sara Talbott when she was in Pennsylvania."

"Right away, boss. I'll call the Pennsylvania authorities for those reports about the attempts to kill Mrs. Talbott."

"Very good. Call Boston, too. See if they have any leads on the hit and run in front of the FBI offices. Oh, and call the Hatboro, Pennsylvania, police to see if they have anything about the attempted hit and run where someone attempted to run her off the road."

"Right away, boss. I'll call the hotel, too, and see if they have a video of whoever tried to get into her room." Margie turned to return to her desk outside Cory's office.

Cory rubbed his stomach. Work was no longer fun, like when he came to work in the DA's office twenty years ago. With each new promotion, he added ten pounds. Nagging stomach pain accompanied the added weight and stresses of the job. Thirty years of crap like this gave him an ulcer, the gift that kept on giving. He popped a Nexium into his mouth and gulped it down with black coffee. Hell, if you got right down to it, the law gave him an ulcer. Why did he go to law school in the first place?

Oh, yeah. To preserve justice.

He sighed. On days like this one, he wanted to take early retirement and move to the mountains he loved. Oh well, it was time to get cracking and figure out who the blazes killed Jackson Talbott.

It would be interesting to see if Philip Martino bothered to show up. It might be even more interesting to learn where Sara Winslow Talbott might be on this bright, sunshiny October morning.

Chapter 24
Sara

I fussed internally the entire way to the Ritz. If Uncle Roberto made the first reservation at the Ritz, I could have spent the night at the Crillon. Damn it.

And then I walked into the Ritz Carlton Paris and swallowed hard. This place was posh, it was swank, it was 'all that and a bag of chips.' Hell, the Ritz was the entire bag of chips, and then some.

The Ritz was gorgeous, even if it wasn't Le Crillon. Built in an eighteenth century private residence, the Ritz Carlton Paris is one of the premier hotels in the world, for good reason.

Uncle Roberto reserved me a regular room at Le Crillon. It was fabulous, and I hated to leave it. In fact, I stole a towel from it.

I handed the Ritz Carlton desk clerk my passport. "*Mais oui, Mademoiselle* Munsterlander. It delights us to have you tonight. A bellman will show you to your suite."

I blinked as my heart began racing. "But I reserved a regular room."

German is not my strong suit, but I struggled to speak French as if I lacked native fluency in the language. That meant I spoke a tad slowly and enunciated every word, as I heard Germans speak French in the past.

He beamed at me. "We upgraded your room as a courtesy. Please, allow me to show you to your rooms."

I think my mouth may have hit the floor. I struggled to quit drooling, and nodded. "*Danke*, that would be *wunderbar, monsieur.*"

I had stayed in five-star hotels before. Not many times, but a few. Daddy loves luxury. He always stayed first class when we traveled. We stayed in lovely hotels, but I stayed nowhere before that came close to the suite at the Ritz Carlton in Paris. It was all I could have imagined, with a cherry and sprinkles on top.

Remember that old television show, The Lifestyles of the Rich and Famous? This place should have been on it. It was swankier than anything I remember ever seeing on it.

Anyway, once the nice man showed Hairy–oops, no longer posing as Georges but as *mein liebling*, Otto–and me to our room, we just stared at it for a few minutes. Then Hairy—oops, now Otto—let out a little yip and ran in circles.

Mama, Mama, Mama, it's so nice! Can we stay here? Can we? Can we? Can we?

No, baby, we go to Italy tomorrow.

But I like it here, Mama! I want to live here! Forever!

You have very expensive taste, little boy. No. We go to Italy tomorrow.

I laughed and laughed. My dog ran circles around the exquisite living room before dropping from exhaustion on the oriental rug in front of the wood-burning fireplace.

How come I have to be Otto now? I liked my other name better.

Which name? Georges? Or Hairy?

He barked and began running again. *You're so silly, Mama. Georges is my fun name for the game. Hairy is my real name.*

But which name would you like? If you could pick?

He stopped running and sat in front of me panting like, well, like a dog. His tongue lolled out to one side as he studied me. *Why? Are you going to change my name?*

I thought for a minute before I answered. *Would you want me to change your name?*

I swear the dog shrugged at me. *I don't care just as long as you are my Mama and I'm your baby.*

He slurped a big kiss across my cheek, and I grabbed him close. *Silly boy, you own my heart. You will always be my baby.*

He slurped another kiss across my cheek. *Sing my song, Mama.*

I laughed. Since he was a tiny puppy, I sang this stupid little ditty to him. My dog adores it.

Hairy Baby, Hairy, Hairy, Baby, Baby, Hairy, Baby, you're my guy.
Hairy Baby, Hairy, Hairy, Baby, Baby, Hairy, Baby, my pride and joy.

Like I told you, it is a stupid song. Who sings to a dog, anyway?

Hairy began barking and running again as I sang. *More, Mama, more. I love it when you sing for me!*

I laughed and sang on and on as Hairy ran around the room and barked. Only Hairy ever asked me to sing. Mom says I sing almost as horribly as my stepbrother, Charlie. My half-sister, Dara, is the singer in the family. She warbles like an angel.

After the song, Hairy and I collapsed together into a pile on the floor. Later, Hairy whispered to me. *Mama, I need to go outside and go potty.*

I laughed again. "Well, let's go take a walk and find you a French park."

He barked. *With pretty French girls?*

"Maybe, baby, we'll see."

We started walking, and it wasn't long before we strolled along the Seine. The sun shone bright, and the air crisp with the promise of colder weather to come overnight. I laughed as Hairy flirted with poodles and raised his leg to pee on the trees. We shopped along the Place Vendome, where I bought another hideous blouse for Fraulein Munsterlander to wear the next day. We ate at an outdoor café before we returned to the hotel, exhausted and relaxed from our Parisian outing.

Tomorrow we would go to Italy.

Chapter 25
Philip

"Have you found her yet, son?"

Philip gritted his teeth. "No, Dad, she seems to have disappeared."

"Bull hockey. She flew from Houston to New York yesterday. A cab carried her into town and dropped her off in Times Square. Didn't you know that?"

"Yes, I knew it. Look, Dad—"

"No, you look. I am the senator. You are supposed to handle this mess. I already checked, and she did not register at any hotel in New York. Who does she know there?"

Philip shook his head. "No one, to my knowledge. Her older sister lived there several years ago. She must have gone somewhere else from New York."

"Brilliant, son. I would never have guessed. My secretary checked the flight manifests for all flights leaving from New York, New Jersey, Pennsylvania, and Boston for yesterday and today. They did not list her on any of them. Any other bright ideas, son?"

"No, sir." Philip sighed and shook his head as he bit his lip in frustration. His dad could be so infuriating. Philip wanted to say more, but he knew to control his words with his dad. Otherwise, he would regret any rash comments he might make to James Martino.

Senator Martino paused before replying. "Find the bitch, son. And take care of the problem when you find her. Don't let her get away again."

"But, Dad, you don't understand—"

"I understand everything I need to understand. Take care of the problem, damn it. If you did it the first time, like I told you to do, we would not be in this predicament now."

Philip rubbed his hand across his eyes as his shoulders slumped. "Yes, sir."

Philip stared out across the Houston skyline. Damn it, Sara, where the hell did you go?

Chapter 26
Sara

Hairy, who I would call Otto on this leg of the trip, and I flew to Naples the next morning. I wore my hideous Fraulein Munsterlander disguise. By mid-day, we arrived in Naples. I slipped into the restroom, and within minutes dowdy Fraulein Munsterlander changed her wig and her outfit. It amazed me what I could accomplish to transform my looks with a slight effort. From Sara Talbott, Attorney at Law, I became the fashionable and lovely Parisienne, Liliana Montrachet. Liliana then morphed into Helga Munsterlander via bone ugly brown hair, a brown business suit, no makeup, a fake mole on my chin, and oversized tortoiseshell glasses.

I changed from poor, unattractive Fraulein Munsterlander into the petite but voluptuous Signorina Mariana Antonietta in the Naples Airport. I removed the fake wart with a sigh of relief and applied fresh makeup. With a fresh pound and a half of makeup on my face, a sexy, long curling, black wig, a skin-tight red Roberto Cavalli dress, the ultimate Wonderbra of all Wonderbras, and the highest, red patent leather stilettos I ever wore (these suckers had to be at least six inches high), I became every man's ultimate fantasy, vivacious and vampy as only an Italian woman can be. I felt every bit as sexy as I looked. Jeez-Louise, I could not get over the cleavage! It was incredible. I never needed implants; I needed a Wonderbra. I sashayed over to the rental agency, where I picked up a sporty little car reserved for Signorina Antonietta, and then drove around to baggage to pick up Hairy. His crate and my luggage just barely fit into the BMW convertible my uncle reserved for our drive south.

Since the day was glorious, I dropped the top on the pretty red convertible. It was only a little more than a half day's drive from Naples to Reggio. I felt confident I could make it to *Zio* Roberto's estate before night. I tied a silk scarf I bought at the airport around my head. The scarf would keep the long wig on my head and the long hair out of my face. I put on my sunglasses, reapplied my red lipstick, and Hairy and I hit the road.

As you travel around Europe, you realize it differs from traveling in the United States. I have never seen guards at the airports in the United States carrying machine guns. That freaked me out the first time I saw it in Italy. It traumatized me when twelve and we visited Calabria the first time. I had never seen armed guards carry machine guns in airports. When we crossed the state line into Calabria, we went through a 'border check,' with guards armed with machine guns, too.

Uncle Roberto warned me the guards would search the car for drugs and contraband. I did not want them to search my bag and find my money, so I hid it under Hairy's bed in his crate. I knew no one would reach inside my dog's crate to check for contraband. Hairy would not bite, but he would make the guards think he would bite. After all, he is a terrier.

At the border, two guards stood waiting as I pulled up at their little hut. The men grinned as I slithered out of the sexy red convertible, with one arching his eyebrows at the other. I knew I looked hot as a fresh-picked jalapeño in the clingy Cavalli dress. I selected the little red Cavalli number to distract these dolts from a thorough search of the car. As one patted down my curves, the other made a half-assed attempt to look in Hairy's crate. Hairy growled at him through the bars on the front door, and the guard jerked his hand back.

"*Signores*, I am sorry, but the dog is not friendly with strangers."

I leaned against the sports car as I joked and teased with the guards for a good half hour before they signaled I could proceed. Hairy growled every time the guard reached towards the crate, and each time, the man jerked his hand back. After the third try, the guard never attempted again to open the crate door, much less to reach inside and check the contents. I tossed my long black hair over my shoulder, waved, blew a kiss to each of the boys, and then Hairy and I started out south towards Reggio again.

We proceeded through the Pollino Mountains, past the Costa Viola to Reggio. I worried we might not arrive until after dark as I drove the twisting, turning route outside of town up the mountainside to my uncle's estate. My uncle lives five miles outside a quaint resort town that faces the Tyrrhenian Sea. Locals call his home Villa San Giovanni. I turned to drive up the narrow, winding road into the Aspromonte.

We arrived as the sky darkened to the coming night. I parked the little sports car and released Hairy from his crate. I bent over and slipped off the high heels and slipped on a pair of flats before I eased out the trunk holding the priceless urn.

It took a couple of minutes for Hairy and me to walk up the curving trail on the steep hillside to my uncle's house. I stopped once to admire the view of the turquoise blue waters of the Tyrrhenian Sea below us in the distance. Hairy ran along beside me, delighted to be freed from the confinements of his crate. He sounded joyful as he barked while I walked up the trail, carrying the precious artifact with utmost care. On the way, I passed two men who were guarding Uncle Roberto's property, armed with Uzi's and shotguns. Both fell back and saluted me as I passed. "*Buona sera, signorina.*"

I smiled. "*Buona sera, signores.*"

Hairy and I arrived at the house after the long hike up the hill. I set the handle of the wheeled trunk down beside my feet, straightened the skirt of my dress, pulled off my scarf and smoothed my hair. I lifted the trunk again before I knocked at the door. When Roberto opened the door, I pushed the trunk over to him.

He took the trunk, a smile playing upon his lips, and wheeled it over to the table inside the door. He pulled me into his arms to kiss me, first on each cheek and then on my forehead. "Are you all right, *cara*?"

Smiling, I nodded and entered the house.

"Did everything go as planned?"

I nodded again and my smile broadened. "Exactly as planned."

Hairy trotted in the house. He jumped on the couch, where he curled into a ball. "I love that little dog, *zio*. He has my heart. You cannot imagine how many times I told Hairy we were in the heart of the storm, but the reality is

Hairy was that calm center of the chaotic mess I lived in for these past few months. I'm the storm. Hairy saved my life more than once."

"You must tell me all about it once you rest."

"Rest assured, I shall. Well, we managed to get here safe and sound."

Uncle Roberto beamed at me. "You did very well, Catareina. I am proud of you."

I smiled back at him again as I looked up at my uncle. "Shall my name be Catareina now?"

"Yes, of course. Catareina Franchetti. After all, you shall be our *Reina Nuova*."

"Ah, I should have realized that. I always preferred my middle name. You really think I did well?"

"*Carissima*, I would not say so if I did not mean it. You did a fantastic job."

I smiled as I relaxed. Uncle Roberto could always soothe my fears. After all, I pulled it off. All of it.

Success felt damned good. It is not every girl who can learn her husband is cheating on her and survive, yet I survived with style and panache. I found *La Sforza* and got it back to Italy. Now, we could return it to the Museo from which the Stelari family stole it and put a shadow on my family's reputation.

I even escaped the people who wanted to kill me, and that was no small trick. In fact, it took a fair amount of fancy footwork to accomplish my escape.

That last day, when Jackson knocked me down the stairs, he said, "You can't win this one, Sara. You are not strong enough to withstand the storm I will unleash on you."

My dog snarled and barked with unexpected ferociousness as he snapped at Jackson. I grabbed Hairy's collar and pulled him to my chest as I arose to run down the rest of the stairs. Jack continued to laugh. I turned to face him one last time at the base of the staircase. "You don't understand, Jackson. I am the storm."

Jackson never understood Hairy could calm the storm within me.

What do you do in the middle of a trial when you learn your husband is having an affair with your client? Suicide was not an option. But murder?

Jackson always swore I had the best poker face he ever saw.

I warned him I would be the storm which turned his world upside down.

I managed Jack's death with such finesse that I was not even a suspect any longer. Philip Martino was the prime suspect, since the DA learned of the repeated murder attempts made on me at the request of Philip's father. On one level, I hated to pin Jack's murder on Philip. I thought I was falling in love with him before I overheard the phone call between his father and him. However, overhearing him talk to his father pushed all thoughts of love and a happy-ever-after with Philip Martino right out of my head. For heaven's sake, the man intended to kill me! The District Attorney had begun a formal investigation about those allegations and about my untimely disappearance. The authorities feared either Philip or the mob murdered me. I chuckled. If they only knew how *la famiglia* was involved.

I was still in Maggie's parking lot when my phone rang. I accepted the call. "Yeah, we're done. I'm leaving now."

She paused for a minute before she replied. "Are you okay?"

"Hell, no, I'm not okay."

"So…" she began.

"Do it."

"Okay, sis."

People always said Dara and I looked enough alike to be twins. No one suspected her. Everyone thought she had gone back to work until we would leave for Montgomery. Everyone except Jackson, and he realized too late the sister on the boat with him was an outstanding shot, where I am terrified of guns. The fool thought it was me until she pulled the trigger, but that was our plan.

I took a deep breath and smiled again. Uncle Roberto was right. It really is quite marvelous to be the Queen.

About the Author

Middleton is a fourth-generation Texan who grew up in San Antonio and now lives near Galveston. She claims she escaped the law and professes to be a recovering attorney.

Middleton writes, quilts, and enjoys her Skye terriers. She loves North Georgia and hopes to build a retirement home in the mountains overlooking the Cohutta Mountains next year.

She has won awards for historical romance from the Pencraft Awards and the Texas Best Book Awards, and Author Shout has recognized her books as 'recommended reads.' While *Heart of the Storm* is Middleton's eighth publication, it is her first mystery.

Middleton loves to hear from her readers. You can contact her at sharonmiddleton359@gmail.com if you have ideas about future plots or other constructive suggestions.

Note from the Author

Word-of-mouth is crucial for any author to succeed. If you enjoyed *Heart of the Storm*, please leave a review online—anywhere you are able. Even if it's just a sentence or two. I want to know if you love it. It could make all the difference and would be greatly appreciated.

Thanks!
Sharon K. Middleton